Time of Grace

Gabriella West

WOLFHOUND PRESS

First published in 2001 by
Wolfhound Press Ltd
68 Mountjoy Square
Dublin 1, Ireland
Tel: (353-1) 874 0354
Fax: (353-1) 872 0207

© 2001 Gabriella West

The Arts Council
An Chomhairle Ealaíon

Wolfhound Press receives financial assistance from The Arts
Council/An Chomhairle Ealaíon, Dublin, Ireland.

British Library Cataloguing in Publication Data
A catalogue record for this book is available from the British Library.

ISBN 0-86327-863-9

10 9 8 7 6 5 4 3 2 1

Cover Illustration: Retna Pictures
Cover Design: Mark O'Neill
Typesetting: Wolfhound Press
Printed in Scotland by Omnia Books Ltd.

Time of Grace

———————————

Gabriela West was born in California in 1967. In the late 60s her parents moved to Dublin, where she grew up. She graduated from Trinity College Dublin in 1988 with a degree in English Literature, and moved to San Francisco to pursue a graduate degree in Creative Writing and other interests. Her stories and essays have appeared in numerous anthologies and literary magazines in the US, and she reviews books for the *Irish Herald* in San Francisco. *Time of Grace* is her first published novel.

This book is dedicated to my grandmother, Doreen Healy
Born in Dublin, 1917

Chapter 1

_A_ugust 1915

No friends or family waited with me on the Holyhead dock on that unseasonably dreary late-August day. Usually I loved the sea — I had grown up in London, so the seaside had always been a treat for my brother Ralph and me — but as I stood there clutching my two battered suitcases, preparing to board the ferry that would take me to Ireland, the chill air clung to me and I shivered uncontrollably.

'Are you not well, my dear?' a matronly woman asked me. I blushed. Did I look as pale and wretched as that? I nodded to her, and she said comfortingly, 'These really are terrible times. We all know someone at the Front, don't we?'

This was not the most tactful thing she could have said. As I fished for my compact and gazed disconsolately at my thin, bespectacled face and dark hair sternly knotted in a bun, I thought not of myself — Caroline Singleton, nineteen years old and going out into the unknown to Ireland, to work as a governess in what might be a futile attempt to gain some independence for myself — but of Ralph, killed in action at the battle of Ypres in the spring of that dreadful year. He had been one year older than I, and glowing with health and exuberance, even on the day he left us. Ever since Mother and I had received the news, I had felt more and more like a ghost myself. It was selfish, I knew, to want him back so that I could be happy, but that was the role he had always played in my life — protective, charming, teasing — and now there was no one to do it, nobody who cared.

My matronly acquaintance pulled a shawl out of her baggage and offered it to me, introducing herself as Mrs Grimsby. I told her my name. Her husband, she said, was a merchant in Dublin, a purveyor of fine wines, and every now and then he sent her back to London to check up on their English shop. It was a little holiday for her as well, she explained. Dublin did get dull. Had I ever been there?

I confessed that I had not travelled much, and mentioned briefly that I was going to be working for an Anglo-Irish family called the Wilcoxes who owned a great house in County Louth, north of Dublin. I would be in charge of their young daughter Amelia.

Her kind blue eyes seemed to take in everything: my shabby luggage, threadbare clothes and small frame.

'I hope you'll be content with your position, my dear,' she said. 'Educating the young is a very important affair. A difficult one, to be sure.'

I nodded hesitantly. I wanted to tell her that I did not have much confidence in my abilities as a governess, but perhaps she could read that in my eyes. Often I did not know quite what to reveal to people. 'You say either too much or too little,' Ralph had told me. 'Either you don't give them enough to go on, and they think you aloof, or you embarrass them with detail.' It was the type of advice he'd often tried to offer me, taking the place of our mother, who had not been well since Father's death, ten years before. We had watched her turn from a happy, active woman into a fragile, demanding semi-invalid. Ralph's death had undone her completely.

'This delay is *most* annoying!' Mrs Grimsby observed, pulling a sandwich from her bag and offering it to me. I tried not to wolf it down too fast. Before Ralph's death, I would not have accepted food from a stranger, but I felt so helpless and alone these days that I would have taken anything from just about anyone. But I had avoided men, always. It had pleased Ralph, but I think he had wondered about it too, wondered if I would ever marry. It seemed unlikely that anyone would want me — poor, educated, but without prospects or good looks.

I was secretly glad of this. I knew I had the strength to live my life on my own without any regrets. I was not maternal. I would never want children, I thought, and certainly not a husband. Perhaps a friend, but I could not imagine what shape this shadowy friend would take. I had had few close girl friends; my mother's social circle had simply been too small, and at school I was the shy, studious one. My teachers had liked me, though. I was smiling at some private memory — a pretty young history teacher patting my cheek and saying I was her best pupil — when Mrs Grimsby touched my shoulder. The ferry was pulling up in front of us. As if some switch had been pulled, the light drizzling rain that had been chilling us stopped, and the sun shone weakly through the clouds.

'The sea is calm,' Mrs Grimsby said with satisfaction. 'It will be a peaceful crossing. Will you have some tea with me, Miss Singleton?'

'Caroline,' I said shyly. 'Yes, I'd love to.'

Passengers began to swarm up the ramp, and we followed with difficulty. Mrs Grimsby sighed as she manoeuvred us into some seats.

'Well, thank goodness we're going to a country where there's no war on. It feels different there. True, a lot of young men have joined up and been killed; but the country just hasn't suffered the same losses. You can see it in the eyes and voices of the people. And they don't *think* about the War in the same way. It's not their affair, not their tragedy. I don't blame them. Grimsby and I are removed from the whole thing, thank God. I'm glad now that I never had a son!'

Seeing the pain and dismay in my expression, she suddenly stopped.

'I'm a talkative old fool,' she said bluntly. I had to laugh through the tears that were beginning to stream from my eyes.

'Your young man?' she guessed.

I shook my head. 'My brother.'

Mrs Grimsby clapped her hand to her mouth. As she apologised, I began to wish I were somewhere else, somewhere safe, instead of on board ship, heading for a new land. But there was nowhere to hide. All I had in this world was in my suitcases and on my back. And inside me.

I did not blame Mrs Grimsby, and I did not blame the Germans for taking my brother away. Instead — and this was something I had not told a soul — I blamed the government. I sympathised quietly with the pacifists whom I saw jeered at on the London streets. I had gone to several peace meetings, just to listen. Even before Ralph had been killed, I had known that 'the cause' was not worth his death. *I must be brave now*, I thought, *but I must not just accept mindlessly the soothing words handed down by the politicians.* My brother was not a hero, and he had not, I thought, done his patriotic 'duty'. What was duty, anyway? Surely one's highest duty was to oneself — and to one's fellow men!

I could not explain this to Mrs Grimsby, who sat dabbing at her eyes and murmuring that time would ease my loss. I wondered if she was right.

The ferry docked at Kingstown, a fishing village south of Dublin. All around us seagulls flew, and men spoke with rough voices, Dublin accents. Mrs Grimsby took a little flask from her pocket and swallowed. She offered it to me, and for some reason I could not say no. My throat burned as I tasted it, and tears rushed to my eyes. 'Irish whiskey,' Mrs Grimsby said with satisfaction. 'Now, dear, is someone collecting you?'

'I think so.... There should be a car.'

I looked about wildly. It was quite black. A street-lamp cast eerie shadows on people's faces. How I wished I were going with Mrs Grimsby to her nice solid brick house on the outskirts of Dublin!

She handed me a scrap of paper. 'My husband's card. If anything goes wrong, you'll call on me, won't you? We have plenty of room; I'll be glad to put you up.'

'Thank you,' I stammered. 'You've been so kind....'

And then she was gone, hailing a cab and jumping into it as if she were a much younger woman.

Someone tapped me on the shoulder, a middle-aged man with a tired, friendly face. 'Miss Singleton?'

I nodded. He took my bags and I followed him rather numbly. My eyes widened as I saw a large black motor-car. I had never ridden in one.

The man, who introduced himself as Carter, the chauffeur, opened the door for me. I climbed gratefully into the leather seat. The inside of the car was comfortable and elegant, like a luxury train-carriage. I felt completely lost; I had realised the Wilcoxes were wealthy people, but to me wealth had meant a few servants and the leisure to throw dinner parties, not this level of material comfort.

'Sir John's a motor enthusiast,' Carter explained as the car purred down the road. 'It's still going to take a while to get to Thornley Hall, Miss, so if you'd like to sleep ...'

'I think I will,' I said with a nervous laugh. I lay back against the seat, watching the dark streets slip by. Soon we were in the countryside; I could no longer see a thing. I closed my eyes to the sound of Carter's gentle whistling. It was a song my mother had liked to sing, 'Loch Lomond'; and as I drifted off to sleep, thinking of Ralph lying dead on that dark, lonely Flanders field, tears pricked my eyes.

> *You'll take the high road, and I'll take the low road,*
> *And I'll be in Scotland before ye,*
> *But me and my true love will never meet again*
> *On the bonny, bonny banks of Loch Lomond....*

Chapter 2

S he was the first person I saw. As I stumbled up the steps, trying not to look at the great grey house looming above me, a young girl holding a lamp stood waiting for me.

I had wondered if the lady of the house would be there to greet me, and had hoped not. I was in no mood for conversation, and I knew I scarcely looked presentable. But this serene young woman in a maid's uniform caught my attention in a curious way. We stood looking at each other. She smiled. Her glance was inviting, and I had the strangest sense of familiarity, as if I knew her from somewhere long ago.

The spell was broken as a portly man came out onto the steps. He must be the butler, I thought, noting the way the maid lowered her eyes submissively.

'Miss Singleton?' the man said. 'I'm Mr Johnson, the butler here at Thornley.' He surveyed me for a moment as I stood on the step below him, shivering, suddenly awkward. 'This is Grace Sheridan,' he continued. 'She'll show you to your room.' He walked rapidly into the house ahead of us, as if he were washing his hands of me. I had not spoken a word.

'This way, Miss,' Grace said in a quiet voice, but I caught in her tone a hint of the salty, worldly-wise Dublin accent that I had heard before at the dock. So she was a city girl. That surprised me, and I pondered it as we walked up a long, spiralling flight of stairs inside the house. The light from her lamp wavered and I watched my footing carefully.

'The mistress doesn't like having the gas-light on after ten o'clock.' Grace spoke in an amused whisper, turning back to me as if we were conspirators. I stifled a giggle. It felt as if we were schoolgirls, sneaking out of our beds for a midnight feast in somebody else's cubicle in a boarding-school dormitory. Neither she nor I had gone to boarding-school, of course. It was something that rich girls did.

Grace opened a door and ushered me into a room with a bed, a desk and a couple of chairs. She put down the lamp and brought in the suitcases, which Carter had left outside. I saw a night-stand, with a pitcher of water and a basin for bathing; a painting of some rural landscape on the wall. There was a cosiness about the room for which I was grateful, and I sat down on the bed without thinking. It was a four-poster with a firm mattress. I felt better immediately.

I looked up at the girl standing opposite me. She appeared to be around my age, perhaps a year younger, with rich brown hair tied back from her face, hazel eyes with long lashes, and soft, almost sensual lips. She was plump, with full breasts; hers was an hourglass figure of the kind which I could never hope to have, but which I sometimes found myself admiring in other women. She smiled again, looking at me with a friendliness and curiosity that almost troubled me. I had expected polite disinterest from the maids and the other servants.

'So you're from London, then?' she asked. Again, there was that absence of formality.

I nodded. 'Have you ever been there?' I felt myself blushing as I spoke, and looked down. It was hard to meet her eyes, for some reason.

'No.' She spoke matter-of-factly. 'I've never been anywhere except Dublin and here.'

'Oh.' I hated this tongue-tiedness; but why should I be surprised? I was completely out of my element here. *And what is my element, anyway?* I thought sadly.

'Miss Amelia shouldn't be too much trouble,' Grace said almost idly, 'if you was wondering that.'

'Oh, good. I was quite worried.'

'Mind you, she can be a bit sly.'

I rubbed my eyes. I had no idea how to deal with an untruthful child.

'But I'll leave you now, Miss, you'll be needing a good rest,' said Grace.

'Thank you, Grace,' I heard myself saying. We looked at each other and she nodded slightly. Still with that intent, curious gaze, she said, 'I'll come fetch you tomorrow, then, to go meet the mistress.'

'Oh, good. So I'll be seeing you again.'

It must be the fatigue, I thought, that was causing me to make these inane comments.

Grace smiled. She had a beautiful smile, I mused, mischievous and daring. 'We won't be strangers. There's not an army of us here, you know.'

'I see.... I thought there would be.'

She laughed. 'I was frightened too, when I arrived. But you'll find everyone here is very nice. Except for a few of the men, and you won't have to worry about them.'

'But you do?'

She shrugged. 'Well, there's those of us who do our jobs here, and there's those of us who feel they own the place and have the right to order everyone else about. But you'll be dealing mostly with the family.'

'I'll have a lot of time alone, I expect.'

'It can be lonely out here,' Grace admitted. 'In the evenings ...' Her face took on an air of melancholy which made it look, to me, all the more appealing.

With her lamp, she lit a couple of candles for me. As I watched her, I thought, *She's taking so much trouble to be kind. Why?* I was a foreigner, someone of a higher social class. I had had fears that, as a governess, I would be cut off from everyone — not good enough for the family, too refined for the servants ever to completely relax around me, stuck in an awkward limbo of my own. Yet this girl did not seem intimidated by me; she was friendly and respectful, someone whom I could talk to. It was a good start.

And that was practically my last coherent thought. As soon as Grace left, I hurriedly undressed, shivering slightly, fell into bed, and went straight to sleep.

I was awoken by the sound of the birds. I lay in a daze, watching the pattern on the wallpaper opposite my bed slowly brighten. It was chilly, and I hugged my blankets to me. I wondered when Grace would knock on the door.

Grace, I thought. What a beautiful name. My own, Caroline, was so dull, so English, so prim. I had never had a chance *not* to be prim — except when I was a child, and Ralph and I would romp in the garden, or go on long unsupervised walks in London. Those walks had been such fun; there had been a sense of freedom, of relief, at escaping our little house in Camden Town. And sometimes we would hop on a bus and ride it to wherever it would take us. Ralph had always said he wanted to be an explorer, an adventurer. I had been thrilled to be his second-in-command. But I could not follow him to the War, of course....

A gentle knock on the door. I started, embarrassed at being caught lying in bed in my thin nightgown. Grace entered with a steaming pitcher in her hands.

'Warm water for you, Miss.'

I sat up, hugging the blankets to me. I put my spectacles on, so I could see her, and to my surprise she walked over to the bed. She leaned over me a little, which for some reason made my face flush.

'How did you sleep?'

'Oh ... very well,' I said nervously. 'The birds woke me.'

'The mistress is waiting for you in the morning-room. I'm to wait outside the door and show you where it is.'

'I won't be long,' I said. I felt myself blushing again and my heart beating faster, even though there seemed to be no reason. *She affects me strangely*, I thought. *It must be loneliness, the new place.*

'There's no hurry,' Grace said. 'In fact, I'd rather you went slowly; there's a lot to do downstairs, and I'm not eager to begin it!'

I wanted to ask her what her duties were, but I felt shy about it. Perhaps she would tell me later. She looked neat and well-turned-out in her black uniform, and I still felt dreary and exhausted. She slipped outside the door, and I got up and wandered over to the night-stand to wash.

As I drew the sponge over my pale, skinny body, a strange image began to play in my mind. I started to imagine what Grace looked like as she washed herself every morning. As I closed my eyes and imagined her slowly sponging her breasts, I felt myself quiver and flush all over. She was so womanly! I pulled on my dark stockings, then my boots, trying furiously to suppress these thoughts. Where had they come from? Why?

I was still trembling a little as I opened the door. When I met Grace's inquiring gaze, I tried to act casually. Perhaps I succeeded. I began to apologise for keeping her so long. Again, she flashed me that mischievous smile; then, to my utter surprise, she put her hand on my arm.

I froze. It was so unusual for people to touch me. Her hand slipped away, but before we started walking, I smiled at her. I couldn't help it.

'Do I look presentable?' I asked.

She was a little shorter than I. Gently, she reached up and tucked a stray curl behind my ear.

I felt my breath shorten. I turned aside, not wanting to meet her eyes.

'I'm sorry, Miss,' she said awkwardly. 'Did I do anything wrong?'

'No,' I said rather abruptly. 'No, not at all. Please ... call me Caroline.'

Grace looked at me in astonishment.

'Does that seem strange to you?' I asked. 'If it does —'

'Not really,' she murmured, 'it's just that most people like to keep up the barriers. They get to call me Grace, but I have to address them as "Miss" or "Madam" or "My Lady" ... I'll call you Caroline when we're alone; I could get the sack for being too familiar.'

'Even with me?' I was incredulous.

'Well, it's obvious that we're not of the same station,' she said, as if explaining to a child. *We're whispering like conspirators again*, I thought.

'But the more important thing is that we like each other,' I said.

Grace looked at me thoughtfully. 'That's true. I do like you,' she said under her breath.

I almost gasped.

'We've got to go now,' she said, nudging me with her elbow. 'The mistress will think I've led you astray.'

For some reason we both smiled, and as I looked into her eyes I thought I saw some hint of knowingness in her expression. *Or did I just want to see that?* I asked myself as we hurried downstairs. On our journey we passed several maids at work dusting or scrubbing, and they did not even look up at us as we brushed by.

Chapter 3

'The mistress', as Grace had called her, looked up with an air of impatience as I entered the room. She was seated at a desk and had evidently been writing letters or doing accounts. She motioned to a hard chair opposite her.

'Well, Miss Singleton,' she said, with that especially haughty accent that Anglo-Irish gentry seemed to have, 'I'm glad to see you ... finally.'

I bit my lip. A sense of rebelliousness that occasionally welled up inside me prevented me from apologising. I looked down at my thin, pale hands. My fingers were long and slim. Grace had large, warm, capable hands....

'I trust you slept well,' Lady Wilcox continued, with an edge to her voice.

I nodded. Summoning up my courage, I blurted, 'Yes, thank you, Lady Wilcox. Grace was very helpful.'

She snorted. She had one of those cold, set faces with sculpted greying hair that made her look (when her face was still) like a Greek marble statue. Her eyes, I reflected, had a

similarly blank look; it was an impassivity that could turn to
cruelty at any second.

'I should have known Sheridan would delay you. She spends
every spare moment she has gossiping with the others. They've
learned to ignore her, I can tell you. Don't let her distract you.
Frankly, Miss Singleton, she acts as if she's above her station.
And she's far too attractive. She won't last long in this occupation. To be quite honest, I often question her responsibility,
her respectability. One slip and she's out. That goes for all the
staff I employ, Miss Singleton! You have *no idea* how difficult it is
to maintain a well-regulated house.'

Lady Wilcox glanced at the papers on her desk, as if consider-
ing her next speech. I swallowed, fighting the unease I was
feeling. Why had I expected this woman to be understanding
and decent?

'I found her perfectly well-behaved,' I said as forthrightly as I
could. 'I have absolutely no complaints. I didn't mean to single
her out in any way; I was just struck favourably by her.'

Lady Wilcox gave me an incredulous look. She paused,
drumming her beringed fingers on the table.

'You haven't been exposed to many of the Irish, I imagine?'

'No,' I admitted.

'You may be in for a surprise, Miss Singleton. One notable
quality they possess is their slyness. One simply can't trust them
or take them at their word, I've learned that again and again.
Sheridan comes from a deserving family — her mother married
beneath her; the father is a drunkard, like so many lower-class
Dublin men — and my friend Mrs James was good enough to
trouble herself about the situation and recommend the eldest
daughter for a maid's position here. But I've learned not to

expect any gratitude for this kind of thing. Respect, Miss Singleton, is something these people do not feel they owe us, for the most part. I would really advise you to keep your distance.'

I nodded, but some anger must have shone in my eyes, for she looked at me sharply, almost suspiciously.

'Now, you'll want to know your duties. Amelia is eight years old. She will be an easy charge for you, Miss Singleton. I want her taught the basics: improve her reading and writing, a little mathematics, French of course, start her on Latin if you wish.'

'Very well,' I said nervously.

'And I shall monitor her progress. You may also accompany her on walks. She likes to go into the woods, and I do allow that. You can teach her the names of flowers and trees if you have that kind of knowledge. Of course, having grown up in London, you probably haven't much experience of nature.'

Her dismissive tone chilled me. In what I hoped was a firm voice, I replied, 'I studied natural history in school, Lady Wilcox.'

'I see,' she said briskly, shuffling her papers. 'Well, come along: I shall introduce you to my daughter. You will be responsible for her lessons from ten o'clock until five, unless I wish to take her out. That doesn't often happen. As you can tell, I don't have much of a social circle around these parts. We do go down to Dublin for the winter months. You will accompany us then.'

I bent my head, pleased at the thought.

'Weekends are free. There aren't many amusements hereabouts, so you may wish to acquaint yourself with my husband's library. And, of course, you will attend church with us in Drogheda, the nearest town.'

I was tempted to tell her that I no longer went to church, but I did not dare. However, a look of dismay must have flitted across my face. Catching this, Lady Wilcox thought for a moment and added, 'I shall excuse you from church for the next two Sundays, as you will no doubt need to recover from your journey; but after that you *will* be expected to join us, Miss Singleton.'

She rose, and I stood up. I tried to force a smile, but her face remained largely impassive. She was an imposing woman. I was not. But as I looked around the room, with its opulence, its airiness, its signs of wealth, I was not awed either by the room or by Lady Wilcox. *She does not seem happy,* I thought. *I imagine her husband neglects her and her daughter does not love her. I won't be broken down by her coldness to me.*

'You seem quite a self-sufficient young woman, Miss Singleton,' she said unexpectedly. I blushed. I saw myself differently, as sheltered, timid, inexperienced.

'I'm glad you're here; it's a pleasure to have a young Englishwoman about the place.'

'Thank you, Lady Wilcox.' I hoped I sounded grateful. I felt more relief than gratitude. Her icy coldness had its limits.

I followed her out the door, trembling slightly. I was on the way to meet my charge. I tried to feel governess-ish. I felt like a fraud.

We passed Grace on the stairs. She was shining the banister, rubbing furiously. She glanced up at me, and her eyes brightened. As Lady Wilcox swept on ahead, I shot Grace a faint smile, and she winked. The smell of wood-polish had never seemed so sweet.

~

Amelia was a good little girl, her curly blond tresses tied back with a bow. Her fixed, curious stare rattled me a bit, but I tried to be pleasant and a little jolly without losing an edge of strictness. Weren't governesses supposed to be strict?

The room that we were in had been designated the school-room. I liked it. It was a sunny, peaceful room with pictures of horses on the walls. There was a blackboard. Amelia showed me a box full of counting-blocks, books, and other instructional games designed for young children. Lady Wilcox pointed out where the paper and pens were kept. She told me when Amelia would take lunch, and I realised that Amelia and I would be dining together.

'You'll take supper in the servants' quarters,' Lady Wilcox said in a bored voice. She moved out of the room with surprising speed. Amelia, who hardly seemed to notice her mother's absence, sat me down in a chair and began telling me about the family. I listened with interest, asking questions and making her laugh.

'You do know that Ireland is divided into thirty-two counties and four provinces, don't you?' she prattled. 'This is County Louth. We're very close to the River Boyne, where there was a famous battle in the seventeenth century. Bad King James was defeated — he was a Catholic, you see. All the Irish are Catholics. All the maids are.'

'Do you like the maids?' I asked. I realised that I had an obsessive turn of mind, but Amelia was quite happy to oblige me.

'I like three of them.' I smiled; children were so particular. 'Grace is my favourite. Who's yours?'

'I think Grace is my favourite too,' I said, smiling. It was absurd: my heart was beating slightly faster at the mention of her name!

'I like you,' Amelia said suddenly. She looked at me rather plaintively, her golden locks framing her stolid little face. 'You're a lot nicer than Nurse. She treats me like a baby and won't tell me anything.'

'Thank you, dear,' I said, smiling. Perhaps children were nicer than adults, after all; perhaps I was lucky to be working with a child. We started our lesson.

~

As the afternoon sun streamed in through the tall windows, I realised that my day was nearly over. It had gone fast. Of course, there had been the interlude with Lady Wilcox in the morning, and I had slept late; but it seemed that I could get used to the rhythm of this life.

The woman who knocked on the door was not Grace, but Amelia's nurse, come to take her up to tea. 'Goodbye, Miss Singleton!' Amelia cried gaily as she followed the tired, matronly woman away. 'I'll see you tomorrow.'

I tidied up the books and pens, feeling rather sad. I could not help comparing my rather lonely childhood to Amelia's pampered one. Of course, Ralph had been a great comfort, but there had been times when I was left alone with my mother, reading to her, bringing her tea; those had been dreary hours as I tried to distract her from her endless pain and worry about the future.

Mother would not miss me, I thought. Her greatest tragedies were the death of her husband and the recent death of her son. I simply had not figured very strongly in her life. It was always a surprise when other people noticed me, when people seemed sincerely interested in my well-being. Like Mrs Grimsby. I smiled, thinking of her, but with a touch of bitterness. If I'd had a strong and loving maternal figure, if my father had not died, I would not be here in a strange house, taking care of somebody else's child.

I thought of what Lady Wilcox had said about Grace's family. She did seem like an eldest daughter, I mused, quietly and efficiently providing comfort and support. She would make some man a wonderful wife.... At this my heart contracted, but I firmly pressed on with the thought. Yes, she would make some man an excellent wife.

I sat at a desk, idly sketching a picture — something I liked to do in my spare time. The face I was sketching was Grace's, I realised with a slight shock. *Oh, well....* I continued the drawing, becoming more and more focused on my task. She had such a pretty mouth!

Suddenly I felt a hand on my shoulder. I started back in surprise.

'Grace!' I said, embarrassed. 'I was just —'

'Just drawing, were you?' Her voice was teasing, thank goodness. I put my hand on the paper, but she brushed it aside.

'It's you,' I said, trying to control my nervousness. 'I'm no artist — I mean, I'm very bad....'

Grace stared at the picture for a few seconds. I tried to read the expression on her face. It was difficult. She seemed serious enough, but not angry or offended.

Drawing up a chair, she sat down opposite me. We faced each other over the desk. I tried to look calm, though I did not feel it. It seemed that I had revealed too much; but perhaps she only saw it as a flattering gesture?

'You've made me look beautiful,' Grace said.

But you are — it was on the tip of my tongue. I could think of nothing to say, but finally I murmured, 'I thought I captured you well.'

There was an even longer silence. I could see Grace did not quite know what to say; neither did I. We just looked at each other for a moment. There was something tremendously open about her gaze. The expression in her eyes was gentle.

'I'm supposed to take you down to dinner,' she said at last.

'Oh, are you my escort?' My nervous joke did the trick: she looked at me rather oddly and smiled.

'The servants eat very well here. We'll fatten you up,' she said briskly. 'Do you see how heavy I am? I certainly wasn't before I came.'

'I don't think I'll ever put on any weight. It just doesn't seem to work.' I realised with a twinge of shame that I was playing on her sympathies — the poor, thin English girl — when in fact her background had no doubt been much, much harsher than mine.

'Can I keep this?' She held up the drawing. I nodded. She folded it up and slipped it into her pocket, a faint smile on her lips.

Chapter 4

The kitchen in the servants' quarters was far too rowdy for my liking. Grace brought me a heaped plate of food and I began to eat with downcast eyes, grateful that no one was bothering to introduce me. We sat at a table with two other maids, both about ten years older than us. They looked a little uncomfortable at my presence, I thought, rather intimidated and inhibited. But I had been instructed to eat below stairs. There was nothing I could do.

Grace's presence was a comfort. Occasionally she would ask a question in a low voice, and I would respond. She nudged me gently with her elbow once. I looked up. A plump man with pursed lips stood by our table. The butler.

'Everything all right so far, Miss Singleton?'

'Oh, yes,' I assured him. He reminded me of an uncle in Manchester, a wealthy man whom we rarely saw, and who had responded grudgingly after my father's death with a small gift of money.

'I see Grace is taking care of you,' Mr Johnson said. There was something sarcastic in his tone. I smiled politely.

Looking up, Grace said, 'Is there anything else, Mr Johnson?' There was an edge of hostility in her voice, and like a whipped dog he turned about and left us, scowling.

I glanced at her questioningly, but she just shrugged. The clatter of plates and the hum of voices, especially from the men, were beginning to bother me. I felt slightly afraid. Did the men and women here dislike me because I was English? I did not know. I thought that trying to be as unobtrusive as possible was probably a wise decision.

~

About a week later, we were finishing dinner when Grace asked me hesitantly if I would like to take a walk with her. I noticed that she was blushing slightly, and I blushed too. I knew that I would never have had the courage to suggest it.

'Oh, yes,' I said at once.

We stepped outside the house. I drew deep breaths. The air was cool, not yet chill, and smelt deliciously fresh. I had just eaten a large meal, and yet I felt full of energy. We began walking down the gravelled drive together, and suddenly I wished (not for the last time) that we could walk out of Thornley Hall together. If only there were some way! The kitchen had been so claustrophobic; it had brought home to me the humiliating fact that I was simply a servant, nothing more, even if I was treated well. I could not leave of my own will. That would signal disgrace.

After we were out of sight of the house, Grace took my arm. Meadows stretched out on either side of us; we were separated from them by tall hedges, long grass and brush. Occasionally a small animal rustled somewhere at the side of the road. Our boots crunched firmly into the gravel. We heard cattle lowing not far away, and the bleating of sheep.

I turned to Grace, my eyes shining. 'We're quite deep in the countryside.'

'You didn't know?' Grace said, smiling. 'If you like the countryside, you'll love it here. I'm going to show you my favourite spot.'

'All right,' I said. I felt younger, suddenly, and free. I had a sudden impulse to run. 'When you were a little girl, did you turn cartwheels?'

'Yes,' said Grace, after a moment. 'I remember. But I wasn't good at it. Not light enough. I can see you would have been, though.'

'I was,' I said with a laugh. 'Ralph and I used to do them for hours.'

I bent my head. I hardly ever referred to him in casual conversation now.

'Your brother? Is he ...'

'He's dead,' I said harshly, eyes averted from her. It gave me a lonely sensation to say it, almost a chill.

'I'm sorry,' she said, after a while. Then, 'It's strange....'

'What do you mean?' I said. I looked at her almost coolly, for I imagined her having several brothers, all safe and well in Dublin.

'My brother Jack is ... well, not in the Army, but it's something called the Irish Citizen Army. I worry about him being arrested.'

'I don't know anything about it,' I admitted. So her brother had joined some rebel organisation, while mine had died for

England. There was some irony in this, I thought, but I could not pinpoint it. I knew that I felt little sympathy for their cause. Freedom was a noble thing, but I thought it could be established by political means. My father had been a supporter of Home Rule for the Irish. But I knew nobody who felt any more strongly about it than that.

'Yes, it must be a worry,' I said. I still felt detached, almost irritated by this tangent. I stole a glance at Grace. She was rather pale.

'I haven't told anybody else here about it,' she said. 'It's not something I tell lightly. You see ... I think there's going to be a rebellion.'

I didn't respond, frightened at the thought of her having this knowledge and, even more, at the fact that she was telling *me* about it.

She sighed. A careworn look had come into her face. As we walked her hand brushed against mine — first once, then twice. Without thinking, I took her hand in mine and clasped it.

She smiled. Pulling her hand away gently, she said, 'Well, you're a great comfort to me, Caroline.'

'Even though I'm English,' I joked, though I wasn't sure it was so funny.

Grace said nothing, but pointed to a stream that had opened up on one side of the drive. We crossed a little stone bridge and sat down on a bench near the water.

'I like to come here in the summer and bathe my feet,' she said.

'It's beautiful.'

'You can take Miss Amelia here.'

'That's a good idea.'

We were silent, then. Looking down at her hand, lying by mine on the bench, I had the strange urge to stroke it.

As if she guessed my intent, she gave me a rather sweet smile. 'You're not the typical Englishwoman, are you?'

'There is no typical Englishwoman,' I said, a little embarrassed. 'I do hope that Lady Wilcox isn't one.'

Grace looked at me warmly. I felt a little frightened. Her gaze made me wonder if my feelings might be returned — if not now, perhaps at least at some time in the future. What would that be like?

'I do like you,' she said, as if to herself. I closed my eyes. The words filled me with pleasure, excitement, and a tiny flash of apprehension. We had known each other for only a few days. How could something occur so fast?

'You've probably brought other people here!' I said.

She looked at me earnestly and shook her head.

'So tell me ... why were you so rude to Mr Johnson?'

She grimaced. 'Can't you guess?'

I shook my head, trying not to jump to conclusions.

'We ... well, he took a fancy to me when I first came. He "paid court" to me.'

There was an angry edge to her voice. She looked hurt, though, I thought, as I listened in dismay. 'One night he went over the bounds. Didn't even apologise. I refused to ever go out with him again. The other maids told me that he has a habit of behaving badly with women. There was a scandal once. He got a girl in trouble. She tried to kill herself.'

She spoke the words simply, but it was clear she felt deeply marked by them. 'They didn't sack him, though. They say the girl lost the baby, and went mad.'

'Oh,' I said. I tried to sound worldly and self-assured, but I did not think I was convincing.

'That's why I don't walk out with anyone here. It's just not worth it. Lady Wilcox hates me as it is.'

'She told me you were attractive,' I said teasingly, trying to get her to smile. She looked so dejected. 'Far too attractive for your own good — something like that.'

'She probably thinks all the lower orders should be ugly — just to please her!'

'I don't blame you for being angry,' I said. 'I didn't like Johnson, and I could see you didn't. I was curious as to why. Perhaps it was intrusive of me. I'm sorry.'

Grace looked up at me. 'No, it helps to talk.'

'You're not alone,' I said. I blushed as I spoke the words. And then I did stroke her hand. The touch of her fingertips on my palm made me tingle all over. It felt so intimate, so lovely. But we kept our heads bent; our eyes did not meet.

We were quiet for a long time. All I could hear was the musical sound of the stream rushing over the stones, and the rustling of the wind in the trees. My heart was beating fast. I loved touching her, I realised; but perhaps she only saw it as innocent, friendly. It was better if she did. I knew that in my head, but my heart wanted more.

We talked no more about rebellions that day; we walked up the drive together in companionable silence, our bodies occasionally brushing against each other. I did not think of it until later that night, as I lay in bed trying to sleep, my mind filled with thoughts of Grace. Her anxiety over her brother was something that I could, of course, understand. I just could not bear to remember the months of anxiety I had endured, the months of waiting and praying — and then the dreadful day the telegram had arrived.

I will try to listen to Grace, I thought, *but we each have battles we must fight alone.* I felt as if a line had been crossed that day. I had never stroked a woman's hand before. How I had wanted to take her in my arms!

I buried my face in the pillow. I had tried so hard to tell myself — I had, at first, truly believed — that what I was looking for in Grace was a friend, a comrade, the sister I had never had. But this desire to touch her, to press my lips to her hand, her hair ... this, I knew, was not what friends or sisters felt for one another. The feelings that surged up inside me when I saw Grace were feelings that, I had always been told, could only exist between a man and a woman.

Yet I knew that, impossible as it seemed, I was falling in love with Grace. And I knew that I could not prevent myself. It was too late.

Chapter 5

The house was in a bustle, as Lady Wilcox was holding her annual garden party. It had been postponed until September, Grace told me, because she particularly wanted her nephew, a young man on leave from the Front, to attend. There would be a cricket match, children for Amelia to play with, and other governesses for me to meet. Sir John was tied up with business at Dublin Castle, the centre for British administrative rule in Ireland, and could not attend.

Several weeks had gone by quickly, and I felt almost content with my new life. London, and my mother, seemed a world away. Thornley was like a rest cure in comparison to the deadening hours spent caring for her in Camden Town. Luckily her neighbour, Mrs Potts, had promised me before I left that she would look in on her every day. I had even received the first letter from my mother.

My dear Caroline,

I trust this letter finds you well, and that you had a safe journey. Things here are much the same. I visit the library, tend to the garden when I feel well enough, and go to church with Mrs Potts. I have been reading over some of your brother's letters. Like your father, he had a gift for words. I don't know if I can ever recover from the loss of my son. I know you lost a brother, but I had so many hopes for Ralph. Now I shall never see grandchildren, I'm afraid.

I was talking it over with Mrs Potts and she agreed that the young today are very selfish and headstrong. Especially the girls, she said. She has three daughters — one works in a munitions factory and the other two are doing other war work, I forget what. They are all walking out with young men and none of them seem to want to get married. Mrs Potts is afraid that they are wasting their youth. They tell her that marriage means babies and they're quite happy as they are. It wasn't like that in our day. A girl was grateful to be married. It does worry me, dear, to think that you may not marry and that you don't seem to regard religion as important. Once that goes, all sorts of modern ideas can creep in. All the same, perhaps this Irish jaunt of yours will help you to see how much you do miss London. I won't say anything about missing me, as I am trying not to be a burden.

I do appreciate having a little more money now you are gone, but really, dear, it's not a question of money. You know that. As Mrs Potts said, it's tragic that these girls think they have to go out and earn their living like men. It sends the wrong message. I didn't dare tell her you were once a suffragette — or sympathised with them, I'm not sure of the difference. Of course, that was just a whim of youth. At any rate, one doesn't hear much about them now.

Your loving mother

My mother's letters always had a rambling air to them, I mused, as I sat in my bedroom on the morning of the party. And yet her words stung. I was somewhat amazed — and a little chilled — by her mention of the suffragette movement. It was true: I had attended a march organised by the Pankhursts in London, three years before, with my brother and my schoolmate Violet. We all very much believed that women should get the vote. I had been forbidden to join the marchers, but Ralph and I and Violet had linked arms and stood in a jeering crowd on the sidelines. My heart had leaped with excitement as I saw a young woman lobbing a stone through the windows of the War Office. She was carted away by two burly policemen. We had not even told Mother about that. She had been scandalised all the same, and looked at me with a pained expression when I came in that evening. I remembered Ralph and me sitting down to tea in high spirits, and my mother in her severe black dress handing me the daily paper, in which there was a cartoon of several grotesque-looking women. The caption underneath read, 'Suffragettes who have never been kissed.'

My face had burned. I passed it across the table to Ralph, who had immediately laughed and said lightly, 'But there were plenty of girls at the march today whom I should have liked to kiss, Mother!' This retort had mollified my mother. She had left us to eat our dinner in peace. Ralph and I had joked about it; he suggested that if I did ever kiss anyone I should tell her immediately. I giggled and said I would.

No wonder Ralph was so cheerful around that time, I thought. He had had everything to look forward to: he was working towards a scholarship to Oxford, he had friends, a loving family, good looks and excellent health. But most of all, and far more than I, he had loved life. I could recognise this now as I felt in myself some stirrings of youth and happiness, some lifting of the gloom into which his death had plunged me.

I was glad, however, that Mother had not mentioned Violet. Violet and I had attended the North London Collegiate School together, along with other serious young girls destined to be teachers and governesses. When I left she had stayed on to take the teacher-training course. She had wanted me to take it with her, had disapproved of my going to Ireland. She saw it as a hysterical gesture on my part, because of my brother's death. She also thought I was abandoning my mother, that it 'looked bad'. This had led to coldness between us.

Mother liked to throw it in my face that Vi was engaged to a young officer. I had only met him once, and had not liked him. He was blond, like Vi, and utterly conventional. It was galling that he was alive while Ralph was gone, but I knew I could not afford to think like this. Ultimately, I pitied them all, even this unfortunate nephew of Lady Wilcox who was expected to show up for a formal social occasion and pay court to young ladies, while his mind must be full of terrible sounds and images. But perhaps I saw things too dramatically.

A knock on the door startled me out of my reverie. Lady Wilcox appeared, clad in pale yellow, a tight smile on her face.

'Miss Singleton, I wanted to let you know that people will be arriving at noon, and that you should make yourself comfortable and, of course, enjoy the refreshments. Do you like cricket?'

'Er — well, I actually haven't ...' I stammered.

'Oh, you must watch the match, then. My nephew Captain Philpott is a fine cricketer. I'm so pleased to be able to see him play myself. The servants will have to play too, we're so short of young men. Now, what are you going to wear?'

I opened the wardrobe and showed her a white muslin dress, the only piece of clothing that I thought might do for this occasion.

'But I don't have a sash,' I admitted.

'Oh, excellent, excellent,' she said, looking at it critically. 'Don't bother with the sash. And a hat? Yes, that's perfect. Yes.... Now, you won't paint your face, will you? I see young girls doing that more and more, and I must say I'm quite repelled.'

She exited the room as swiftly as she had come in.

~

Lady Wilcox need not have feared that I would be a flamboyant, distracting presence at her party. I slipped shyly downstairs at the appointed time, plainly dressed, with only a touch of powder. Traps clattered up the drive and car tyres crunched on the gravel, and as I walked out the door I was fascinated by the sight of elegant women stepping down from motors, unwinding dusty motor-veils, kissing their hostess on the cheek, or sometimes on both cheeks, as the men stood around idly, lighting cigarettes. The air was full of 'darlings' and effusive welcomes. Young women wore short-sleeved frocks like mine, but with blue or rose satin sashes and flowers fixed to their chests, and glossy hair pinned loosely under delicate hats. Everybody seemed to know everybody. I watched the scene from a distance, with a strange sort of ache.

I felt someone at my shoulder and turned my head slightly. It was Grace, holding a tray of drinks. She smiled at me.

'Pretty, aren't they?' she said in a low voice, looking at the young women.

'Oh, I wasn't really —'

'Yes, you were,' she said teasingly. 'That's all right.'

I laughed nervously.

'D'you want a drink?' she asked. 'Go on.'

'But I don't think —'

'Yes, go on,' she said. 'The first one should be for you.'

I took one of the elegant, fluted glasses of champagne.

'I wish we could both have one,' I murmured. She smiled and gracefully made her way through the throng.

I gulped the drink quickly. I had never had champagne, but I was grateful for the sudden lessening of tension I felt. I noticed that the drinks were for the men and the married women: young ladies were expected to refrain. But Grace had made sure *I* got one.... The sun had burst through the clouds, and as I wandered down the lawn where the guests were mingling around a long table I felt a sense of exhilaration. I was free. For the first time in my life, I felt that I could do as I liked. Of course, I couldn't; it was an illusion, I was being watched like a hawk, no doubt. But still, I thought, for this moment, for this precious moment ...

'Excuse me.' A sharp-faced girl poked me in the side with her parasol. Coming down to earth, I gazed at her curiously.

'I'm Vera. Vera Lee. I believe you're Amelia Wilcox's governess?'

'Yes. Caroline Singleton.'

I set my glass down on the table, noticing her glance at it, and we shook hands formally.

'I'm the Keanes' governess. Two girls — quite a handful.' She gestured to two plump sisters who were giggling over a young man in cricket flannels. 'I really think they shouldn't have been brought today. They're too young for all this flirting and carrying on.'

'I suppose it's their mother's decision,' I said vaguely. I found Vera a bore. I wondered where she was from and whether she was a clergyman's sister.

'I'm from the Wicklow area. Greystones,' she proffered. 'I do miss it, I must say. Only an hour on the train to Dublin.'

'I still haven't been to Dublin,' I told her. 'Except the evening I arrived, in the dark.'

'Really? Well, my brother went to Trinity, so I was always up in Dublin going to temperance lectures, plays and so on. There's absolutely nothing here, don't you find?'

'Yes, but it's restful, isn't it?' *I really do feel peaceful today*, I mused. I knew I was a little tipsy, too, but I liked it. It seemed to ease my nerves.

Vera scowled. 'Yes, I suppose it is if you live in a huge house like this. In the Keanes' place I have to share a room with the servant girl.'

I couldn't help smiling.

'Do you find that funny? How odd. Well, it's even worse: she's a Catholic and says the rosary every night before bed. Sometimes I can't stand that horrid mumbling. I feel like throttling her.'

I glanced around for Grace, but could not see her.

'Perhaps we could meet at church on Sundays? I presume you go to church in Drogheda.' I looked blankly at Vera for a minute until I remembered that Lady Wilcox had mentioned that Drogheda was the nearest town. I had actually learned about it in a history class at school, because Oliver Cromwell had carried out a brutal massacre of the townspeople there when he was Governor of Ireland in 1649. Apparently the Irish had never forgotten. But I didn't expect Vera would want to go into such matters.

I shook my head. 'No, I actually haven't — not yet, at any rate. I've only been here a couple of weeks.'

'And you haven't asked Lady Wilcox?'

'Well, no. I'm not ... terribly religious.' Actually, I had been hoping that Lady Wilcox had forgotten.

Vera looked at me in surprise. Then a certain pitying look flashed into her eyes.

'My mother was reproaching me for it in a letter today, as a matter of fact,' I said rather uncomfortably.

'Don't you miss it? For one thing, it's the only place to meet people like us.'

I paused. I supposed I should try to befriend this woman, but I felt I had nothing in common with her. I was still warmed by Grace's flirtatiousness — for it had been that, hadn't it? Nothing about Vera interested me.

'Have you seen the shrubbery?' I asked, dipping a strawberry into a bowl of thick, sweetened cream. She shook her head.

'I think I'm going to take a stroll there. Would you like to come?'

I hoped she would say no, but she seemed glued to my side. We walked together into the shade and comparative quiet of the shrubbery. Quite soon we came across a group of three portly women sitting on a rug together, eating sandwiches.

Vera clapped her hands. 'Oh, I must introduce you! These are my friends Bertha, Doris and Eliza.'

The women smiled and nodded to me.

'Sit down, Vera, and tell us the latest gossip,' one of them said. 'She's so sharp, you know.'

Vera collapsed eagerly onto the rug. I knew that as soon as I moved on I would probably be one of the subjects of her gossip — I had told her I wasn't religious! Well, never mind, I thought. I smiled at them and wandered deeper among the laurels and rhododendrons. The shrubbery itself seemed to tail off as I moved further into the sun-dappled wood.

It was deliciously warm. I could still hear the partygoers shouting in the distance — it was peculiar how the upper classes seemed to need to shout at one another. And yet so little was said. I sank down against a tree and rested my head on the bark. I would bring Amelia out here to sketch, I decided; there was plenty to draw, and I did not think it was good for either of us to be cooped up inside so much. Even though high summer had passed, the weather was still lovely. What did the Americans call it? Indian summer. Everything seemed to float around me, and I was glad I had not sat down with the other women, for in this pleasurable state of tipsiness I was capable of saying exactly what I felt.

I was dreamily examining a leaf when I heard footsteps. A young man in flannels was coming in my direction, on his way back towards the throng. He was smoking a cigarette. We smiled at each other. He had a pleasant, angular face with dark-blond hair.

'Rex Philpott,' he said, surprising me. 'I think I saw you last night.'

'Caroline Singleton,' I said. 'I'm Amelia's governess.'

'Ah, yes.'

He paused as if not sure whether to go on, tapping another cigarette into his palm.

'I suppose you don't smoke? Beastly habit.'

I stood up. 'Well, as I had champagne today for the first time, I might as well smoke.'

'Mmm,' he said pleasantly, lighting one for me. I noticed that his fingers trembled slightly, and when I glanced at his face I saw that his light-blue eyes were unfocused. He blinked often, as if trying to clear his vision.

We smoked for a few minutes. I coughed a little, but found that if I took short puffs it was surprisingly soothing and pleasant. I knew I was still under the lulling influence of the champagne, for I found myself wanting to tackle a subject that was on everybody's mind these days, but which was almost never touched on in polite conversation.

'Well, I suppose I can't ask you how the War's going,' I said. 'It seems that it's much the same.'

Rex Philpott nodded. 'Nobody ever asks. You're the first person who's mentioned it today.'

I shrugged. 'My brother was killed, so I talk about it when I get the chance.'

'I'm sorry to hear that,' he said. He sounded genuinely sorry. 'What was his name?'

'Ralph. I'm sure you wouldn't —'

He paled. 'My God. Ralph Singleton?'

'Yes!' I stared at him in shock. Hearing my brother's name on his lips was strange and disconcerting. 'You knew him?'

'He was in my regiment. I never expected —' He paused for a little while and then said in a low voice, 'I was his commanding officer. I wanted to write after it happened, but I was wounded myself. We lost so many.'

I put my hand on his arm. I seemed to need to hold on to something, or someone. I felt myself reeling, and I could see that he was none too steady himself. I wondered how much he had been drinking today to calm his nerves. Yet it never occurred to me to doubt his words. I was thrilled that I had been given the extraordinary luck to meet someone who had fought beside my brother.

'Did you join up at Oxford, like Ralph?' I asked.

He nodded. 'Yes. I wish I had known him at Oxford. We were in different colleges, and of course I moved with the sporty set.' He touched his flannel shirt and said with a slightly mocking air, 'I'm still playing the game.'

I wanted to ask him how Ralph had died. Nobody ever knew; one just got a telegram and wanted to believe that the end was swift. I had thought about it many times, wondering why he couldn't have been wounded and sent home, why a young man who seemed so lucky should have received no mercy. I had not told Vera this, but I had believed in God for most of my life, up until the point when my brother had been snatched away.

'It was a filthy mess,' he said bitterly. 'But if I had written, Caroline — may I call you that?'

I nodded.

'I would have told you how much we all liked him. He just went in there and did what he had to do. And full of jokes. Full of life.'

'How did he die? Do you know?' I asked, clearing my throat and looking Rex in the face. I wanted the truth, and I felt I was strong enough to hear it now, six months after Ralph's death.

He paused and looked down. I could tell that it was enormously hard for him to unearth these memories, that he was keeping himself sane out of habit, upbringing and temperament, and that these things were only just enough. I sensed a fragility much greater than my own.

'I held him after he died. It was quick, Caroline. One minute he was standing up, saying something to me — we were in a foxhole together, you know — and the next ... a bullet came. He fell back and I crawled over to him. He was gone. I stayed with him until the medics came. Then we got orders to march towards the enemy lines. It was pouring rain. I thought, *This is it.* I really felt my number was up. I kept tripping and falling in the mud. So did everybody else. Men next to me were being shot to pieces. I felt a burning in my leg, looked down, saw the wound, and collapsed. I was lucky not to drown in the mud.'

Tears slid out of my eyes and I bowed my head on his shoulder. I felt the warmth of his breath against my hair. We stood together for a while. I felt that my brother was with us — it was a strange sensation. A comforting one.

'I can't really tell you what it's like over there,' Rex said suddenly. 'But coming here — being in Ireland like this — it's as if it were a dream.'

'Like a brief respite from hell, do you mean?' I murmured, stepping back a little. I was a little ashamed of my tears and I wondered how I must look. Yet I felt cleansed by them. Everything was very clear and, as yet, not terribly painful. I had the oddest impression that Rex Philpott and I were supposed to meet. He seemed like an old friend already.

He looked surprised. 'Nobody seems to know, or want to know, what it's like over there. I suppose they don't want to believe that sort of horror can exist. But I can tell you, it's blown all my old ideas about King and Country out of the water. At this point, I'm doing it for *them*.'

'The men?' I said.

'Yes. My men.'

He looked around rather wildly at the peaceful wood.

'But all of this — you begin to see what isn't real. The chattering women out there — my aunt, blithering on about cricket — it's all a sham. I looked at her servants yesterday and I thought, "They'll stick knives in your back one night." And they should, if they had any pride.'

He smiled bitterly. 'You must think I'm mad.'

'No,' I assured him, though I had begun to feel jittery myself.

'I don't believe I'm going to survive this. I certainly don't deserve to, above anybody else.'

I didn't know what to say. He lit another cigarette for me and one for himself.

'It's going to change everything, this war,' he muttered. 'I don't see that this nonsense can go on, all this....'

He looked straight at me suddenly, with a clear and intense gaze.

'You don't look like him.'

I met his eyes. It occurred to me that he found me attractive. I felt very straightforward with him, as if we were comrades. It wasn't romantic, but I was drawn to him, as I could tell my brother had been.

'Ralph was very good-looking,' I said, 'and people loved him, but he never had anyone special, as far as I know.' It was a question phrased in the form of a statement, and I hoped Rex would respond.

'Things happen quickly at the Front,' he replied.

'Do they?'

Our smoke ascended to the trees. Perhaps he had loved my brother, as I loved Grace; perhaps nothing had been said.

He blushed.

'Yes. You shouldn't worry too much about your brother in that way.'

I felt an enormous sense of relief, of childlike happiness: at least something had gone right for Ralph in those last days. My face must have glowed, for Rex gently put his hand on my shoulder. He looked vulnerable, and I knew he had told me more than he had ever intended. I sensed that in the next second he would kiss me and I felt suspended, locked in his gaze in a way I had never experienced, nor expected to. He had given me so much. I felt myself leaning towards him, wanting to erase all distance between us. Our lips met in the briefest touch.

'Rex, dear!' It was Lady Wilcox herself, breaking in on us like a smiling demon from quite a bit away. 'Aren't you coming to the match? We're all waiting.'

'Sorry, Aunt Julia,' her nephew said briskly, abandoning his cigarette and moving a few steps in her direction. 'I was just talking to Miss Singleton about the War. It turns out that her brother and I fought together.'

'I see,' she said, casting a look at the still-burning cigarette in my hand. 'Are you coming, Miss Singleton?'

'In a moment, Lady Wilcox.' I could hear my voice quaver and hated it. They moved away. I stood leaning against the tree, trying to conjure my brother's presence back. But he was gone.

~

I had retreated to my room after the cricket match, which had dragged on for what seemed like many hours, and which I knew I had to endure as stoically as possible. I felt Lady Wilcox's cold eyes on me many times. After he had been bowled out, Rex had sauntered past me, dropped to one knee, and ventured under his breath, 'I say, Caroline, may I write to you?' 'Of course,' I'd replied, and he'd given me a grateful look. I wondered what those letters might contain — more details of my brother, perhaps, if I was lucky? But I had a presentiment that I would get a letter soon, not from him, but from someone else, saying he was gone. I hoped not.

The alcohol had worn off. I felt the sadness of it all: my brother's quick, meaningless end, Rex's disintegration, my inability to help him, and my own aching sense of loss, which I feared would never completely heal. To keep myself from feeling utterly black, I was sketching my brother's face. As I drew, a million little memories came back to me and I was completely absorbed. I barely heard the door open.

'Caroline,' said Grace rather breathlessly, 'look.' She came in with a flushed face, carrying a bottle of champagne. 'I was clearing up and found an unopened bottle!'

'Oh Grace, I'm not sure I should,' I said at once. 'Just the one glass you gave me earlier made me tipsy, and —'

'Yes, I noticed you disappearing into the shrubbery,' she said teasingly. 'I heard all the gossip about your conquest. Is that him?'

She came and stood by my side.

'No, that's my brother,' I said. 'They served together in France. I found it out today. That's what we were talking about.'

She put her hand on my shoulder. I let it rest there.

'Don't be sad,' she said gently.

'You must think it's morbid.'

'No, I don't at all.'

She used a towel to open the champagne and filled my tooth-mug to the brim. I couldn't help laughing.

'Would you like to draw me?' she asked, as we shared sips from the mug. 'I have the rest of the day off.'

'Well, I ...'

'I posed for an artist in Dublin once or twice. Not in the altogether,' she added.

'You'd better lock the door, then,' I said. My body had begun to buzz with a peculiar kind of nervousness. What was she up to? Her words had summoned up the unfortunate image of her lovely body draped over a sofa, being leered at by a lecherous artist in spectacles. *Perhaps I am the lecher here,* I thought ruefully.

Grace locked the door and began taking off her heavy, dark uniform. I tried not to stare too much as she unbuttoned her blouse. Soon all she had on was a cream-coloured shift, which did not come to her knee. She had peeled off her stockings and her legs were bare.

'How would you like me?' she asked.

I bit my lip, not sure what to say. 'Well, you could lie on the bed ...'

She lay on my bed, on her back, one leg over the other, with her hands behind her head. The angle of her arms accentuated the line of her breasts. As I looked at her, with a flushed face, I imagined peeling the thin silky fabric from her body. What I could see was beautiful.

'You know, when I was a kid,' she said casually, 'there was a huge scandal in Dublin because they used the word "shift" in a play.'

'I'm not surprised,' I blurted out. I began to sketch her, more out of nervousness than anything, using firm, rapid strokes.

'So nothing happened with your man in the wood?' she queried.

'You're not supposed to be talking,' I responded.

'Ah, you don't mean that,' she murmured.

I laughed despite myself. 'Grace, are you jealous?'

She looked at me seriously. 'Maybe I am,' she said, after a while.

I had not expected that she would be so honest.

'You know you don't have any reason to be,' I said softly.

She nodded, and seemed to drift into her own thoughts. I continued sketching as the sky slowly dimmed outside. She lay very still, a slight smile on her lips.

Everything is planned, I thought to myself. Grace's warmth seemed to stem from the same desire that I had felt in the wood, and that Ralph must have felt in those dark and dreary days before he died: the desire to connect with another person, even very briefly, in a situation where so much disconnection exists, and where the rules dictate otherwise. *If I hadn't come here*, I realised as I worked, more steadily now, *I would never have met Captain Philpott. I would never have known that my brother was loved before he died, that he found someone. That is the most important thing in life*, I thought: *to have someone who understands. So it was Fate that drew me here.* And to find Grace seemed like Fate as well, working towards some end that I couldn't yet know. I only wished I could trust that it would be good.

'Do you believe some things are meant to be, Grace?' I asked.

'Yes,' she said. 'I really do.'

Chapter 6

*A*melia was soon devoted to me. Each day she bounded into the schoolroom, all eagerness and cheerfulness. With such a dedicated pupil, I became more confident and more imaginative in the lessons I set her. She particularly loved tracing maps, and could do this for hours. While she drew, I daydreamed, feeling like a foolish schoolgirl. I dreamed of little things: running my fingers through Grace's hair, kissing her, feeling her breasts press against mine.... I constantly thought about purity, wondering how it had eluded me, how from the beginning my feelings had been impure and unwholesome. I had imagined myself to be a fairly pure and wholesome person, and I had always congratulated myself on not falling in love, not being tempted to sin with another person. But a member of my own sex! How could I possibly ...

Even at school, I had never experienced the adolescent crushes or 'pashes' that the older girls often seemed to inspire in the younger ones. There had been friendships, but for some reason — perhaps because I had felt nervous about bringing friends home to the depressing atmosphere of our house — they had never reached the 'special' stage that the other girls sometimes whispered about. And I had wondered what that intensity would be like, but had been resigned not to experience it; I had thought of myself as rather plain and cold, unlikely to create feelings of attraction in another.

So I had never expected to be seriously tempted. I had always assumed that nothing I would ever want to do would seriously transgress the moral codes of my middle-class upbringing, even though I believed that there was a higher code than the one I had been taught in school and at home, a higher allegiance one owed to oneself and one's own feelings. But then one could go very wrong, couldn't one? I asked myself. One could behave scandalously, be completely immoral ... and lose one's reputation, the respect of friends and family.

But I'm alone. The thought came into my mind for once as a delicious relief. *I'm accountable to no one....*

Many times in the first few weeks after my arrival at Thornley, as I stood in front of Amelia's glossy, bowed head and watched her lips pressing together in concentration, I had thought that what would save me was the fact that Grace would want nothing to do with me in that way. At the most she would want a friend. And I should be grateful for that. But naturally she was an innocent girl who would never even have *dreamed* of the things I had been contemplating. Maybe she had a young man back in Dublin, and she simply had not mentioned him; why should she? We were still practically strangers!

Lately, though, as my feelings for Grace had deepened and come to feel more natural to me, I had questioned why I was being so hard on myself. Wasn't I allowed to love? When men and women were involved outside marriage it was called 'living in sin', but often women lived together and it was seen as deep friendship. Could Grace and I ever live together? Surely she would never want to. I did not dare to ask her whether she saw a future for herself as some man's wife; yet it did strike me as odd that she never mentioned the possibility, never gossiped about men. They seemed to hold no fascination for her.

As if she had her own doubts about my precarious moral state, Lady Wilcox brought up the question of church with chilly promptness the day after the garden party. I was to attend service with the family at St Barnabas's in Drogheda, while the servants, I soon learned, all went to the local Catholic church. There was no chance for me to meet Grace on those Sundays in town. We seemed to have come to a silent agreement that it would attract too much attention. I reluctantly renewed my acquaintance with Vera Lee, and on those dull Sunday afternoons in Drogheda we would sit in a tea-shop and I would tell her about London (she expressed an interest in the Royal Family) or visit the windows of a millinery so she could look at hats. On the second Sunday that we spent together, I managed to slip into a shop and buy a box of paints and an easel. It cost nearly all the money I had brought to Ireland with me, but it was worth it. I wanted to paint a portrait of Grace from the drawing I had done.

Vera was most curious about my purchase. 'You're going to paint for your own *amusement*? How odd. Sometimes I do think you're quite the bohemian, Caroline.' She gave a brittle little laugh.

'I want to do some studies of the house and grounds,' I told her. It was not exactly a lie: I planned to paint a whole series of pictures at Thornley — I would certainly have the time, and it would be much-needed practice. I had excelled in art at school, but of course I had to think of money, and Miss Peabody, the headmistress, had gently discouraged me from applying to an art school. 'Girls from good families are doing it now,' she had admitted, 'but it's not exactly practical, is it, Caroline? I know your poor mother's situation. And, besides, you have a gift for teaching.'

She had seen me as a younger version of herself, I always thought, a learned and virtuous lady dedicated to the instruction of others. But being with Vera brought out a different side of me: rebellious, tomboyish, artistic, unconventional. I wished I had had a more shocking life, so I could tell her wicked tales of my past, but I had to be content with casually mentioning French novels that she had barely heard of but that she knew were 'immoral'. Sometimes I would luridly sketch the plots of these books, which Ralph had surreptitiously supplied me with during his university days, while Vera went into little squeaks of protest at the tea-table. *Madame Bovary*, for example, sent her into a tizzy of outraged propriety, as did Zola's *Nana*.

'I don't wish to hear about these fallen women, Caroline,' she would say priggishly. 'I have enough of that to worry about when Bridget, the servant girl, comes in after an evening with her young man. She insists on telling me the most revolting details. I'm sure one of these days that girl will get in the family way.'

She said this with self-righteous satisfaction, pursing her thin lips. I could imagine her pumping poor Bridget for stories late at night, seeming sympathetic and open-minded. Sometimes I had the suspicion that she was trying to lead me on to greater and greater indiscretions, but I dismissed this as being too far-fetched. Still, I was careful never to speak about Grace. I tried not to discuss Lady Wilcox, either, much as Vera seemed to want me to; I found I could not speak about her without a tone of bitterness and dislike creeping into my voice. 'At least she leaves you alone,' Vera said enviously. 'Mrs Keane is always breathing down my neck. And Lady Wilcox is a real *lady*.'

~

Soon it would be too cold for Grace and me to go for walks. I treasured the brief days, and it seemed she did too, for she took every opportunity to see me. September passed into October, and the leaves began falling from the trees.

Grace often came to my room in the evenings now. She would watch me paint by the light of a flickering candelabrum. As I painted, she would talk, curled up on my bed. She told me about her poverty-stricken childhood in Dublin, her brief schooling, how her father's chronic unemployment and fondness for drink had marked her family, how she hated the contemptuous way she had always been treated by the upper classes — how Lady Wilcox had grilled her about her morals at their first meeting, for example, and seemed unwilling to believe a thing she said. We discussed the fact that we had never had close female friends. Grace said that only having brothers might have made it more difficult. She said she'd always been criticised for being too much of a tomboy; that before she developed she'd had a boyish figure. We laughed at that.

'And I still do,' I said.

'I like that,' she said. She was watching the progress of the painting, which was slow — I wanted to do it just right. 'What are you going to call it?'

'*Grace Reclining on Bed*,' I said. We giggled.

'What about *Grace Reclining on the Artist's Bed*?' she suggested playfully.

'Even more accurate,' I said, blushing. She seemed to like catching me off guard; but, as ambiguous as her words sometimes were, I did not feel confident enough to act on their seductiveness. And what would I do, anyway? I liked the thrill her words produced in me, but I felt a nervousness too. I swallowed, and continued to paint. The girl in the painting was looking down shyly, away from the viewer. An enigmatic smile played on her face.

~

Another evening Grace seemed very tired, so to cheer her up I told her something that I had blurted out to Vera the previous Sunday after church.

'I told her I was a suffragette,' I said, rather proudly. 'Did you know that, Grace? I went to a public meeting, three years ago, where women were throwing stones at the War Office and smashing shop windows on Oxford Street.'

'And what did Miss Vera Lee think of that?' Grace inquired in a sarcastic tone. She didn't seem to like Vera or approve of my association with her.

'Oh, she was horrified. She said that over here in Ireland those ideas aren't half as popular, that Irish women aren't militant and aggressive. And I have to admit that she's probably right.'

'Mmm,' Grace said with a grimace. 'Well, that just shows how much Miss Vera knows. Course, she's a good little Protestant from Greystones, so she doesn't know a damn thing.'

I paused in shock at her tone, paint dripping onto the floor. Hurriedly, I rinsed the brush. It unnerved me that she would criticise Vera so blatantly, even though I was not particularly fond of Vera.

'There's a woman in Dublin who everybody's heard of — except West Britons like your friend Vera — called Countess Markievicz. People call her Madame. She married a Polish count, but before that she came from gentry folk in Sligo — her maiden name was Constance Gore-Booth. She doesn't hide any of that. But about six years ago, when I was thirteen or so and my brother Jack was twelve, she started a youth group called the Fianna Éireann. That means "warriors of Ireland" in Irish — something else your friend wouldn't know. Anyway, she taught Jack and all the young Dublin lads to shoot. She's a great shot.'

'So she's your hero, is she?' I said. I couldn't help a note of sourness from coming into my voice.

'Everyone loves her. She's a socialist and a republican. She's so committed to the struggle. She has the Fianna going down the street, whistling rebel tunes at the policemen, these big beefy fellas swinging batons.' Grace laughed, remembering. 'Jack had so many stories. They'd train every week — in uniforms that were thrown together from any old thing, and caps that they robbed off Baden-Powell's Boy Scouts!'

My brother had been one of the first Boy Scouts, but I did not say so. 'And now?' I asked.

'Oh, Jack's in the Citizen Army now. It's mostly made up of working men, and some women too. It's tiny compared to the

Irish Volunteers, which has thousands of men from all over the country. We're Dublin only. The Countess is one of the leaders of it; James Connolly, the trade unionist, is the president. There's a place called Liberty Hall, on the quays, where they train. A big banner hung outside says, "We serve neither King nor Kaiser, but Ireland." The police are always comin' by and rippin' it down.'

I noticed for the first time that when Grace became impassioned she dropped her final g's. Perhaps I had been too much with Vera lately, for it grated on me.

'Why don't the authorities suppress these organisations?' I asked.

'They don't dare,' Grace said with satisfaction. 'And they don't believe we mean what we say. We're doin' it all right under their noses.'

I rinsed and wiped my brushes. I was unable to work when I heard this troubling tone in her voice — a tone of defiance that seemed to exclude me. This was her world, then. I listened to what she was saying, but I could not find a common ground between our childhoods — hers so rough, deprived, and shot through with a strange undertone of degradation. It was poverty that did it, I thought, the same poverty that had been all around us in Camden Town. But my genteel mother had kept us safe from the worst of it: there had been food, heat, a servant girl to help out when I was younger, books and music.

'I'm surprised you're working here,' I said, trying to keep my voice casual. 'If you feel so strongly ...'

'There's no work in Dublin. That's the reality of it. I'm keeping the whole family going with my wages. Did you know that, Caroline?'

I shook my head.

'It's the one thing me ma can count on. Da will never work

again — he's too far gone with the drink — and my brothers work here and there, but there's no steady work; they're sacked as often as not. Catholics get the shite jobs, if you'll pardon the expression.'

I sat down on a chair opposite her. She was tense, over-wrought, looking at me with a frown. It was a side of her I had not fully glimpsed before: an alien Grace whom I did not quite understand or even like, if I was honest. *Perhaps I just don't want to know*, I thought, *because my people have caused this suffering. And that's the one thing she truly believes. So how can she care about me, seek out my company the way she does? Why does it seem that, despite the fact that I have more in common with Vera, I don't like Vera, and despite the fact that I have almost nothing in common with Grace, I want so much from her?*

I forced myself to question her about the Countess, this obviously fanatical woman with whom Grace seemed so besotted. I was troubled by the jealousy that her words had stirred up inside me. Could she see it?

'How old is the Countess Markievicz?' I asked.

'Oh, she's an older lady, in her forties by now. She's tall and thin and wears little spectacles. But she looks lovely in uniform with her gun. They wear dark-green uniforms, the Citizen Army.'

I found myself breathing easier, despite the uniform comment. I had imagined her to be a beautiful young woman.

'She's so brave!' Grace went on. 'She's been beaten up by the police more than once. Whenever there's a rally in Dublin, you know, the police come out in force and crack heads.' She sounded wistful, and I imagined her sadness at missing all the drama and excitement that was apparently going on in Dublin under the surface.

'So she comes from a landowning family,' I mused. I was not trying to bait her, but this discrepancy had troubled me.

'She was even born in England. But that doesn't matter.' Grace was airy.

'So as long as people believe the right things, the accent doesn't matter, or anything?'

'Nobody cares about that, because she has a good heart. She even goes into the slum tenements and does the washing for people and plants flowers outside.... She used to be an artist when she was young, went to art school in Paris.' Grace's tone was dreamy. 'I know all about her. I even found out about her sister Eva — not many people know this....'

I waited.

'She lives with another lady, in England,' Grace said, blushing. 'In Manchester. They're suffragettes.'

'That's where my uncle lives,' I said, for want of something better to say.

Grace got up to go, smoothing down her uniform as she stood in front of me. We were silent for a minute. Then I murmured, 'Do you think it's wrong, two women living together like that?'

'No,' she said flatly. 'Why would it be wrong?'

'Well, if they ... if they were more than friends. I'm not suggesting that about those two.... I mean, I don't know.'

'I don't know either,' Grace said, smiling. 'We'd have to ask the Countess, and maybe even she couldn't tell us.'

'Or wouldn't,' I joked, desperately relieved at the way my words had been received. I got up, and we stood facing each other.

'Can I have a candle?' Grace asked.

I pulled one of my candles out of the candelabrum and gave it to her. Our hands lingered around the exchange. It reminded me of the first night, when she had lit my candles with her lamp.

'Good night, Caroline,' Grace said.

October was passing into November. Grace did not have much time at the weekends, as I did, so I took Lady Wilcox's suggestion and buried myself in Sir John's library. I could sit by the fire there and escape into a book. Besides the volumes of military history, there were some unexpected gems: a volume of W.B. Yeats's lyric poetry, for example. In Yeats's yearning for his aloof beloved, I found traces of my own longing and confusion. I was still not sure what I wanted to do, or what Grace wanted from me.

Even after all this time, I had not met Sir John, but Grace told me one morning that he would be here the next day.

'He's an advisor to Augustine Birrell, the Secretary for Ireland,' she said. She was sitting and watching me fix my hair. Glancing at myself in the mirror, I saw her looking at me with an odd intensity; but when I turned around quickly, I thought that I was wrong. Her face was relaxed, if solemn.

'I don't know much about Irish politics,' I said. It was my way of trying to ask her not to talk about them, but she invariably did these days. I saw that she was obsessed with the current political situation, caught up in it in a way I could not truly understand. Even after all she had told me, I still found it strange that she should not feel, as I did, that momentous events were outside her control. I had stopped reading about the War, for example.

Nothing had come from Captain Philpott and I did not want to ask Lady Wilcox about it.

'You don't *want* to know,' Grace said thoughtfully. She seemed disappointed in me. I could feel it.

I shrugged. 'It's not my country, Grace.'

'But you're living here.'

'Yes, but nothing important is going to happen. It's all talk. I suppose at the end of the War they'll have to figure out what to do about Ireland. Until then, it seems idle to speculate.' I bit my lip, realising how arrogant I had sounded.

Grace looked at me, and her eyes were cold suddenly. 'You've no stake in what happens, no interest, but I do! My brother sends me letters all the time. I tell you, the rising is on its way, and he's committed to fighting. When we go back to Dublin for the winter, I'm going to be in the thick of all of that. I'm just telling you now.'

I did not know what to say. I felt as if she was drifting away from me. My greatest fear was that she would no longer want to associate with me. I had made clear my disinterest in the country's struggle for independence, which I could not take seriously anyway. The Ireland I had experienced in my short time here was far too stable and comfortable under the British crown for a rebellion! I came and sat down on the bed, my face turned away from her, pale and miserable, angry at myself for feeling such a presentiment of loss.

I felt her sit down beside me on the bed; and then, to my astonishment, she leaned against me, drawing my head down onto her breast. She held me in her arms and pressed her head against mine. I felt her warm breath on my face. I closed my eyes. *If only I did not have to get up and go to Amelia, if only she did not have to return downstairs.....* We could be caught now, and the scandal would be enormous. But I didn't care. And neither, it seemed, did Grace.

'I want us to stay friends,' she murmured.

'But do you think we really can?' I said. 'It has meant so much to me ... it's meant everything.'

'I know,' she said softly. She released me, and I drew back. We looked at each other, not understanding, perhaps, how to resolve this impasse.

A sharp knock on the door sent Grace flying off the bed. I stood up, frightened. She opened the door and Johnson the butler was outside, looking at us sardonically.

'Are you finished with Grace, Miss? She's needed downstairs. As you may know, the master comes back tomorrow, and it's all hands on deck.' His voice was loud, and his politeness seemed false and rather threatening.

'Yes ... she was helping me fix my hair,' I said breathlessly.

He pulled a watch out of his pocket. 'Weren't Miss Amelia's lessons supposed to begin at ten?'

'I'll go up there straightaway.'

As he closed the door I heard him say in sharp, nasty tones, 'You'll pay for this later! I've had enough of your dawdling and wasting time. I don't know what you do for her, but it must be something good!'

I sat down on the bed again, staring blankly at the window. How symbolic it was that the view looked out onto an enclosed courtyard. *This will end soon,* I thought suddenly. *And when it does, you'll want to have something real and concrete to remember. You'll want to know whether she really cared. Otherwise none of this pain will have been worth it.*

~

Grace had been set some punishment that evening and did not appear at dinner. I ate sparingly, wondering if it was just my imagination or if the stares of the other servants were stonier than usual. A plump blonde scullery maid and her friend, a spiteful-looking brunette, sat near me and conversed in low tones, punctuated with brief bursts of laughter. My interest was piqued by the sound of Grace's name, and I listened carefully.

'So he's still mad for her — well, everyone knows it, and she leads him on something terrible. Even goes so far as to become fast friends with her uppers; maybe she thinks that'll help her keep her position. Well, I have it for a fact that he's going to give a report to Lady Wilcox that'll send her packing. He'll say she's been stealing, trying to fill our heads with her nationalist ideas — well, you know the way she talks sometimes....'

The blonde snorted with laughter. 'She puts on airs, thinks too much of herself. Thinks she's royalty, does she? I mean, my uncle knows her da and says he's a common drunkard, and if it's not drink it's loose women, if you know what I'm sayin'.'

'Oh, I do. Worst of it is, she may be staying on. Johnson says he'll make sure she either gets the sack or gives him what he's been waiting for all this time. And she's the type that would do it, she's no saint. Just thinks she's too good for *him*.'

'... Always gets his way,' the blonde put in knowingly.

' ... Heard he's not half bad; at least he knows what he's doin', unlike some here....'

More giggles, and they passed on to something else.

I felt sick. The colour had drained from my face. They were

all against us. *Surely Grace would not surrender to Johnson out of fear of losing her job. It would not be worth her honour, would it?* I thought. The very idea of her having to give herself to that man to buy more time was sickening. But no — I was assuming far too much. What was clear was that our little idyll was coming to an end.

I pushed my plate aside. A walk would do me good. As I opened the heavy front door of Thornley Hall, the bleakness I felt inside was so icy that I welcomed the sudden gust of cold air. I buttoned my coat and pulled on my gloves. I would walk and walk. This time, I would go through the woods. I had waited for Grace to take me there, but she had never wanted to. I wondered about that now. Perhaps she feared being seen with me there, feared that people would gossip....

As I walked quickly down the drive, I cursed the Wilcoxes. Perhaps serving the rich could bring nothing but unhappiness. Of course, I loved Amelia, and recognised her genuine sweetness. But she would be brought up to be a 'great lady' like her mother, to distance herself from all lower forms of human beings.

Grace had been right. Six weeks of eating rich food had put weight on me. I felt larger, stronger. I had probably never been so healthy in my life. I had also never been quite so unhappy. I had begun to miss London, foolish as that seemed. Perhaps I only remembered the good things, I mused: having tea and cakes with my mother and Ralph in a café for a special treat; going to see a moving picture — a cowboys-and-Indians western — and having Ralph tell me approvingly afterwards that I was the kind of girl who could enjoy these adventurous things, that I wasn't prim and proper and vain, constantly primping and crimping, like the girls who showed interest in him. He had never loved a girl. *How sad*, I thought, as tears finally gushed out of my eyes. I had turned off into the woods, and I leaned against a graceful elm tree and sobbed like a baby.

She would return to Dublin, and perhaps she too would die; and it would all be for nothing. And if she survived it, she would hate me for being one of the English, even though I had few patriotic feelings and was not part of the governing class. They would put down any rebellion easily; I did not understand why Grace felt so hopeful. Perhaps determined rather than hopeful.... I rubbed my face against the silky bark of the tree. I felt so powerless.

Chapter 7

---

*T*he knock on the door the next morning gave me a brief rush of hope. 'Yes?' I answered eagerly. But the woman who entered was the plump blonde maid from the night before. Without looking at me, she said, 'I've brought your hot water, Miss.'

'Thank you,' I said shakily. 'Is Grace not ...? I expected Grace.'

'No, Miss, she's been given other duties.'

There was an ominous ring to that. I wanted above all to keep the girl talking, so I found myself asking recklessly, 'Where is she?'

'She's been assigned to the kitchen,' the maid said in dismissive tones. 'Will that be all?'

I could see that I had tested her patience, and I nodded miserably. She walked out, closing the door a little more sharply than necessary.

Her rudeness to me was not surprising, I reflected, given her dislike of Grace and her obvious distrust of me; but it was the kind of treatment I had expected, dreaded, when I came here. To be subjected to it now, when I was so vulnerable, was very painful. I felt close to tears.

~

Amelia was in a playful mood, which only increased my own sense of isolation.

'You look so sad, Miss Singleton,' she said at the end of the first lesson.

'I'm sorry, Amelia. I'm just tired.'

'Well, I have wonderful news for you. Can you guess?'

I looked at her blankly.

'Mamma told me last night that we're going to Dublin shortly! Papa has come up today to make arrangements. You're coming, and we're taking the maids — some of the maids. We're taking Grace. We always go to Dublin for the winter, you see.'

'Oh....' I said. I smiled at her. 'That *is* good news.'

'You've no idea how much fun things are there! You can take me to the park, Miss Singleton. I love feeding the ducks in Stephen's Green. I can show you my favourite places. And Mamma said you may take me to museums!'

She was practically jumping up and down in front of me. I felt a kind of relief: a new chapter was beginning for Grace and me. But had Grace heard? I knew that I had to tell her as soon as possible, had to find out what this would mean for *us*.

'Aren't you happy, Miss Singleton?'

Amelia was looking at me wistfully. It occurred to me that she must sense that she had failed to make me glow with happiness. It wasn't her fault, I thought, that only one person could do that now.

'Yes, dear, I think it will make our lives a lot more interesting,' I said, though I knew I sounded hesitant. 'It's the best news I've had in a long time,' I said more honestly.

She beamed.

~

At the end of the day, another surprise: Lady Wilcox appeared in the schoolroom, along with Amelia's nurse. 'Go along with Nurse, now,' she said to Amelia, who skipped off cheerfully.

'You've heard about Dublin, Miss Singleton?'

'Yes, Lady Wilcox.'

I was sitting and she remained standing. I wondered why she was there, but I felt too numb to be frightened.

She smiled at me, though I found her smiles lacked real warmth. *Perhaps that isn't her fault*, I thought.

'Miss Singleton, you've been with us for a couple of months now. I want to tell you how *pleased* I am with your instruction of Amelia. She seems much changed, much less flighty. I had hoped she would become more earnest, and she tries to earn your approval, I think, by concentration on her studies.'

'I — I do find her a very willing pupil,' I said awkwardly. 'She's still so young, of course....'

'Yes, but as we both know, Miss Singleton, youth is the time to mould minds. You have the task of shaping someone's character by your example and by teaching. I think you are doing a tremendous job.'

I blushed and looked down. Her praise was unexpected, and, I thought, rather undeserved. But I sensed that she was grateful to have found somebody to take Amelia off her hands.

'You see, Miss Singleton, one of my duties in overseeing staff is to balance the good and the bad. Perfect conduct is, at the end of the day, probably impossible. Excellent conduct is an achievable standard, however.'

Lady Wilcox paused, and I felt wary, suddenly.

'I have had reports of your ... friendship with Grace Sheridan. It has even been suggested to me that there may be some kind of undesirable intimacy occurring under this roof. But I simply can't believe that of you, Miss Singleton. I considered leaving Sheridan behind this time, but I realised that she could do greater harm here unsupervised, especially given her propensity for attracting the attentions of others. Johnson, however, *will* remain here. What I'm saying, Miss Singleton, is that I'm sure that in Dublin you will be able to form more *equal*, more intellectual, companionships. And I will be watching Grace's behaviour very closely indeed.'

I swallowed, trying not to appear agitated. 'Yes, Lady Wilcox.' I forced the words out, looking up into her eyes with what I hoped seemed like the respect she would consider her due. I tried to suppress my defiance and anger.

'And your salary, Miss Singleton. I was remiss in not arranging some form of payment before. I will pay you in two parts, once when we reach town and once at the end of your first year. Does that seem fair?'

'Yes, Lady Wilcox. It seems quite fair.' She was paying me twenty-five pounds a year. It occurred to me that I might not be there at the end of the year to receive my second payment. The thought gave me an odd thrill.

She smiled again, rather tartly. 'I hope nothing I've said has given offence.'

I hesitated. It would be unwise to try to defend Grace, even to mention her. I had to pretend that nothing very much had been said.

'No, not at all,' I replied. *If she could read my mind,* I thought, *my bags would be packed and I would be summarily dismissed. Her high opinion of my moral character would certainly change!*

And yet, as Lady Wilcox left the room, I did not feel ashamed of myself. Even if the servants — probably Johnson — had gossiped about us, they knew nothing of the strength of our feelings. I felt more loyalty to Grace than to Lady Wilcox and I was comfortable with that. But it was painful to have to be so secretive. And it did occur to me, as I walked downstairs to dinner through the silent, dim house, that I might have made a very profound mistake in trusting Grace.

~

At dinner I looked for Grace, but I did not see her. The servants were talking about the move to Dublin, and the ones who were not going were griping about their lot.

After I cleared my plate, I got up as unobtrusively as possible and wandered over to a door through which I had occasionally heard the rattling of pans. The food was served in there and brought out on big trays. Grace was behind that door, I guessed.

As I opened it, a cloud of steam seemed to emerge and settle into my skin. A figure poked her head out, large, stern, clad in an apron.

'What might you be wanting, Miss?' The tone was not helpful.

'I need to see Grace,' I faltered.

The door opened further, and I ventured further in. It was a huge, crowded, noisy space, and in my nervousness I could hardly make out the faces of the women who stood around the table, chopping and mixing.

One figure stood at the far end of the table, her head down, lost in her own private world.

'Grace!' the cook yelled harshly. 'There's a young *lady* here to see you!'

The girl looked up. It was Grace, and as she approached me I saw that she had been crying. Her face was pale and her eyes were shadowed. She looked exhausted.

'What is it, Caroline?' she asked. Even her voice sounded defeated, and a little distant. She's given up, I thought. It did not occur to me until later that she had used my name in public.

'You haven't heard? We're going to Dublin!' I said urgently. 'You're coming too; Lady Wilcox told me expressly. I have to see you! When can I see you?'

She shook her head. 'It's best not. They're watching me. I'm glad about Dublin — I didn't know. But any mistake I make now ...'

'Oh, Grace, what does it matter?' I said impatiently. Nobody could hear us, I was sure, with all the clanging and clattering that was going on. 'The point is that we're going — and Johnson won't be! You're safe now.'

'Not for a few days,' she said stubbornly. 'You don't understand —'

'He wouldn't dare touch you now, Grace.'

She shrugged, then looked up at me wistfully. 'Maybe.'

'I'm going to the woods. Will you meet me there when you get off?'

'I can't. I'm not supposed to go out.'

I stared at her. It had never been clearer to me that she had her own priorities, her own secrets. Was she no longer willing to take risks for me? I had no right, perhaps, to ask that of her. But I wanted her to care enough about me that her own safety didn't matter to her! I didn't have the patience to wait for Dublin, I realised, and she was probably right to be cautious. But I felt bitterly disappointed.

'Well, that's the news,' I said, turning away. I looked around as I reached the door. She was still standing there, staring at me. As if I were a ghost, someone from another world. *I am*, I thought, as my eyes lingered on her. *Too much separates us. She'll never come to me, and I can't pursue her forever. It may be time to give up.*

~

As I wandered down the drive the sky darkened around me. We would be in Dublin for Christmas, I thought. I wondered what kind of a celebration that would be, in the bosom of a strange family. Would Lady Wilcox give me a gift? Probably. But it would mean nothing, since it would not be a gift from an equal to an equal.

Grace and I might not stay friends after we reached Dublin. Certainly that was what Lady Wilcox expected. Perhaps she only tolerated my friendship with her maid because we were deep in the country and I had no one of my own class to associate with.

In Dublin, though, it would seem more glaring. And Grace would have friends, she would go visit her family....

The idea of losing Grace was hard to bear. She had not been just a little trifle for me, I thought sombrely as I reached the woods. She had meant everything to me. I had hoped ... well, just how idle my hopes were I was beginning to see. I had read her warmth, her friendliness, her ability to touch me both physically and emotionally, as something completely different. Suddenly it occurred to me that she had been involved with Johnson all along, and that what I had perceived as a cruel abuse of power on his part was actually something more like a lovers' quarrel!

I hated myself for doubting her, but I sensed that she had not told me everything. The maids' gossip had presented her in such different colours. Was she avoiding me now because she had sworn to Johnson that she would not associate with me? The jealous butler.... I grimaced, but my heart ached. It all seemed so unnecessary, so sad. I felt betrayed.

I had walked quite far into the woods, and had reached my favourite tree, a silver beech. It was tall and graceful, and the leaves had turned a deep red. The white bark that gave the tree its name was particularly appealing to me. I would miss the woods.

I sat down on a little bench. I was shivering, but no matter. The solitude was a relief. Grace had been my only true friend, I thought, and now I wondered how true she really was. I sighed, and began whistling a little song, trying to distract myself from my misery.

To my surprise, my song was echoed by another whistle, somewhere in the wood behind me. I stood up, terrified suddenly. I heard a tramping sound; then a dog rushed out of the undergrowth, a brown-and-white hound. To my astonishment, the animal was closely followed by a bearded man swinging a stick.

'I like a good whistler,' the man said jovially. His accent was English; he had pleasant brown eyes in a rather worn face. 'I believe you must be my daughter's new governess, Miss Singleton.'

'Sir John,' I said ruefully, making a small curtsey in his direction. He waved his hand.

'No need for that nonsense! I hear you're a modern woman; you've been making full use of my library. Excellent. No point in having the books if nobody reads them.'

'I — I've been trying to read about modern Irish history,' I said, feeling like a scared schoolgirl and hating it.

'Ah yes,' he said. 'A melancholic subject, to be sure.'

'I've heard talk of some troubles — some possible insurrectionary activities.' I tried to use language that Sir John would respect.

He glanced at me shrewdly.

'We're not entirely certain that such a thing is out of the question. There are a number of secret and not-so-secret revolutionary groups, as you may know: the Irish Citizen Army, the IRB, the Irish Volunteers, the Fianna.... Even the intellectuals like W.B. Yeats and Lady Gregory are having some influence on public taste. There's a nostalgia for the Celtic past which seems utterly absurd on the face of it, given what we've done for the country, yet these things do have a strange power. But you won't find this in the history books; it's all quite a recent development.'

I nodded.

'But what's your interest in all this, Miss Singleton? Are you a sympathiser?'

He said it lightly, but I knew I had to be circumspect.

'I'm an observer, Sir John. I'm far too English to really understand the Irish, I feel.' I could not keep some bitterness out of my tone.

He laughed, digging his stick into the earth.

'The problem is, they understand *us* all too well. I think we *have* been guilty of some insensitivity, Miss Singleton. There's no doubt the populace is rather discontented, but there's also an incredible amount of ignorance to contend with. The kind of peasant philosophising that goes on nowadays is really very annoying. Luckily, we're not exposed to any of it up here, which is why I spend as much time as possible at Thornley. My wife and child feel somewhat marooned, no doubt. Well, you'll be coming with us to Dublin; I'm sure you're pleased about that. It's not quite London, I'm afraid.'

'London's a grim place nowadays.' I looked down, wondering if he knew about my brother's death.

'The whole of Europe is,' he said gently. 'Enjoy your time in Ireland, Miss Singleton. I realise that governessing is not a rest cure, but I don't think we've overburdened you.'

'No ... I'm grateful for your kindness,' I said in a small voice. Sir John looked gratified, touched his cap to me, and called his dog to heel.

'You must be a night owl, Miss Singleton,' he called back to me after he had gone a few paces. 'Don't let it get too dark before you return!'

I sat musing, glad that I had met him, surprised at his evident decency. Yet he did not really understand the very people he was ruling, nor did he see why he should! That kind of arrogance was indeed very English. I wondered if I, too, had been guilty of arrogance....

The second surprise of the evening was a pair of hands placed over my eyes. I squirmed, and opened my mouth to scream. A hand clapped over my mouth, and I looked up into Grace's flushed, smiling face. Pulling her hand away, she sat beside me on the bench.

Chapter 8

'*A* bit unnecessarily violent, don't you think?' I felt a little angry, and rather haughty. 'So you had a change of heart?'

'I'm sorry,' Grace said simply. 'I thought about it and realised I was wrong. It can happen so easily, getting sacked and sent home in disgrace. You don't know.'

'You're right, I don't,' I said, not looking at her. 'Why should you be acting so guilty? You've done nothing wrong.'

'I've ... I've stepped out of line. That's what Johnson said, and he's right.'

'With me, you mean?' I still did not look at her.

'Yes.'

'You're right, it's not worth the risk.' I felt myself speaking coldly, and could not help it. 'I suppose the pleasure of my company doesn't make up for any of this.'

'You know it does,' Grace said. She stared off into the wood, shivering. 'I should have brought a shawl.'

I felt impatient. 'I haven't tried to entangle you in anything, believe me.'

She looked at me impassively.

I blurted out, 'I suppose you don't want to be suspected of immoral conduct!'

'I don't think my friendship with you has been immoral,' she said.

'Well, perhaps my feelings for you *have*,' I said. 'I'm sure that changes everything for you. If we're going to stop being friends, let's do it sooner rather than later. I'm afraid of getting hurt.'

She looked at me in astonishment. 'How can you speak so coldly? I — I know what you're talking about, I think, and I didn't have any intention of stopping....'

A blush rose to her cheeks and she averted her gaze. 'I hoped that I meant something to you.'

'Of course you did! You still do, for that matter. But I haven't seen you in days, and you were going to let that continue —'

'We have to be very careful now,' she said.

We sat in silence for a while. I felt my heart beating rapidly, and when I looked at Grace I could tell she was breathing hard — out of nervousness, no doubt. I touched her hand. She clasped mine in hers.

The touch of our flesh broke some spell that had been holding us apart. She leaned against me, then raised her head and sought my lips. For the first time, but as naturally as if we had done it hundreds of times, our lips met.

I had never kissed anyone, and scarcely knew how. But the warmth of her mouth drew me in. At last we paused for breath. I gulped, not knowing what to say, only wanting more. As if she guessed this, Grace knelt on the bench beside me, and we clasped each other, kissing more wildly and fervently. She began to use her tongue, and as it entered my mouth I groaned. I ran my hands over her shoulders, pressing her to me, stroking her hair, wishing we were naked and in bed together.

'Grace,' I whispered.

Her eyes were lit up with pleasure and a kind of tenderness. With a smile, she removed my glasses and put them carefully down on the ground. Then she pulled me down into the fallen leaves. She began unbuttoning her blouse, pushing my hand inside her clothes so that I could feel her breast. I sighed in frustration, anticipation, amazed at how soft and silky her skin felt to my touch.

We kissed for a long time. As we lay pressed together, our breasts touching, our mouths locked, I felt as if I would swoon in ecstasy. She was so heavy, so solid, so warm and fluid somehow underneath my hands. I wanted her on top of me, so I rolled over. She had released her hair and it hung about my face. The feel of it brushing against my face and neck was exquisite.

At last she raised her head.

'Caroline ... I want to be with you tonight.'

I couldn't think. I gazed up at her dreamily. She had never looked more beautiful. With her hair down she was a goddess, I thought, a Celtic goddess, enchanting and strange.

'I love you,' I said, looking into her gentle hazel eyes. 'Grace, I love you.'

She smiled, a little mysteriously, I thought.

'I can't imagine more pleasure than you've given me tonight,' I murmured.

'There's so much more,' she said. Her voice sounded throaty, and I smiled at it. I drew her down to feel her lips upon mine once again.

'I know. But we have time, don't we?'

'Why not tonight?' she said insistently. 'Once we're in Dublin the rooms are too close. Here you can lock your door, nobody can hear a thing.'

'Have you had lovers here?' I asked. She was silent. I could tell she was hurt by my question.

'I don't mind if you have had,' I said. 'Why should I judge you?'

She sighed, and ran her finger gently over my lips. 'I've never felt as much for anyone as I have for you. That's why I ... I think we should be together while we can. But ... if we're caught, we'll both lose our places. That's the risk, and maybe you don't want to take it.'

I thought for a second about the effect it would have on my mother, but she was curiously far away, in a distant land.

'I'll take the risk,' I said.

'I'll make it worth your while,' she whispered into my ear, biting my earlobe gently. I shivered in delight. Each sensation made me crave more. I now understood the concept of an 'erotic awakening', which I had read about in so many forbidden French novels. It was happening to me, and it was wonderful.

I sat at my dressing-table. In front of me was a scratched mirror, and I observed myself dreamily. I had lit some candles and had put on my nightgown. With my hair down around my face I looked like a schoolgirl, I thought, still thin and undeveloped and painfully needy.

But something was different now. My eyes were glowing; they were a bright, almost dark blue. My lips looked puffy and fuller, somehow. I ran my tongue over them, thinking of how she had tasted this evening. *Oh, Grace.* What if she didn't come?

My heart was thudding against my chest, and I could not think. All I felt was anticipation, nervousness, and a kind of desperation. I hardly knew what I was doing. It amazed me that I cared so little for my own reputation, for what others might think or say. What would Ralph have thought? He had told me that a young man had made advances to him once at Oxford. He'd said that he was drunk and that for a second he had been tempted. But he'd refused. Still, when he had spoken about it to me it had been in matter-of-fact tones. I'd wondered, at the time, why I wasn't shocked. Now I knew that he had followed his desires at the Front and guessed that he would be pleased for me.

I wanted Grace, and it seemed so strange that she wanted me too. I had never dealt with this before, never had to wrestle with feelings of attraction for 'the wrong person'. *What if Grace is the right person?* I thought, staring at my reflection as if it were a different woman looking back at me, a wiser one with more knowledge of the world.

I felt more than heard the knock on the door. Something in me shuddered.

'It's open,' I said.

I did not look around, but I heard her latch the door. I felt her hands on my shoulders. As she bent over me I saw in the mirror her beautiful brown hair covering my breasts. Twisting around, I kissed her almost harshly. She was cold, and I wanted to warm her with my mouth.

It happened so fast, and yet infinitesimally slowly. I felt transformed, and I did not stop to question my actions, but pushed her down onto the bed. When she gasped, I felt a surge of desire so strong that I was afraid I was losing my sanity. In a few seconds, it seemed, we were both naked. Without even covering us up, I began to kiss her, every inch of her body, caressing her with my hands. Her passivity spurred me on to greater passion. I felt more in control than I had a few hours earlier; something had changed between us. She was surrendering to me this time.

It gave me great satisfaction to sense her pleasure as I used my tongue on her, to hear her low moans and gasps, to watch her arch her back, to feel her fingers in my hair. There was something so intimate, I thought, about wanting to taste a lover's body, to savour her. As she convulsed against me, calling my name, I knew I had given her what she needed.

Tears rolled out of her lovely eyes. I kissed her eyelids, wrapping my fingers in her hair, thicker than mine and with a slight curl. Our bodies were damp with perspiration, and oddly enough, I loved the sensation.

'Don't cry, Grace.'

'I'm sorry, it's just ... I didn't expect ... You were so *wild*, Caroline.'

I beamed. 'I didn't want you to do all the work, as you always have to. Was I too rough?'

She shook her head. Nestling against her, I felt her heartbeat begin to slow. 'No; I wanted that, but I didn't know how to ask.'

We held each other tightly. I rested my head on her breast, feeling tired and satiated, and immensely happy.

Then, gently, she rolled over so that she was on top. As I looked intently into her eyes, noticing how flushed she was, I also began to feel the delicious sensation of her body moving against mine. Kissing my breasts, she began a sensuous rhythm, her hair spreading over my face as she moved. The bed began to creak. I felt faint with desire, my breathing ragged, wanting only for her not to stop. I held her tight against me, her face in my neck, my eyes closed, and then a quivering sensation spread throughout my body. 'Oh God,' I moaned, as I collapsed back on the bed, my face burning, my heart racing.

We kissed and kissed, working each other into an absolute frenzy. I felt her push her fingers inside me, and could not stop myself from crying out. She took me roughly, and I begged for more.

'You are so beautiful,' I whispered to her, as we lay together in exhaustion. 'Why me? How could someone like you choose me?'

'Because you're good and kind and sweet,' she said softly, 'and you treated me special from the beginning.'

'You treated *me* that way —'

'I just knew, as I saw you come up them steps —' She stopped and corrected herself. 'Those steps — that you was someone I could trust. And then later, when you said to call you Caroline, I just thought, "Well, if you can say that to me I must mean something to you." And I was glad. But then when we were sitting by the water and you were comforting me, I wanted to kiss you.'

'I wanted to, as well,' I said. 'I thought it was just me.'

'I was almost going to do it. But then I thought you might take offence. I just wasn't sure.'

'It's hard to be sure,' I said dreamily. My body, usually tense, felt totally at ease. I stroked her arm, immersed in her lovely white skin. 'This has all happened very fast. I suppose that's your style, not mine.'

I said it teasingly, but she looked hurt suddenly. 'Do you think I'm easy? I suppose you do.'

'No, I don't. Of course not.'

'You can ask me ... If you've anything to ask me, now's the time,' she said with difficulty.

I didn't know what to say. I didn't want to ask the hard questions — who she'd slept with, when she'd started. It was clear to me that she was sexually experienced, but I did not regard this as any of my business. I knew I was a jealous person, and I did not want to open a can of worms; I had no interest in knowing names, in knowing who had been 'the first'. I had not even been the first woman she'd been with, I was sure of that. I was surprised and rather dismayed at how much I did not want to know, but after a few moments of uncomfortable silence I said, 'Did you ever ... with Johnson?'

I could tell how nervous Grace was, and I was sorry I had asked.

She turned her head away. 'Just once. It was when I first came. When I told you he took advantage of me ...'

'He assaulted you?' I could feel the rage beginning to build inside me. 'How could he?'

'It was ... well, I finally let him. He was obsessed with me. And after he'd done it he let me alone.'

'That's awful.' I felt almost physically sick.

'He wasn't the first,' Grace said grimly. 'He knew that, so he thought it didn't mean anything to me. But I haven't been with very many, Caroline. I don't want you to think —'

'It really doesn't matter to me. Honestly.' It didn't, at that moment.

I held her, and she hugged me tight.

'See, I told you were kind and good.'

'So are you, Grace. You've been good to me. Better than I deserve.'

'No, not better that that. You deserve it,' she said. 'Are you too tired now?' She was kissing me again, and I felt an urgency behind it. 'I want you to know that it's never been like this with anyone. I never even came to climax before. That's hard to say.' She blushed, but pulled me to her more intensely. 'I can't get enough of you.'

We made love slowly, almost hesitantly, our desire just ahead of our exhaustion. I felt like a sputtering candle, flaring up only to burn low again. The strangest thing was how tender we were with each other, yet I craved her teeth on my skin. My nipples felt bruised, my lips swollen.

By the time we had finished I could hear the birds starting outside my window, and we were bathed in grey light.

'How will you work today?' I asked. 'You'll be so tired....'

'So will you,' she said, laughing. 'We'll sleep well tomorrow and catch up.'

My face fell at the thought of a night without her.

'We'll do this again?' I said anxiously, 'before we go?'

She nodded, stroking my cheek. I lay beside her, knowing she would have to leave soon and dreading it.

'We can't just stop here,' she said. 'Even though it would be safest.'

'I can't be prudent now,' I said. 'It's too late for that.'

She smiled.

Chapter 9

The next morning, I was slumbering deeply when I felt her hand on my shoulder. There she was, back in uniform, the circles under her eyes the only hint of our night together. That, and the tender look she gave me.

'I gave you a little extra time,' she said. 'You do have to hurry now.'

I sat up. Suddenly I threw my arms around her, and we embraced passionately. We said nothing for a few minutes as we held each other. *We feel so* right *together now,* I thought.

'I love the fact that I see you first thing every morning,' I murmured.

'That might change in Dublin, but I'll try to keep doing it. It's nice for me too. My heart was in my mouth going back to bed last night.'

'But nobody saw you.'

'I was yawning this morning and they looked at me strange; but I said it was working in the kitchen, that I wasn't used to that. And they feel it isn't right what Johnson did.'

'Are you back to normal duties now?'

'Yes, thank God.'

'And will you consider being with me one of your "normal duties"?'

'More like a special duty,' she teased. Our faces were still close together as we whispered to each other. My heart was beating hard.

'I'm in love with you,' I said. The words just came out; I felt terrified immediately. But I continued. 'I'd do anything for you. Make any sacrifice.'

'I hope that won't be necessary,' Grace said, looking at me intently. 'I want to be with you as much as I can, believe me. And what you said about love ... it's not so easy for me to say it, but that doesn't mean I don't feel it.'

We kissed, and she ran her hands over me under my nightgown. It gave me a delicious shiver. I pressed tightly against her, aware of how much I desired her, fearful that she wouldn't want to continue.

'Please, Grace,' I said softly. 'Just quickly. Please?'

I knew that I was begging, that I should be ashamed, but I so wanted her to say yes. I lay back down on the bed. To my astonishment, she lowered herself down on top of me. She had a way of moving herself against me that brought me to climax very quickly. My body, still sensitised from the night before, responded almost too fast. I clung to her, tears falling from my eyes. 'Oh God,' I said helplessly. 'God....'

At last she pulled away, smoothing herself down. Her face was very serious as she looked at me, and I was afraid she was angry. I said nothing, feeling self-conscious about what I had said, what I had done.

'Caroline,' she began, and then stopped. Her voice was unsteady. 'Caroline, we can't do that every morning....'

'I know,' I said, not looking at her. 'I'm sor—'

She laid her finger across my lips. 'Tomorrow night. All right?'

'Yes,' I said breathlessly.

'That'll be it for quite a while, so let's make the most of it.'

I nodded. The look we gave each other was one that conspirators must use, I thought. Now Grace had two big secrets that she hid from the outside world: her involvement in the struggle to free Ireland, and her love for me. I only had one, yet nothing more momentous had ever happened to me.

After she left, when I was bathing myself, I thought of her hands on me and inwardly swooned. I was learning about passion: that it demands fulfilment, satisfaction, again and again. I hoped the day would never come when Grace would deny me, because I thought it might drive me mad. *So the perfectly rational Caroline Singleton has come to this,* I mused wryly. And yet I was a little frightened, for I sensed that Grace was still holding back.

The day passed slowly, and since Amelia's high spirits were exhausting, I decided to take her out for a walk. We bundled up in coats, and because she insisted, I took her to the barn so that she could see the cows. It was strange to walk past brawny men who tipped their caps to me, strange that walking with Amelia granted me automatic respect. Amelia picked handfuls of hay to feed the cows; I smiled at her need to feed animals. *Adults lose that desire, for the most part,* I thought. I did not particularly love animals, being a London girl, but I enjoyed seeing Amelia in her element. She took me to visit the henhouses next, and was allowed to keep a warm brown egg. 'Nurse will boil it for my breakfast tomorrow!' she said with glee. 'Oh, look, Miss Singleton. There's Grace.'

I turned around. Grace and another maid were coming towards us. I stood by Amelia, blushing, and Grace approached me shyly.

'What are you doing here?' she asked, just as I queried, 'Out for a walk?'

'Well, once again I'm being asked to do "special duties",' she said with a grimace. 'We have to iron sheets before we go, so that when we come back in the spring, they'll be ready to use.'

'That doesn't make sense. I thought some maids stayed here.'

'Not many. Anyway, we've been sent to the wash-house to collect them.'

'I want to go!' said Amelia, tugging my arm insistently. 'You should see the wash-house, Miss Singleton.'

'No, Amelia, I don't think your mother would approve of that,' I said without thinking. Looking back at Grace, I was surprised to see a coldness in her expression. I trembled. The other maid walked on, waving to Grace, who said, 'Be there in a minute.'

Turning back to me, she said, 'I used to bring Amelia to the wash-house. That's why she remembers going there.'

'Oh,' I said. 'I just assumed Lady Wilcox would object.... Isn't it smelly and hot?'

Again, Grace looked at me coldly. 'It smells of disinfectant. There's nothing unhygienic about it. Course, the English are cracked about that sort of thing.'

'Cracked?' I said.

Amelia tugged at my arm again.

'I'm sorry, Amelia, it's time to go in,' I said sharply. Grace shrugged and muttered that she would see me later, then. *We're both so tired*, I thought, and I wondered how she would get through the rest of the day. I watched her figure recede, feeling an aching start in my chest.

I asked Amelia to wait, which she did, pouting. I ran after Grace. She had reached the corner of some low buildings, and no one could see us. She turned, her face impassive.

'You don't want to be with me during the day, then.' I was shocked and moved to see the glint of tears in her eyes.

'Grace ... I just didn't want to mix Amelia up in this. I mean, she might notice.'

'What could she notice?'

'She notices a lot,' I said. 'And Lady Wilcox knows something.'

'Lady Wilcox?' She looked at me in disbelief.

'Yes. She told me that she had heard rumours that we might have formed an undesirable intimacy. I didn't want to tell you because I thought you had enough to worry about.'

'What else did she say?'

'Well,' I faltered, 'she did say that she was going to watch you closely once we got to Dublin.'

'Oh, that's very nice!' Grace was suddenly blazing with anger. 'And naturally she told you that *you* were doing an excellent job. It's always the same!'

'You've had other governesses before, then,' I joked, trying to make her smile, but she looked at me as if I were one of the enemy.

'You don't understand how it feels — always being under suspicion. Then you wonder why I won't take risks. I take *all* the risks, Caroline.'

There was a silence. I knew what she said had a lot of truth to it, and I felt guilty and miserable, yet at the same time resentful. Didn't she know I was on her side?

'You'd better go back to Miss Amelia,' Grace said, not meeting my eyes. 'I might go lie down instead of going to supper.'

'I might too, then,' I said. The thought of eating alone was terrifying.

She shrugged.

'Grace, let's not fight,' I pleaded. 'It was all going so well.' I suddenly had the strangest foreboding that she had had second thoughts. 'It's not over, is it?' I blurted out, my voice rising half-hysterically.

She looked at me with a little more warmth.

'No, but you hurt me just then. You get to sit in a nice room all day, while I'm worked half to death. And then you won't even take time to spend a few minutes with me. Maybe you don't want to talk, maybe you think that all I'm good for is —'

'No,' I said fiercely. 'That's not true. You know it's not.'

'I know one thing,' Grace said. 'You won't talk about what's really going on in this country. If you ignore that, you ignore everything about me. All you care about is what I can do for you in bed.'

I blushed, feeling a sense of shame well up within me.

'I'm not using you,' I muttered.

'Oh, I think you are.' She looked me straight in the face. 'For all your talk of love. You're as bad as a man. The minute you get it, you want more, and that's *all* you want.'

I shook my head, too stunned to respond. From behind, I heard Amelia say tentatively, 'Miss Singleton?'

I spun around. She was watching us curiously, a slightly apprehensive look on her face. In her hand she still clutched her egg.

'Amelia must get back,' I said to Grace in what I knew was a cool tone. 'Will I see you tomorrow?'

She looked down, then nodded. 'Have a good rest.'

To my astonishment, she reached out and put her hand on my shoulder for a moment. It seemed to vibrate, and I stared into her eyes.

'I'm sorry,' she whispered. And then she was gone.

~

I lay on my bed, staring at the ceiling. I had told Amelia's nurse I was going to lie down, and she had said that she would have some food sent up to me. I had told her I would go without supper, but she had insisted. So I had eaten my soup and was trying to sleep. Sleep would not come.

If Grace was right ... No, Grace couldn't be right. But I knew that my reaction to her words had not been one of complete disbelief. It was true that what I had felt that morning was largely compounded of lust, need and desire. It was just all so new to me, and I could not help asking for more, even though it was unreasonable. I realised that now. When had I stopped being able to exercise restraint?

I turned over and hugged the blankets, thinking of Grace. My body was unruly, I thought, and I saw no way to tame its desires. Then the tears came. I missed her so much, and I could foresee only sadness and loss as I envisaged my future with her. We were too different, and would perhaps grow less tolerant of those differences. I had seen a harsher side of her today, and she had seen an aspect of me that I was ashamed of.

Yet we *were* lovers. I smiled at the thought and, strangely enough, felt my eyes closing.

~

I woke early the next morning to find her snuggling against me. Her warmth spread through me, and I stroked her hair. We did not kiss.

'How long have you been here?'

'Not long. I wanted some time with you.'

'Well, you have it.'

We said nothing for a while. I resolved to say nothing about our plans for that evening. If Grace did not mention it, I vowed I would not pressure her.

'I'm sorry I said you were as bad as a man.'

'That was what hurt most,' I said playfully.

'Be serious.'

'Nobody's ever said that to me before. I didn't understand how you could accuse me of that. Then I looked at my own behaviour and I saw how you must feel. I never want to make you feel used. We don't even have to ... be together in that way.'

'You're more passionate than me, maybe. I like that about you, so it was wrong of me to turn it against you. I thought you'd be angry with me.' She spoke in a wistful, vulnerable way that I loved.

'No, how can I? I'm so glad you came, that you've forgiven me.'

'There wasn't really anything to forgive.'

'What you said about me not wanting to know about Ireland....' I began. 'Well, maybe that was true. But I know there's not a lot you can tell me. You can't give away secrets. I know that your brother is involved in a group that will take part in a rising, if there is one. And I have to believe you when you say there's going to be one. But — forgive me — it just doesn't seem real to me. Any of this. Perhaps the War in France is not particularly real to you, and I don't hold it against you. Isn't it normal that we keep things from each other, that each of us has her own life, in a way?'

She remained quiet for a long time, thinking. I waited anxiously for a response. Her arms were still tight around me, her head on my breast.

'I don't think you understand what an independent Ireland might be like.'

I shrugged.

'It would be a republic. A socialist republic. Men and women would have equal rights. Have you heard of Patrick Pearse?'

I shook my head.

'He's a schoolteacher in Dublin. He runs an Irish school called St Enda's. My brother and I heard him speak at the funeral of a Fenian leader called O'Donovan Rossa, two years ago. He gave a speech that fired up the crowd. He said that the British had made a huge mistake when they left us the graves of our patriot men and women, that Ireland unfree would never be at peace. After he heard Pearse speak, Jack knew that he had to get involved, and I did too. We didn't tell our ma and da. They wouldn't understand. Then lots of things started happening. Eoin

MacNeill formed the Irish Volunteers and they began training every week, right under the noses of the English. They're still the biggest group we have. He's more of a moderate, though.'

'So Pearse is somehow involved with the rising?'

'He's the brains behind it. He's an amazing man, Caroline. Very shy, but very fierce. His whole life is dedicated to the idea of freeing Ireland. You see, every generation has tried. It started with the rebellion of 1798, then Robert Emmet, the Young Irelanders, the Fenians, and now us.'

'But do you think ...' I paused, wondering if I could ask this. 'Do you really think it would change your life so much? Wouldn't you still have to work?'

'As a maid, you mean,' she said in a subdued voice.

I said nothing.

'What I do now means *nothing* to me. As it is, a few rich families, mostly English or Anglo-Irish, hold all the wealth in this country. Do you realise that at the time of the Famine in the 1840s, almost half the country died or emigrated? They were peasants, so nobody cared. And the English did nothing. So you see, if we have the power to rule ourselves, we'll be our own responsibility, and I have to believe that we'd rule ourselves with more compassion then they've given us over the years.'

'You're talking about the redistribution of wealth,' I mused. It was a slogan that I had often heard bandied about in London. 'So I'll be out of a job too, eh?'

Grace laughed gently. 'Caroline, what will I do with you? You take nothing seriously.'

'I do take you seriously, Grace.' I said this with all the sincerity I felt. 'I just don't understand what you're doing with me, an Englishwoman.'

'I don't think of you that way. We have English people involved in the struggle. Some Englishmen have been involved in getting us guns. Even a man who was knighted by the English has helped us — I can't tell you his name; he has contacts with the German Government, who also want to help us....'

'But most Dublin people, for example — they don't know much about all this?'

She shook her head. 'They know about as much as you do, love. Which is going to be a bit of a problem.'

I coloured. Her use of 'love' was very charming.

'I'm open to knowing more. And I will support you. I have no particular loyalty to the British Government since my brother's death.'

'That's right,' she said quietly. 'You've suffered. And you've learned from your suffering.'

'I suppose so,' I said.

'I've learned a lot from you. You seem strong. Let's both be strong so that neither of us has to take the man's role.'

'You say things to me that seem so ... so bold, Grace.'

'I know, Irish women are supposed to be pure and good.'

'Londoners are said to be more worldly, but I feel you know more than I — about life, and loving.'

'Oh, talking about that,' she said teasingly, looking into my eyes now, 'are we still meeting tonight?'

I smiled, weak with relief. 'If you'll still have me.'

'I'd never back out now.'

She flung her arms around me, and we kissed, but still sparingly, as if reserving energy for later. I knew I would make it up to Amelia today for what I considered an 'off' day yesterday. My first responsibility was to Grace, my second to Amelia. *Or, I* wondered, *should my first responsibility be to myself?* Grace seemed so trusting, and I wondered how many other lovers all over the country were spilling secrets in their passion at this moment. Presumably Dublin Castle, with its huge spy network, was busy processing all this information. But that was my cynical English view, perhaps, of a situation that was extremely Irish in its volatility.

'When we get to Dublin,' Grace said dreamily, 'I'll take you to plays at the Abbey Theatre. Once you hear these ideas and see the drama of them, you'll see what I'm getting at. I want you to love Ireland.'

'Can't I just love you?' I said, caressing her face.

'It's a start,' she said, closing her eyes and becoming very still. 'You're good at that, don't stop....'

We were in our own little cocoon now, and the outside world faded to nothing.

Chapter 10

---

*D*ublin changed everything, though it was a while before I realised just how much would be different.

I had said a perfunctory farewell to Vera after church, explaining that I did not have time to take tea with her as we were leaving so soon and I needed to pack. To my surprise, she sniffled into a handkerchief and said that she would miss me. She recommended several shops in Dublin that I must visit. There was little to say. I presented her with a shilling volume of Oscar Wilde's *The Importance of Being Earnest* as a keepsake. She looked at it oddly. 'There's an interesting portrayal of a governess in it,' I said, trying not to smile. 'She's called Miss Prism. She falls in love with the vicar.' At this Vera brightened visibly.

I had some hopes that I would be able to ride down to Dublin with Grace, but they were quickly dashed. The maids had been sent on ahead in carriages to get the house ready. Instead, I sat with Lady Wilcox and Amelia in the back seat of the car. It was mostly a silent journey. Sir John seemed rather preoccupied; he barely spoke to his wife and child. Amelia was tense with excitement. She had also been more subdued with me in general since our meeting with Grace out of doors. This distressed me, and I felt a little shy and apologetic around her.

I assumed that Lady Wilcox was annoyed by the informality of the arrangement, for I sensed irritation in the way she sat stiffly upright, her hands clasped in her lap, staring straight ahead. Perhaps, I thought, she had wanted to avert the horrifying possibility that I might sit in a carriage with Grace, our legs pressing together, conversing in whispers. I imagined this alternative journey and my heart ached with yearning. We had been together once more, as Grace had promised, but I had felt upset as she left me that night. I'd tried to hide it, since it seemed unreasonable: what, after all, did I expect? But I had come to realise that, where Grace was concerned, I was not reasonable.

As the car bounced down the drive away from Thornley, a sense of foreboding came upon me. I didn't know if I would ever see the house again, for, given the furtiveness of the way I was living, I had had to adopt a 'carpe diem' philosophy that felt unnatural to me. Our happiness seemed so fragile, dependent as it was upon Lady Wilcox's blindness. In my darker moments, I did not expect it to last. I looked out at the little creek where Grace and I had sat just a few months before, and remembered stroking her hand. How I wished she had kissed me then, how I wished we had had more time.

As we drove through fields and small towns, as we passed thatched cottages and horses and carts, I did not see any outward signs of desperation on the faces of the people. Yes, the men looked gaunt and shabby, and the women mostly cast their eyes down, pulling their children to them; but there was little hostility toward us, just a stoic resignation. I certainly did not believe I was looking at a country on the brink of revolution. But perhaps when Grace looked at this scene she saw something else.

'I've heard that the slums in Dublin are quite bad,' I said finally, to break the silence.

Lady Wilcox glanced at me incredulously, while her husband acknowledged my question. 'They're among the worst in Europe, I'm afraid. Tenement houses filled with starving, ragged children, most families living in only one room. There isn't enough work for the men.'

'Miss Singleton is a very politically aware young woman,' Lady Wilcox observed, a hint of acid in her voice. 'In my day, young women were simply ignorant of these things.'

'You don't want your daughter to grow up ignorant, I hope,' Sir John said.

'I certainly don't want to raise a socialist. I'm afraid misery and want are eternal problems. Some people just wallow in their own squalor. There's not much one can do for them.'

'I don't think we've tried very hard.'

Lady Wilcox made an angry sound, then stared pointedly out the window. It seemed strange to me that they were having this discussion in front of Carter, the chauffeur, who was presumably not supposed to listen. I did not feel that I was really included in the conversation either.

Later, I tried another tack. 'I heard that Ireland was nearly given Home Rule a year ago, but then the war broke out.'

'Yes,' Sir John said. 'The Home Rule Bill did actually pass in the Houses of Parliament. A military group in the North called the Ulster Volunteers formed in response to that threat, to keep the North British at any cost. And then the Irish Volunteers were started in Dublin by a man called Eoin MacNeill — to defend the South from the Ulster Volunteers in case Home Rule is granted, supposedly. It sounds a little farcical, but we do have to monitor these developments. I suppose you've heard the saying, "England's difficulty is Ireland's opportunity"?'

'No,' I admitted. 'I hadn't.'

'Well, it refers to the fact that a lot of England's energy is going towards the War, and there is a certain vacuum here at the moment, and quite a lot of discontent, which I suppose is why this nationalistic Sinn Féin movement has gathered so much steam lately. But I really feel that there's no need to be alarmist. We've weathered worse times before this — all the Parnell rubbish.'

Rubbish? It was the first time Sir John had said something that disturbed me. I settled back in my seat. I knew that Charles Stewart Parnell had been an Irish MP who had fought hard for Home Rule in the 1880s, pressuring our Prime Minister Gladstone to submit the first Home Rule bill to Parliament. He had also won some improvements for poor Irish tenant farmers. Then, I'd heard, he had been brought down by a scandal — it was discovered that he was living with a married Englishwoman, Kitty O'Shea. He'd been drummed out of politics and died soon afterwards, of a broken heart, some said.

'I really *don't* think Irish politics can be said to be interesting,' Lady Wilcox said in freezing tones.

I asked no more questions after that, but I felt that somehow Grace had been vindicated. These people had no interest in what was going on around them, no real fear that anything serious could occur to topple them from their places of power, no sense that anything was *wrong*. I despised their complacency.

~

Dublin, I learned, was divided into north and south sides by the river. We passed by Nelson's Pillar and crossed the Liffey over a broad bridge. I admired the tall stone or brick buildings and the wide streets.

'That's the General Post Office,' Amelia said, before we reached the bridge. A few minutes later she burst out, 'And there's Trinity College! Grafton Street is the best shopping street, Miss Singleton.'

It was so busy. I glanced around in awe, taking in as much as I could. There were some large, marble classical buildings, many eighteenth-century brick buildings, and masses of people. Most streets were cobbled, so we jostled our way through elegant squares to our destination.

'And this is our street,' Amelia said with satisfaction. 'We're near the canal. May she take me walking by the canal, Mamma?'

'I suppose so,' Lady Wilcox said in a bored voice. 'Miss Singleton won't find much excitement here, after London. There's certainly a quantity of water of various sorts, and a plentiful variety of parks. Little culture, however.'

The car drew to a stop, and I got out, staring up at the tall Georgian house that was to be my new home.

'I hope you won't mind an attic room, Miss Singleton?' Lady Wilcox inquired. 'I didn't want to put you upstairs with the *servants*, but we're so pressed for space ... I'm sure you understand. My cousin Arthur, who died in India while in the Civil Service, often stayed there. You'll find the room is full of some of his things.'

~

Lessons had been cancelled for the day, of course, so I sat in my room and contemplated unpacking. The room was, as Lady Wilcox said, full of an odd, dusty assortment of imperial bric-a-brac, including a yellowing elephant's tusk on the wall and a tiger-skin rug by the bed. A photograph of the middle-aged Arthur in his pith helmet was still up on the mantel. He stared out at me with a look of bemused arrogance. It was strange, but I felt lonelier here than I had in the country, and at the same time much more restless.

My small room looked out onto the park in the middle of the square, and seemed noisy. Horses' hooves, shouts.... I curled up on my bed and closed my eyes. I had not seen Grace, though I had met the Wilcoxes' city butler, Jones, a fellow Londoner. Lady Wilcox had mentioned that I need not take dinner in the servants' hall; I could either have it brought to my room or dine with the family. This thought had sent me into a spasm of anxiety. Both options would be awful. I liked being alone, but night after night, staring at the four walls of my room? Yet having to converse with Lady Wilcox and her guests (or, more likely, stay silent) was a terrible thought. My clothes and appearance were so plain....

I realised that I was in danger of drowning in self-pity. Perhaps, I thought, I could at least buy some cheap prints to hang on my walls, to try to lend an artistic atmosphere to the room; a Vermeer would do nicely. I particularly liked the *Girl with the Red Hat*. I realised why: she reminded me of Grace. All of Vermeer's women had a quiet power, I thought, quite unlike the haughtiness of the Lady Wilcoxes of this world. Some were pure, some seemed less so, but they were all quite real, and sensitive....

A timid knock on my door. I sat up, smoothing my hair, reflecting on how travel-weary I looked.

It was Grace. She slipped in the door smiling, her smile deepening as she heard me gasp with joy.

We embraced.

'Do you see this?' she said teasingly, pointing to a rope that hung down near my bed. 'You're supposed to pull this if you need anything from us.'

'But *you* might not come.'

She covered my hands with her warm ones. 'You're cold. I'm going to build you a fire. I asked Mr Jones if I could, and he said yes. I would have done it before, but we've been so busy.'

She knelt in front of the fireplace and began to crumple newspaper and stack kindling.

'This room hasn't been used for years, that's why it seems a bit ...'

'Forlorn,' I said. I sat on the bed watching her work, burying my bare feet in the soft rug. The sight was a pleasure to me, though a somewhat guilty one. 'I could learn how to do that.'

'Ah, no. We couldn't have you dirtying your hands. Besides, I like doing it.'

She shot me a smile. I smiled back, amazed at her cheerfulness.

'You seem happy.'

'I'm back in Dublin, amn't I? And away from oul' Johnson and those bad memories.'

I felt a pang. 'Well, there were some good ones, I hope.'

'There can be here too,' Grace said steadily, dusting her hands and looking me in the eye. 'You'll get used to it here, Caroline.'

I nodded. 'I'm a city girl, so I suppose I will.'

'I'm going to fetch some coal for you now.'

'Wait one minute,' I said. She came towards me hesitantly, and I stood up and pulled her against me. My lips sought hers, and suddenly we were kissing wildly, our lips burning. She thrust her tongue into my mouth, and we collapsed on the bed. I almost stopped breathing.

She got up and ran to the door, pulling the bolt across with aggressive force.

'The fire's not lit,' I said, laughing. 'At least, the fire over there isn't.'

I couldn't believe what was happening. She came back towards me, and we lay together for a moment, breathing hard.

'We don't have long,' Grace said. She began undoing the buttons of my dress, almost lazily, it seemed. 'I can't undress, but you can. I wish I was your lady's maid, then this would all be easier.'

'I'm not exactly a lady, Grace,' I murmured. Her hands were touching me seductively.

As I let her make love to me, I wished I could make as much noise as I wanted to. That in itself was so utterly *un*ladylike, I thought. But her caresses made me want to scream. There I was, lying on the bed, her head between my legs as she pleasured me in what was becoming a more and more expert manner. As I trembled against the edge of the bed I stroked my own breasts, pinching my nipples. I was drowning in ecstasy. Suddenly, I climaxed with a gasp.

I felt light-headed. 'You are so ... incredible, Grace,' I murmured, pulling her up to embrace her.

'I like it when you praise me,' she said softly. 'I wanted to make you feel better.'

'I do, I do.' I began to giggle, pushing my head down into her bosom. 'Oh, Grace ... I can't do anything without you. I'm addicted to you.'

'That's all right,' she said. The touch of humour in her voice made me laugh again.

'Well, it's not all right. I'm not sure how long you're going to be with me.'

She said nothing for a while, holding me close, stroking my hair.

'There won't be anybody else — it's not as if ...'

'Oh, I know, but politics can separate people, and you've never really ... I'm sorry, Grace, I just hoped you might consider ... well, some kind of a future together.'

My words sounded apologetic, and I did in fact feel guilty for asking anything of her.

'Now what kind of a future could you and me have?' she said gently.

I stiffened, my face going pale.

'Some kind of plan, you know, to be together one day....'

It sounded feeble. I recognised that, but I desperately wanted to hear something reassuring.

Grace sat up and began fixing her hair, smoothing down her dress. Her eyes were lowered, and I felt that she could not answer me, could not give me what I wanted to hear.

'I'd better go get the coal now,' she said, still not looking at me exactly.

I began to button my dress. With each button, I felt as if I was closing up some part of myself that had been briefly liberated.

'All right,' I muttered. The swing from joyousness and pleasure to disappointment and sadness had been so abrupt that I really did not know what to say, or even feel.

Grace left the room, and I sat down on the bed again, wide-eyed, trembling. It reminded me of the way I'd felt when we got the telegram about Ralph. My mother had gone into immediate hysterics and shut herself away. I had sat in my bedroom, feeling the same sense of bewilderment, emptiness and despair.

I cannot allow her to do this to me, nor should I inflict this pain on myself, I thought. *She'll never commit to me; the most that we'll ever have is this — stolen moments of intense pleasure and then having to part, again and again. If I can bear these terms, I should accept them; otherwise we should stop now.*

It was just that there seemed no way to stop.

Chapter 11

At Thornley, I had not really felt like a governess, in a curious way. Now I most definitely was 'Amelia's governess', and my feelings for Amelia became tinged with a resentment I could not prevent. Her needs — not just for learning, but for being 'seen' around town — were paramount. Lady Wilcox made sure that every day we went out, either for a walk, or to shop, or to visit Amelia's friends. Amelia was not in the least shy, and I was often left chatting stiffly to another governess or nursemaid while the two children prattled away, impervious to the cold.

My days had become very busy. Lady Wilcox was now taking a radically different course with me: at Thornley, I had been encouraged to keep to myself, with large amounts of free time; here I was expected to be sociable yet demure, a young Englishwoman of relatively good family whom Lady Wilcox could exhibit like a prize cabbage.

Meanwhile, I hardly saw Grace. This new turn of events was terribly upsetting, and sometimes I did not know if I could bear it. I came to realise that, if she chose, she could become invisible. Her life was below stairs, and there was no necessity for our lives to connect at all. They did not connect now, and I scarcely knew how to handle this. I felt that my outward appearance was deceptively calm: inside I was seething, tormented and bitterly hurt.

All I had asked for was what anyone would have asked for. Yet for some reason she had found it threatening! I could see why she could not envisage a life together; we both had to support ourselves by working and living in other people's houses. Yet there was no reason, I thought, why we could not both be shop-girls, or typists: I could see that more and more women were working now, and I had begun to hunger for independence. The irony seemed to be that, while I desired independence on a personal level, Grace desired it for her country, on a national level. And that, I thought, was even more hopeless, more quixotic.

Sometimes I mused bitterly that neither of us was going to achieve her dream. Generations of Irish people had hungered for freedom. And generations of women had been oppressed: we were not even allowed to vote! We were also not permitted to live independently, like men. *All I want is that,* I thought: *an economic self-sufficiency that will give me a chance to be with whomever I choose....* How I wished I had talent, could be a writer or painter, could assume a mask of eccentricity and have people accept me as I was.

I felt Grace's absence from my life as a personal betrayal, and I smarted from the blow. Each morning, another maid would bring me hot water; if I told Lady Wilcox I would dine in the schoolroom, another maid would respond to my summons. It was never Grace. The idea of venturing down to the servants' hall, since I had never seen it, held particular terror. And what if Grace ignored me, snubbed me? I was sure my manner would reveal everything.

At night I dreamed about her, tossing feverishly. In the morning my pillow would be soaked with perspiration or tears, I was not sure which. I could feel myself becoming shyer and more withdrawn, less interested in helping Amelia learn, though full of gratitude for the daily contact with somebody innocent and playful. I plunged myself into new topics of learning for a time, but would just as quickly lose interest, and be surprised when Amelia maintained her enthusiasm.

I felt terribly guilty. Firstly, I had had an illicit affair with a social inferior (this was the way Lady Wilcox would see it); then there was the fact that it was an 'unnatural passion'; and thirdly, I was allowing my obsession with Grace to overwhelm me and cause me to lose interest in my duties. I had ceased to be an effective teacher, I knew. I had ceased to *feel*. I was certainly not as trusting as I had been, nor as kind. I had never seen my love for Grace as evil before, but now I felt like a fallen woman, one who had been used and tossed aside, one who had allowed herself to be exploited sexually. It occurred to me that this was what Johnson had done to Grace, and she had repeated the pattern. But who had seduced whom?

It was the fact that she ignored me now. I could not understand it. The few times I'd seen her I had been in Amelia's company, and Grace had averted her eyes from me and chatted to Amelia. I had been afraid to say anything, standing there trembling and pale. I had felt the strangest urge to reach out and touch her.

Sometimes I pondered the idea of passing a note to her through Jones, the butler, who was always exceptionally civil to me. Yet the fear that the note might fall into the wrong hands was too great. Several times I attempted to write a letter, but I found the strength of my emotions getting the better of me. I would either start sobbing and abandon the attempt, or begin scrawling accusations and questions that grew increasingly more maddened and bitter.

I had started to keep a journal — out of necessity, for fear of going mad if I did not express myself — and found myself writing disquieting passages:

I suppose it was all just a game to her. She seemed sincere, but if she had truly loved me she would never have abandoned me like this, without even a word. Oh God! I miss her so much, the way she felt against me, the way she kissed me for what seemed like hours. Sometimes at night I feel like going into the servants' sleeping-quarters and throwing myself upon her. If I were a man I would probably —

Then I had broken off in disgust at myself, chastising myself for my anger.

~

Looking back, I consider this period the worst time in my life. After the first few days, I had begun to realise that it was not just a phase: Grace really had decided to stop seeing me. The days passed into weeks. My anguish continued, and sharpened at Christmas, when the only sight I had of Grace was at the ritual of the servants coming in *en masse* and being given presents of money. I noticed that Grace looked thinner and more serious, and we did exchange one glance, but I could not read any meaning into her look. It all seemed to happen so fast. Time was either curiously speeded up or strangely slowed down.

Lady Wilcox asked me if I needed to take time off to see my mother. I responded dully in the negative. The idea of journeying to London now was unappealing to me in the extreme, nor did Mother expect me to come. I had not had a letter from her in a long time. And besides, the city was being bombed in zeppelin attacks. Lady Wilcox looked pleased. It seemed strange that she had not noticed my mood; but then, so much escaped her notice. She had not picked up the mood of the country either!

I went by myself to a play at the Abbey Theatre, which had been founded about ten years before by the poet W.B. Yeats and some of his Anglo-Irish friends, including the playwright Lady Gregory. The play was *Cathleen Ní Houlihan*. It was about an old woman who personified Ireland, and I found myself curiously gripped by it, drawn by the lyrical, sorrowful language and the fatalistic yet hopeful theme. Ireland was everywhere, the play seemed to say, carried safe in the hearts of the people. Ireland could manifest itself at any time.

I noticed the way the people around me watched the show intensely, gasping and applauding at certain points where the language grew most forceful. I went home thoughtfully, wishing I could have seen it with Grace, knowing she would have explained it to me better than I could possibly understand it by myself. It took me back to that wonderful afternoon in the woods when she had leaned over me with her hair down, like a goddess, something wild and free in her gaze that captivated me completely.

I began to attend the Abbey regularly. Sometimes I saw Mr Yeats himself, his tall lanky frame and trademark monocle somehow charming, though his combination of shyness and arrogance prevented me from approaching him. Once I noticed him in the company of a haughty yet radiant woman in black, her face and figure classically formed.

'That's Maud Gonne,' my seat-mate whispered to her friend. 'He was in love with her once, maybe he still is — did you read the poem "No Second Troy"? She's married to Major McBride now.'

I purchased Mr Yeats's two most recent books of poems at a bookshop the very next day, and read the poem carefully. It was about a man who is in love with a woman whom he compares to Helen of Troy; her beauty is mythical and the effect she has on people is both wonderful and terrible, terrible because *she cannot help being who she is*. The phrase 'being who she is' rang and rang in my mind. *Perhaps the greatest love is made up of forgiveness and understanding*, I thought. *But it must take time.* Obviously Yeats's early bitterness had passed.... I read on and on, marking the poems I liked most. It was one of my few pleasures.

~

I had started to teach Amelia French, in response to a request from Lady Wilcox, and she was enjoying it.

I tried to explain to her the difference between saying to someone '*je t'aime*' and '*je vous aime*'. The example was listed in our lesson book, so I could not avoid it.

'When you're speaking to an older person you should always use *vous*, unless they allow you to use *tu*. *Tu* is more intimate. So if you were speaking to a friend, you would say "*je vous aime bien*". It really means, "I like you." "*Je vous aime*" would mean, "I love you."'

'But why would you say *vous* to someone if you were saying you loved them?' Amelia persisted. 'If you loved them, Miss Singleton, why would you not use *tu*?'

'Well, it's not polite, Amelia. For example, even though you like me, you call me Miss Singleton.'

'Yes, but that's because everybody else calls their governess Miss. And Mamma would get angry if I didn't.'

'Sometimes you just have to do what everyone else does, Amelia.'

She noticed a heaviness in my tone, and looked up curiously.

'It must be difficult for you, Miss Singleton. You don't have anybody to love here.'

I blushed.

'I think we should get back to work, Amelia,' I said feebly.

'I thought you were going to make friends with Grace.' It had obviously disappointed her that I hadn't.

'Well, I ... I do like Grace, of course.' My words came out strangled.

'*Vous l'aimez bien*,' Amelia said playfully. 'You like her. Isn't that right, Miss Singleton?'

'That is grammatically correct, Amelia,' I said. 'Thank you; you addressed me formally, using *vous*. You're picking up French very well.'

'I even speak it with my friends!' Amelia said cheerfully. I felt a curious pang, and then a burst of anger at myself for being jealous of a child's friendships. I was so friendless and alone, even Amelia pitied me. But my plight was not uncommon. Being a governess was like being a nun; people gave you the same mixture of respect and patronising pity. You had removed yourself from the mainstream. You couldn't complain.

Chapter 12

---

*O*ne Saturday afternoon in March, I was sitting beside the
pond in Stephen's Green, watching Amelia feed ducks.
She loved the mallards, with their green shiny heads, and could
stay there for hours. Various other children played around her; I
had nodded to a few other governesses or nursemaids whom I
knew, but had tried very hard to avoid company.

I had been in Ireland for over six months, I mused, and what
had I achieved? Certainly not the happiness that had seemed so
tantalisingly close.... I had begun to wonder if I should return to
England. Perhaps I could get a post with a nice middle-class
English family, I thought, where I would be one of them, not an
outsider. It would all be very ordinary and pleasant, and I could
forget the troubling events of these past months. Perhaps I could
even meet a nice young man and do the expected thing ... but
then, weren't all the nice young men off being slaughtered at the
Western Front?

Rex Philpott came to mind, and I wondered why he had not
written. Perhaps he had thought better of it, realising, of course,

that we were of different classes and had very little in common. Maybe he had found another lover. The thought bothered me, somehow. *If he were to visit on leave and court me now,* I thought, *I would probably accept him — but it would be out of desperation and loneliness, not love.* In a way I was glad not to be tempted.

I had written to the headmistress of my school, who had recommended me for the post at Thornley, asking her to notify me if any other offers came in. A sudden rescue would be such a relief, I thought. Or perhaps now that I was in Dublin I should look up Mrs Grimsby; maybe one of her friends needed a governess. I did not know how I could explain leaving the Wilcoxes, though. Everyone would think I was mad.

I was enjoying the weak sun, and looked up, startled, as somebody blocked its path. Grace was standing in front of me. Amelia, seeing her, waved, and smiled at me, as if to say, 'Now you have someone to amuse you, Miss Singleton.' I met Grace's eyes as coolly and neutrally as I could, then looked away. She sat down beside me on the bench.

'Remember the last time we sat on a bench together?' I inquired. 'Perhaps you've forgotten.'

'No, I haven't forgotten that.'

'Really? But you seem to have forgotten my existence over the past few months.'

I still didn't look at her.

'I had to do that. I'm sorry.'

'Oh? One of your revolutionary chums told you to, I suppose.'

'I can understand you being angry.'

'Yes, I'm angry.' I spoke in a low voice, and the words rushed out. 'You betrayed me, and I don't see how I can ever trust you again. If just the thought of us having some future together is so repellent to you, then you should never have started anything with me. How was I to know that I couldn't ask for that? It's what people do, even people like us.'

'People like us?' Grace said, looking out over the pond with what seemed to be a faint smile.

'Yes, people who love their own sex. But I forgot: you probably don't consider yourself anything of the sort!'

She said nothing, playing with the catch of a little bag she was carrying. I stole a glance at her, but her face revealed little of her thoughts.

'Well, it doesn't matter. I'm going to look for another position. Obviously you'll stay on here until your precious uprising happens — and then what? You'll leave, I suppose. Will the Wilcoxes ever even know what they harboured in their midst?'

She shook her head.

'It's so deceptive, don't you think? How can you stand to work here, anyway? The rest of the staff are firmly royalist, as far as I can see.'

'I don't associate with them much.'

'That's right. You think you're too good for them.'

'No, I just don't have anything in common with them.'

Her calm responses infuriated me. 'Well, I suppose there's no point in expecting any remorse from you.'

'I *have* felt guilty. Of course I have. It's just — there's been a lot of planning, and I really wanted to keep you separate from it. I felt that I couldn't carry on a romance with you while this was going on. You wanted so much from me.'

'Of course I wanted a lot from you! I loved you, Grace. It was always so simple.'

She smiled. 'Simple for you.'

'Oh, don't give me that nonsense!' I snapped. 'But I suppose you were right to end it with me before I became completely besotted with you.'

'Is that all gone?' she said, turning to me. Her eyes, green mingling with brown, looked at me imploringly, and I caught my breath.

'How can you ask? You've ignored me for so long ... I thought you wanted to break with me, and I've tried to forget you.' My voice, sounding wretched to my own ears, seemed to wring some pity from her. She looked at me with compassion, tenderness.

'No.... I should have explained, but ... I haven't forgotten you. I wanted to see you all this time, but I couldn't allow myself. I couldn't risk the possibility that I'd tell you something that would get into the wrong hands.'

'That doesn't make sense. I hardly ever question you, and never ask for specifics.'

'I know. But I so much wanted to tell you everything. It was my weakness, not yours. Because ...'

I stared at her.

'Because I love you so much.'

Her words shocked and thrilled me to the core. I bent my head, and Grace put her hands over mine, exclaiming at their coldness. She spoke soothingly to me, which made the tears that had filled my eyes spill over. They splashed onto her hands.

'Listen, it won't be long now,' she whispered. 'Something will happen next month. I'll leave the Wilcoxes about a week before, and I'll tell you where I'm going. It won't be home, it'll be a safe place. That way you'll know where I am.'

'You're not asking me to join you.'

'How could I ask that?'

I shrugged. 'You don't think I'd be strong enough, I suppose. Or you're ashamed of me.'

'No, not ashamed. Quite a lot of our supporters have grand accents, you know.' She spoke teasingly, but I still did not smile.

'So I'll know where you are,' I said wearily. 'Well, that's better than not knowing. Forgive me for not being overwhelmingly grateful to you.'

She was silent. I heard Amelia cry, 'I'm getting cold, Miss Singleton,' and I stood up, noticing how my bones ached.

'It's a damp city,' Grace said.

'And you haven't been there to light my fires,' I said in a low voice.

She nodded, looking up at me, shielding her eyes against the sun. 'Would you like me to come tonight?'

'I don't know,' I muttered. The thought frightened me, and I bit my lip. 'Don't do it for my sake.'

'Would you bar the door?'

'I just don't know if I trust you now. I'm sorry.'

Amelia came running over to us, her face flushed. 'Hello, Grace!'

'Afternoon, Miss Amelia,' Grace replied in calm tones. *She's good with children*, I thought.

'Did you come to see Miss Singleton?'

'No, I was walking past and got a big surprise.'

'I hope you gave her something,' Amelia babbled. 'Whenever I quarrel with my friends I give them something to make up.'

'That's a nice idea, Miss,' Grace said. She smiled at me and turned to go. I watched her walk away, rather stunned, and could think of nothing to say to Amelia.

'Why didn't she walk with us?' Amelia asked.

'I don't know,' I said. 'Perhaps it's her day off.'

'Oh, yes, it probably is. Last year, she introduced me to her brother. He came around on one of her days off. He's such a handsome fellow. Pity he has such a low occupation.'

'What does he do?' I asked distractedly.

'Oh, he works as a barman. One of the maids told Nurse. At a public house called the Cloak and Dagger. It's supposed to be quite rough.'

'You shouldn't know about public houses, Amelia.'

'Well, I've never been in one, Miss Singleton,' Amelia confessed, as if this proved her virtue. 'Have you?'

'Now, Amelia, don't be impertinent,' I said, smiling. She was so much easier to deal with than Grace, and I loved her for it. 'Let's go back to the house and I'll read to you until tea-time.'

'Oh, good!' she exclaimed, clapping her hands.

Chapter 13

I could not shake off the sense that something was about
to happen, about to go terribly wrong. A certain fatalism
in Grace's manner had alarmed me. She seemed like someone
who was quite certain that plans were underway, someone who
was 'in the know'. I felt the fear that comes from not having
been told the full story, yet glimpsing snatches of the truth.

And with us ... Although Grace's words had been kind and
tender, had rekindled my hopes, I was not sure what she really
intended. I still did not feel as if she saw me clearly, as if she was
focusing on me. Perhaps she never had. I was just a part of her
life, wasn't I? whereas she was everything to me! We were too
different, I thought as I lay on my bed, my boots off but
otherwise fully clothed. The irony was that Grace *seemed*
sensual, rather simple, not a typical revolutionary by any means,
whereas I with my intense personality would seem to be the
ideal fanatic for a cause. I smiled bitterly, thinking of how her
caresses could drive everything out of my mind. I had never
imagined I would set my hopes on another human being. Was it

more foolish, more futile, than setting one's hopes on an impossible patriotic dream?

Better to be rational, I concluded, and I would try. I would not let her seduce me tonight, though the thought of being intimate with her caused me to tremble inwardly and my cheeks to flush. I still wanted her. How could I not? I loved her, but I would hold back; I would not say it.

It was about midnight, and the house was completely silent. The only sound came from outside my window: the occasional clip-clop of horses as people returned late from the theatre or a show. Once or twice I heard a woman's laugh, low and seductive.

I turned restlessly, pressing my face into the pillow. At that moment a knock came on the door. I got up reluctantly, not sure that I wanted a long *tête-à-tête* where I would have to restrain myself from touching her.

I unlatched the door. Grace slipped in, her flimsy nightgown covered by an over-garment like a coat, her feet bare. She jumped noiselessly onto my bed, and I sat down beside her, but not too close. Her eyes were shining, her hair was down. I felt I could hardly speak, choking as I was with mixed emotions of love, anger, resentment, desire.

'I'm sorry, Caroline,' she said in her wonderful low voice. I looked at her. 'I'm so sorry.'

She took my hand and began stroking it. I remained still, not pulling my hand away, yet trying to signal a disinterest I did not really feel.

'So, Grace,' I said finally, 'why did you want to come here?'

'Just to tell you that I'll be leaving soon.' Her head was bent and her hair brushed over my hand. I secretly thrilled to the touch. 'You mustn't tell a soul. I can trust you, can't I?'

She sounded so excited. *No wonder she's animated,* I thought with a pang. Her dreams of winning freedom from the British had obviously reached a new level — they were about to become reality. I still didn't quite believe it. It seemed like a childish game, which might have deadly consequences. The English were not going to be happy about an uprising in Ireland during wartime, when patriotic fervour was supposed to be at its height.

Grace began to whisper to me. I listened in horror. What she was doing, I realised, was telling me the way the rising would take place!

'One of our influential friends has been raising support from the Germans. He'll land with German troops somewhere on the coast of Kerry. Other Volunteer groups will rise around the country. In Dublin we'll seize five or six important buildings, including the General Post Office on Sackville Street. That's where Mr Pearse will proclaim the Republic. And the date has been set — it's Easter Sunday. Jack is *so* ... I've never seen him like this. He really believes in it, Caroline. He's willing to sacrifice his life. They all are! That's the power of it.'

'I see,' I said after a while. Then, 'Aren't you afraid, giving me these kinds of details? I'm not Irish, you know.'

'But I trust you,' she said, looking at me sincerely. Her big, earnest eyes glowed. 'I trust you, Caroline. Most of the fighters don't even know the day has been set. But Jack's close to Mr Pearse, and he told me.'

'He doesn't even know about me, does he?' I murmured.

'Jack?' Grace said blankly. 'Well, he ... No, I haven't told him.'

'What would he think?' I inquired, not bothering to hide the bitterness in my tone. 'I suppose he'd think less well of you.'

She was silent for a long time. I wondered dispassionately how she would get out of this one.

I saw her face redden. She looked at me fiercely.

'I thought you understood. The revolution comes first for me. It has to. When you talked of a future with me, I just couldn't imagine it. Not here.'

Swallowing my hurt, I spoke as firmly as I could.

'It seems possible to *me*, Grace. But I think we'd have to go to England. Women live together there and nobody blinks an eye. You'd hate it, though, wouldn't you?'

She paused for a while. I could tell she wanted to please me, yet saw no way of doing so.

'I can't leave my country, especially after what's going to happen. But, Caroline, who knows what the future holds? Things may be different. If it all fails, if Jack is killed, if the leaders are executed, then I may just decide to leave for good, go somewhere like America.'

'America?' I said in disbelief.

'Yes, Irish people have been going over there for decades. It started after the Famine. We do well over there, you know, in Boston or New York.'

'I don't think I could go to America,' I said flippantly. 'Not even for your sake, Grace.'

Her eyes flashed and she pulled her hand away. 'Well, you've got a nerve trying to get me to go to England! You want it all your way.'

I lay down on my side, turning my head away from her. I was amazed to realise that I wanted her to go. It seemed that our lives had branched off already — that there was no possible path for us to travel together.

As if my physical reaction was too painful for her, Grace moved to huddle against me, stroking my hair, kissing my neck. I was filled with tenderness, despite myself. *Perhaps*, my body signalled, *one last time....* I hoped that she did not have the same idea, for her touch was so seductive I knew I could not withstand her.

I turned my head, only to see that her beautiful white breasts were bare. I groaned.

'Oh, Grace, no....'

'Yes, my love,' she murmured. She looked at me pleadingly. I wanted her to beg me to go on. To my astonishment, she did.

'Please, please, I'll die if you don't!'

I felt the same way.

'This should be the last time, then,' I said, almost coldly.

Her eyes filled with tears. 'Oh, don't say that!'

She began to remove my clothes, then pulled me down on top of her. It was like the first time in my bedroom at Thornley, although this time I tried to savour every moment of it. I had never seen her so transported, so frenzied. Her whispered endearments spurred me on. My roughness seemed to drive her to ecstasy.

After we had both climaxed, we lay weakly against each other. I did not move to stroke her hair, and she made no loving gesture towards me. This would bother me later, I thought, but seemed curiously apt now. After all, it had been the last time.

I felt a strange aloofness from Grace. Perhaps, I mused, my earlier angry thoughts had not been completely dispelled. I wondered what she was thinking, her face buried in the pillow, but made no move to ask. I hoped, though, that it was not of earlier times in her life when men had used her callously and her own passion had betrayed her.

She looked over at me finally, her eyes weary and sadder than I had ever seen them.

'Usually I can tell you love me when you touch me,' she said softly, 'but not that time.'

'You enjoyed it anyway.' The words came out before I could stop them.

'Damn you,' she said, in the same low tone. 'How do you think it feels?'

'I don't know,' I replied, covering myself up with a sheet. 'But you've never loved me. You've always held back.'

'I've given you everything!' she retorted.

'But you won't give me any promises.'

'How can I? Don't you think I feel guilty? I do. But, Caroline, I'd feel worse if I went off with you and let down the Countess and my brother. I'd regret that till the end of my life. I have to be a part of this. You don't understand, you think things are grand just the way they are. You don't know what it's like to have grown up living under the heel of the English. To feel their scorn. To know your family or neighbours could starve and no one would give a damn. The cause is bigger than you and me. It means more. I'd feel the same if you were a man, it's not because of that —'

I shrugged. 'Well, I'm glad I've been of use to you. I've given you a bit of sexual pleasure now and then. I can't say I regret that. But don't expect me to give you my heart as well. It's not a fair exchange.'

I felt I was being cruel, but I could not take back what I had said, nor did I really want to.

Grace sat up and began dressing, her body still glistening, pale and enticing. I inhaled her odour for what was surely the last time. I felt a hard ache of misery inside my chest, yet did not speak.

'You won't spill a word of what I've told you,' she said sharply.

'No.'

'I won't be here much longer, so you won't have to run into me again.'

'I see.'

Her hair was all wild around her face. As she touched it, her mouth trembled. She gazed at me.

'Can't we part friends?'

I reached out and stroked her face. She looked at me calmly, sweetly. We stared at each other for a charged moment.

'I love you,' she said.

The reverberations of this seemed to ring around the room. I wanted to seize her in my arms, but somehow could not. It was not the answer.

Finally I said slowly, 'You know I love you. If you ever need me ...'

'If you ever need *me*,' she said, whispering, 'I —'

But her words were interrupted by a sharp knock on the door. We both stared at it, struck dumb with shock. The door, which I had not latched properly, swung open to reveal the stern figure of Lady Wilcox, holding a candle in one hand and a piece of paper in the other. It was a telegram. I pulled the sheet up to my chin. Grace slipped off the bed, holding her coat firmly around her.

Lady Wilcox's eyes pierced us like those of that mythical beast, the basilisk.

'My word!' was all she said at first. She seemed more shocked than angry.

'I can explain, madam,' Grace faltered, but Lady Wilcox gave a sarcastic laugh.

'You'll explain *nothing*! Would you kindly pull the rope by your bed, Miss Singleton? I am going to instruct Mr Jones to send Sheridan packing with a week's wages and no reference.' She stared at Grace. 'I want you out of this house forthwith. I have never seen *anything* so beastly and detestable. I had my suspicions, but this ...'

I pulled on the rope. A minute later, a scared-looking maid put her head around the door. She scuttled off to find the butler.

'Miss Singleton,' Lady Wilcox said tersely, 'the reason why I had to *interrupt* you was that a telegram has arrived for you. Read it, please.'

Under her angry gaze I pulled on my nightgown, which had been lying in a crumpled heap at the foot of the bed, and scanned the telegram. I was so numb that nothing could have surprised me. The telegram was from my uncle. It read simply: 'Your mother very ill. Doctor says she will not last. Come home at once.'

I handed the telegram to Lady Wilcox, who read it quickly.

'I see. Well, this is terrible news, Miss Singleton. I hope you understand that I cannot have you under my roof any longer. My child is young and impressionable. I am afraid that there can be no doubt of what you were doing, and I see that you don't try to explain it. Very well. I shall give you the rest of your year's wages and a short reference, and bid you adieu. You must say goodbye to your *friend* now. You shall stay tonight, but she leaves this instant. These wretched, shameless Irish girls!'

Once again I saw Lady Wilcox as a curiously Greek figure, impassively meting out justice. I shivered, unable to think, unable to feel. I glanced at Grace. She was looking at me anxiously. Would I ever see her again? Did she expect me to contradict Lady Wilcox's comment? I said nothing.

Mr Jones appeared at the door, looking grave.

'Goodbye, Caroline,' Grace muttered. 'I'm sorry. I'm sorry about everything.'

'Where will I find you, Grace?' I quavered. 'I'll come back.'

'Maybe you should just leave Ireland for good,' she said sadly. 'You don't want to get mixed up with me.'

'Excellent advice!' Lady Wilcox snapped. 'Very well. I'd like Miss Sheridan to leave the room now.'

Grace looked at me as if she was waiting for a final answer, a clue to my feelings; but I was too stunned by what had just happened, and too aware of Lady Wilcox's building impatience, to know how to respond.

'Goodbye, then,' I whispered.

She disappeared, stony-faced, followed by the bewildered Mr Jones.

Lady Wilcox turned to me, her voice softer. 'I'll have Carter take you to the boat in the morning.'

'I'll find my way,' I said sullenly, humiliated.

'I feel partly responsible, of course. I should have dismissed Sheridan years ago. She was never any good.'

'I don't agree,' I muttered.

She snorted. 'Do you really think this means anything to her? She's ruined you, you foolish girl. I don't understand how you, a young Englishwoman of good character, could allow yourself to be intimate with a little hussy from the streets like that. That something as sordid as this could happen under *my* roof is beyond belief. Only in Ireland, I suppose.'

'I'm in love with her,' I said. The words came out defiantly, and I meant them. I tried not to let her words sting too deeply, not to let her shame me into tears or pleading for my position. It was all over.

'A woman in love with another woman?' A redness crept into Lady Wilcox's cheek. 'Love, my dear, takes time. It flourishes in marriage, with the bearing of children. Sheridan is a vicious and depraved girl who has corrupted you. You will see it that way yourself someday.'

'Never,' I told her; but the sudden painful beating of my heart signalled uncertainty, despair. I put my head in my hands.

Chapter 14

*A*s I watched the misty coastline of Ireland recede, I felt a deep pang of wretchedness. I wept, standing by the rail. *Oh, Grace....* I did not know if I would ever come back. And how would I explain my dismissal from the Wilcoxes'? Maybe it would be better to say nothing, to pretend that they had allowed me time off. I thought of my mother too, but vaguely. She had been ill for so long. It did not quite sink in that she was dying.

I had not been allowed to say goodbye to Amelia. I felt a little rush of fury at this. Poor child! She had been so fond of me, and now she would never know why I had left. Perhaps they would invent some stupid lie. Yet surely she would wonder at the fact that Grace and I had both gone. Probably she would wonder about it for the rest of her life.

The train journey seemed endless. I tried to read, but could not concentrate. I had sent a telegram to my uncle letting him know my arrival time. I did not really want to see him, but I cursed myself for my ungratefulness. He had been taking care of Mother. I had not had to do it.

The stout, annoyed-looking man who met me at the station was only barely recognisable to me. He frowned at me for a minute, as if displeased.

'Well, here you are,' he declared, as if waiting for me had been a bore. 'Your journey went well?'

'How is my mother?' I asked distractedly, as we climbed into a cab.

'Not good,' he replied. 'The doctor says she can last for only a few days more. It's a fever, and her heart is weak. She insisted on seeing you, so I sent that telegram. To be honest, I expected her to die before you arrived.'

There it was, that blunt Manchester talk. I nodded, giving him the minimum of my attention.

'And your post in Ireland?'

'It ... has been interesting,' I said, my heart in my mouth.

He snorted. 'Why don't you just find a husband and stop this shilly-shallying around?'

'That's easier said than done, Uncle.'

He glared at me. 'I suppose you think my advice is worth nothing!'

'Not at all. I enjoy my independence, however. Earning my own money.'

'Well, there's not a lot of it, is there? Eventually you'll see reason. The young these days are so impractical, so unsettled. Your poor brother always refused to come work for me. I don't know. I'd be willing to settle some money on you if I thought you'd be able to start a small business, but you don't have the head for it.'

I ignored him, dreading the arrival at our house.

~

Mother was prostrate, pale and thin, a flush on her cheeks. Her breath was ragged. I sat down by her bedside apprehensively. This brought up memories of Father's death; before that, we had all been a happy family. First Father, then Ralph, then her....

'Caroline,' she murmured. 'I'm sorry.'

'Sorry for what, Mother? Don't be silly.' I talked to her soothingly, as if she were a child. And yet my mother had never really seemed anything else. She had grown up in an era when women were supposed to stay children. She had never understood me.

She said nothing for a while, and I thought she might have drifted off.

'I'm sorry that ... I wasn't better to you these past years. You have been unhappy.'

My throat tightened. I tried not to sob.

She coughed, and her whole body shook.

'I've left you some money. It should last you a year or two. Settle down somewhere — make friends. Will you?'

I nodded, tears streaming down my face. 'Don't leave me, Mamma,' I said, like a child.

She clutched my hand. Her voice was weak, her speech slurred.

'I'll be with your father at last. And your brother. Don't forget, darling, you have a long life ahead.'

The nurse my uncle had hired tapped me on the shoulder. 'She needs to rest now.'

I got up, feeling close to collapse. I made my way to my old bedroom and threw myself on the bed. When I woke up, eight hours later, I was told that my mother was dead.

My uncle, surprisingly, was in tears, raving about how beautiful she had been when my father, his brother, married her.

He had been drinking, I noticed. I drank with him. It was whiskey and soda, the kind of thing middle-aged men drank at clubs, but I didn't mind. He seemed indifferent too. It was the first sign I'd had that he had thrown up his hands: he wasn't going to insist on being a paternal figure. He would do the minimum and leave with a clear conscience. I didn't blame him.

'I don't know who to ask to the funeral,' he said. 'Are there any friends of yours?'

'There's Violet,' I said numbly.

I had had a letter from Violet around Christmastime while I was in Dublin, to say that her fiancé, Gerald, whom I barely knew, had been killed in action. The letter said almost nothing and I hadn't responded. I didn't know why. I remembered how she had helped me after Ralph died. We had still been close, then. But now the thought of seeing her bothered me somehow. Perhaps it was the thought that she had once seen me sobbing, in despair, weak and dependent on her, since there was no one else. I had secrets now, and could not be weak.

'But I don't know how to reach her. It would take too long to get hold of her.' I knew my uncle would not insist, or question my evasion.

'It's best to get these things over with,' he muttered.

The funeral was just my uncle and myself and Mrs Potts, standing by a grave in a vast London cemetery while we listened to the standard sermon from a clergyman I did not recognise. My mother was buried next to my father, and the sight of his untended tombstone caused my tears to flow yet again. My uncle touched my shoulder and sighed.

I saw him to the train station, since he had to get back to his business. He told me that he had talked to the family lawyer and made sure things were in order, and he thought I could handle my affairs myself from now on, but if I ever needed any advice he would certainly provide it, since he was technically my guardian. He spoke the last words rather gloomily.

I thanked him for all he had done: hiring the nurse, sending the telegram. At the thought of the telegram, and my own humiliation and fear at Lady Wilcox's intrusion, I dissolved into tears. My uncle looked puzzled. I could see he did not understand this strange young niece of his, who had fancy notions, who alternated between calm defiance and childish grief. He looked forward to going back to his solid northern city, to his plump wife and dull daughters.

London was different. I had only been gone for half a year, and was not sure at first what had changed, or whether the change was merely in me. It was grimmer. The newspaper headlines jumped out at me every day as I walked past the shops in the shabby, half-deserted streets of Camden Town. Wounded soldiers limped in the streets; men who had stayed behind had a furtive look. Some nights there were air raids. I stayed in the house in the evenings, reading by the light of a single lamp with the shutters closed. I felt as if I was in prison. The peaceful, sunny London of my youth was just a memory.

During those dark days, I sorted through my mother's clothes, jewellery, and letters, not with any great objective, but with a need to look at and touch her things. Much of it she had already given away, it seemed; the lovely dresses I remembered her wearing when I was a child were gone. I read through a stack of love letters to her from my father from the 1890s. They seemed unbearably innocent, from a time when settling down in a little house with one's beloved was the ideal of bliss. My father teased her about the children they would have — this was after they were engaged, of course. He thought that they would have a brainy boy and a beautiful, sentimental daughter. 'We shall sit around the fire in the long winter evenings and drink cocoa and read Dickens,' my father proposed. When I came to phrases like 'my shy, sweet rose' and 'my adored one', I began to understand how a girl who had been starved of love and approval — as my mother implied she had been by her high Victorian mother, who had given birth to fifteen children, eleven of whom survived — could drown in a love like this, could believe that if she centred her life around this one man, her luck and her future could change. No wonder she had spent so much of my childhood at the piano, singing sad, sentimental songs, while my father looked on benignly from his armchair. That had been her model of domestic bliss — to draw love in from an admiring onlooker. And, of course, the prettier, gentler and purer one was, the more love would be elicited.

It made more sense to me now why my mother had been so deeply saddened and disapproving when I became interested in the women's suffrage movement at the age of sixteen — the age when my mother was learning to be a lady and demurely lower her eyes under men's approving looks. How could she have identified with women marching near the government buildings in the streets of London in 1912, shouting 'Votes for women'? My mother had never marched, never shouted in her life. She had seemed to draw quietly away from me in those years, to turn even more of her love on Ralph, who was not the perfect son by any means, but whose boyish charm sweetened her days. I could not make her laugh as he could, for wit in a girl was, after all, unseemly. She did not want to discuss modern ideas, and it actually seemed to upset her that I was in school and learning science and maths like a boy would. She saw a hardness in me, an unwillingness to be defined by others. But my father had always rewarded my seriousness and my intelligence with his attention and warmth. *Perhaps that was the unforgivable sin*, I thought: *perhaps she had not expected him to care about his children, to care about anything but her*. It must have come as a great shock that he had supported my education, that he had sent me to a good school and made her promise to keep me there as he was dying. She had kept her promise, though.

Yet she had never had a real friend, so how could she have been a friend to me? I thought of many things as I tried on my mother's bracelets and necklaces, stroked the one fur coat that hung in her wardrobe, rummaged through her powders and creams and perfumes. This was all that was left. I did not want to discard these things immediately. I could not do that. But I knew that the one thing she had said to me on her deathbed was what remained with me now. She had told me to take the money, to settle down somewhere and make friends. I saw that as a sign that she envisaged me living an independent life with a close and dear friend by my side. She had not wanted me to exist in perpetual loneliness. *In the end*, I thought, *she knew I had to make my own choices. And perhaps she had an inkling that I would never love a man the way she loved my father*. I could not imagine what she would think of Grace, but as I knelt on the floor of my mother's room I knew that I wanted Grace there with me, that if she could be with me all my desolation would turn to joy.

I had moments when I thought Grace was gone from my life and I would have to resign myself to that fact. At other times, vivid memories of being with her, even at that last strange meeting, would flood over me. She had told me she loved me, and I had felt that she did, even in the odd way she had asked me not to come back, as if she had already put me through too much.

I had propped the picture of her against the wall in my room. She was what I saw every morning when I awoke, and I spent many an hour looking at her and going off into a reverie. Sometimes I said to her silently, 'Wait for me. Wait for me.' There was little hope of forgetting her this way, I knew. And, much as I sometimes tried, I could tell it would not work. I would have to see her again one more time, and then I would know. But the thought of Ireland frightened me, and I could not make up my mind to go back just yet.

As the weeks passed, I changed my mind about meeting Violet. I sent her a note at her parents' house, and a few days later the postman dropped her reply through the letter-slot. It was exciting to get a letter. I read it eagerly. She suggested meeting for tea in Tottenham Court Road the next day. She expressed sorrow at my mother's death, but seemed to imply that the great tragedy of it was that I had not been with her during the course of her last illness.

I frowned at this, but remembered Violet's odd maiden-aunt quality. She had always been a little fussy, a little bit of a stickler for convention. At the same time she had been such *fun* sometimes. I remembered her lovely blond hair, which she wore pinned back at school, as all the girls did; but sometimes, when we were alone in her bedroom, she would loosen her locks, sighing at their heaviness, and I would plait her hair, inventing strange styles, or just run my fingers through it. At this memory I blushed slightly, for Violet had not been an excitable, feminine kind of girl and we had always kept away from any embarrassing demonstrations of affection. But she had been my best friend.

It was strange: now that I was separated from Grace, I seemed to hope for more from Violet — hope that perhaps we could talk freely about our lives and about our plans for the future. I even imagined us setting up house together in a little flat in London. If I stayed in London, it was what I would choose to do. Would Violet want that? Perhaps she longed to escape the suffocation of her home now; and I knew her mother thought me sensible. Meeting her for tea was the first step, I thought, and just possibly we would come to an understanding.

I rather enjoyed the ritual of being back on the London buses, climbing the winding stairs to the top deck and relaxing into a comfortable seat.

'Where to, Miss?' said an unexpected voice.

I looked up in surprise. The conductor was a young woman, her cap fixed rakishly and her skirts descending only to the knee. She wore thick stockings and boots.

I told her and paid. She issued me the ticket. She had a very calm and pleasant face, so I ventured to ask her how long she expected to be working for the bus company.

'Oh, only till the end of the War, Miss. When the young men come home they won't have need of us no more.'

'That's a pity,' I said.

'That's the way it is, though, Miss,' she said, shrugging. She gave me a quick impish smile and moved away. I fiddled with my ticket, hating myself for being reminded of Grace. It would not do. She had told me not to come back. This was my country, after all, England. I wondered why it seemed different since I had returned, why I did not feel part of it.

Lyons Corner House was full of chattering women in hats. I looked around for Violet and saw her in a corner, her face in shadow. She stood up and pecked me on the cheek, exclaiming, 'Caro, darling,' in her deep, drawling voice. It was nice to be greeted by a good friend, but as I ordered tea and a sticky bun I could not help noticing that she was looking me over rather coldly, as if sizing me up.

'You don't mind that I started, do you? I'm *so* exhausted.'

'Yes, you must be. You're working?'

'Darling, how clever of you to remember. Yes, I teach a class of small children until three every day.'

'Do you like it?' I inquired.

Violet shrugged. Her face seemed permanently set in a scowl of weariness, and she was thinner. She took a cigarette case out of her bag and placed it rather pointedly on the table. Then she extracted a cigarette.

'You smoke, Vi?' My voice must have sounded shrill, because she gave me a long, appraising look.

'Yes, lots of girls do now. We're modern women, you know.' She sounded sarcastic as she spoke the last words. 'But you wouldn't know, would you? Lost in the wilds of Erin.'

'It's really not like that,' I said hesitantly. 'Not primitive.'

'Oh, I see.' She paused. 'I thought there might be something wrong with the mails.'

'The mails?' I had been brought my tea, and I poured myself a cup while thinking this over, wondering if she meant Irishmen.

'Yes, you know, so that letters get lost.'

'Oh.' I blushed deeply and, looking up, was shocked by the sudden flash of anger in Violet's eyes. 'Yes, I'm so sorry I didn't write after ... I just didn't quite know what to say. I'm sorry about Gerald. It's a terrible thing.'

'You should know just how awful it is,' she said in a low voice.

'I do. Of course I remember. And I'm so grateful for the way you helped me. I should have written.' I was sure she could tell I had not liked Gerald much; he had been a public-school boy with all the prejudices of his type, and I had wondered what Vi saw in him, and been jealous when she talked about him endlessly, repeating witticisms that I did not find funny but was expected to laugh at.

My words sounded stilted, and she did not acknowledge them in the way I expected her to; instead she took a deep pull on her cigarette and stared at me curiously.

'You've changed,' she remarked.

'Changed?' I faltered.

'Yes, I expected you to look quite the old maid.'

I bit my lip. 'Vi, that isn't very nice!' I felt she sensed that I had had a love affair. But how could she? I swallowed quickly. 'I suppose I should be flattered.'

'Yes, you're looking well,' she said in a low, rather deadened voice, so that I took no pleasure in the compliment. 'It's been three months since Gerald died, nearly four. We were supposed to get married on his last leave. But my elder sister was marrying, so Mother convinced me to wait for his next. He didn't get one, of course.'

I nodded, looking at her sympathetically. She was the fourth of five daughters, and had always had to wait for everything. To the outside world the family presented a united front. Only I had ever seen behind the playful, joking façade. The sisters were bitterly competitive.

'Are they all married now?' I asked.

'Oh, all except Emily and I. She's fifteen.'

'Well, that should be all right for a while, then,' I said, trying to tease her.

She frowned. 'You know, at this point I really don't think I'll ever marry. I'm going to join that whole wretched generation of girls who lost a young man in the War. I can't think of loving anyone else again. Let Emily be the next. I don't care. I'll just be the family spinster. Someone's got to be.'

'Vi, I was going to ask you about that,' I ventured. 'I was thinking of getting a place in London — you know, in the middle of things. I'm debating whether or not to go back to Ireland.'

'You should never have gone,' she said bitterly. 'I was sure it was a mistake.'

'It wasn't a mistake,' I retorted. 'I don't regret one minute of it.'

She looked at me speculatively. 'What did you get up to there? I can see it in your eyes, you know.'

I shook my head. 'Vi, I'm not hiding anything from you.'

'I can always tell when you are,' she said with a sly smile. 'So ... you lost your post?'

I stared at her, flushing, taking the comment as a bad joke. 'Can't you let me finish?'

'Oh yes,' she drawled. 'You were thinking of getting a flat in London. And what — you want me to live with you?'

'Well, yes,' I said. 'It would give us independence, which I'm sure you could also do with now.'

'You know,' she said, thoughtfully, 'I'm not terribly excited about independence, really. I was looking forward to marrying, being a wife and mother. I really wanted those things, Caroline. And now you want me to leave my family, which has always been very important to me, and risk my reputation, just to make the point that women can live together?'

'No, not just to make a point.' I felt irritated and confused, and puzzled by her mention of risking her reputation. 'You don't understand.'

'I don't think *you* understand. I would never have done what you did — deserted your mother when she was so ill.'

'She'd been ill for years, Violet.'

'Yes, and you wanted adventure. So off you went. And it seems like you found something, didn't you, Caro? I knew when you didn't answer my letter. I could tell something was up.'

I looked at her closely. Suddenly I realised. She knew. Lady Wilcox had gossiped, probably to the headmistress at our old school, with which Violet was still connected. She knew that I'd lost my post, and why.

We sat in silence for a moment. I felt sick with fear and embarrassment. Why had I thought it wouldn't get around? I had been naïve, horribly naïve. I swallowed some more tea, my eyes downcast. Well, I wouldn't be ashamed. I looked up. Violet was staring at me again, a mixture of pity and disgust in her eyes.

'Why did you do it, Caro?'

'Do what?' I asked, nervously gulping my tea.

'Ruin your reputation. For a *servant*.' Her tone was withering. 'I almost didn't come here today. If Mamma had known about the scandal, I could never have associated with you. But Miss Peabody has been very discreet. The only person she told was me. I believe she mentioned it because she needed to find out if I had any knowledge of it. Of course, she felt terrible about giving you such a glowing reference. She was quite disgusted. I told her I had the strongest contempt for what you'd done. It was horrible. I couldn't believe it at first, but I do see that you've changed.'

'How dare you lecture me?' I found myself saying. My voice had risen and I watched Violet glance around to see if anyone had noticed.

'How dare I? I've always had the strongest respect for morals. The strongest. As much as I loved Gerald, we never did more than kiss!'

I clenched my hands. 'Don't blame me because you didn't go further with Gerald.'

Now it was her turn to be enraged. She glared at me.

'You've always wanted to be different! You're like these unconventional girls I see coming out of the Slade Art School, their hair cut in a mop, looking like men! Probably living with men for all I know. It's disgusting, deviant. I've done my best to keep clean and my fiancé died in the War, like so many of our best young men — including your brother! Think of your brother, Caroline. Don't you have a responsibility to him to lead a good life?'

'Yes, Vi, and I *have* been living a good life. I've found out what love is —'

'And the only excuse would be if it hadn't been physical!' she blurted out. 'But you were caught *in bed* together. It's the worst thing I've ever heard.'

'You told me once that your uncle got a housemaid pregnant in the nineties,' I said stubbornly. 'That seems worse. He compromised her *and* he ruined her life.'

Violet was silent, angry, stirring her tea in such an agitated manner that I feared the cup might break.

'It must be true what they say about Ireland,' she said after a while.

I didn't respond.

'They don't have any morals over there. They're waiting to stab us in the back. You know, Caro, the filthiest thing you can be is a traitor to your country. Conscription was introduced here in January, and they couldn't even implement it over there because they were afraid the Irish might rise up.'

I sighed. I knew about conscription, and I also knew, from reading the papers, that the authorities had been disappointed by the unexpectedly large numbers of men they'd had to exempt from service due to ill health from decades of poverty and malnutrition. It seemed sadly ironic to me. Violet had moved far from the days when we used to discuss votes for women and better conditions for the working class. Our families were liberals, and I'd thought we shared a common ground. But her people were much more upper-middle-class than mine; there had been so many friends to whom I had never been introduced, parties to which I had not been invited. I had accepted this and never complained, and in the months before I left for Ireland Vi would poke fun at the 'stuffy' events that she'd had to participate in, the dull young men she'd had to meet. But then she fell for one of them and she began to change. It had started to sink in that the girl sitting opposite me was no longer my friend.

My reflective silence seemed to aggravate her even more; she suddenly burst into a tirade.

'You've lost all your ideals, haven't you? You don't care about England. You're completely selfish. Like this new breed of beastly, deviant writers that have cropped up, who call themselves conscientious objectors. You've heard what that shirker Lytton Strachey said at the Hampstead Tribunal last month, when he was asked what he would do if he saw a German soldier attempting to rape his sister?'

I tried to look interested, but I could feel my cheeks burning with anger at Violet's self-righteous accusations.

'He said, "I should try and come between them."'

I smiled; then, as the unexpected joke sank in, I began to laugh nervously.

Violet jumped up. 'I've nothing more to say. Nothing. I hope you find some way out of the quagmire that you're in. Please don't attempt to write to me or contact me again. If you'd shown some *speck* of remorse or shame ...'

'What?' I asked her. 'Would I be good enough for you then? I'd qualify for rehabilitation?'

She glanced at me contemptuously and flounced out of the tea-shop.

~

I was wandering in a daze. It hurt to think that I had lost Vi after so many years, and it stung to think that she saw me as immoral. How much more horrified would she be if she knew of Grace's political affiliations? Yes, perhaps I had betrayed everything her beloved Gerald had stood for, I thought caustically, but I didn't care.

The next moment, though, I felt as if I were about to faint. I had respected and admired Miss Peabody, and to think of her hearing the news from Lady Wilcox.... I wondered why Lady Wilcox had done such a vengeful thing. *You never get away with anything of this sort*, I thought. *You have to be made an example of.*

I looked up, finding myself on Gower Street. I drifted among the University of London buildings. Here was the Slade, the art school Violet had alluded to. I was sure it was not a den of iniquity, but my glance lingered on the elegant stone façade. A group of students emerged, laughing and chattering. Two broke off from the others. They passed me, deep in conversation, arguing, it seemed. The young man had dark hair and was short and pale; the young woman was boyish, with a shining mop of blond hair and a charming, plump face. She wore a paint-stained shirt and *trousers*. I could not help staring. As they walked by I heard her say, 'But, Mark, you don't think there's anything really wrong with the Bloomsbury crowd, do you? You don't think the fact that Lytton prefers men is beastly? I don't see anything wrong with it. I like him.'

The young man snapped, 'Oh, for Christ's sake, shut up about Lytton! No, I couldn't care less if he likes men, it's the way you seem to be so infatuated with him these days....'

As they wandered into the distance. I looked after them wistfully. They seemed the very epitome of modernity to me. Was it possible that they were discussing the same writer that Violet had mentioned? What a strange coincidence! Educated London was such a small circle, really.

I wanted to be part of that circle, I decided suddenly. Really a part of it. Why had *I* never considered the Slade? Because it was impractical and unconventional, and no one in my family would have dreamed of suggesting it. I simply hadn't allowed myself to think of university or of art school as a reasonable goal.

The more I understood of life, the more I realised that things happened because people had an idea, a vision, and stuck to it no matter what. I'm going to come back here and be one of them, I thought, taking deep breaths of spring air in the London afternoon to try to calm my dizziness and exhilaration. But first, Dublin. I wanted to see Grace again. If what she had told me was true, things were about to explode.

Chapter 15

Returning to the house with this resolve in mind, I was idly flicking through the post when a letter addressed to me at the Wilcoxes' house in Dublin caught my eye. Lady Wilcox had written 'No longer here. Please forward' across it in bold black letters. I took the letter into the sitting-room and curled up on the sofa to read it. The only noise in the airless room was the ticking of the clock, but soon I was deaf to that.

It was from Rex Philpott, the first letter I had ever received from him. The return address of a nursing home in Folkestone, Kent, was printed on the letterhead.

Dear Caroline,

Forgive this horrid scrawl. I wanted to write to you to let you know that I am still alive — if barely — and am told by my nurses every day that I am on the mend. I was hit quite soon after returning to France and pretty badly smashed up. This is the first time I've been able to put pen to paper. My mother insisted upon parking me here — I feel rather an old fogey, as I'm surrounded by seventy-year-olds complaining about their hearts. *It would be so delightful to have a visitor, especially one under thirty. Perhaps my aunt will be decent enough to give you a summer holiday in a few months and you could pop down to see me then. Caroline, I have thought about you often since we met. It is a memory that has stayed with me when so many other memories seem to have oozed away. Funny about the old brain cells, isn't it? I'm off the morphine now, but I must admit it has done my neuroses the world of good. I feel quite uncomplicated for the first time in my life. It would be jolly to hear from you. I hope you're enjoying Dublin.*

Yours,

Rex

And Lady Wilcox had never said a word about him, I mused, touched by the almost childlike tone of the letter. She must have known *months* ago what had happened. What an icicle! Perhaps she had kept it from Amelia too, for surely Amelia would have been concerned and wanted to write to him. A devious woman....

It made sense to go see Rex before I went to Ireland, I thought. After all, I didn't know how long I would be staying there. I wanted to see him. It was a strange feeling, for I had only met the man once. It was the imploring, beckoning tone of the letter that worked on me like a charm, especially after Violet's rejection. I would take flowers and a box of chocolates and make him feel better for a little while.

~

The next morning on the train, moving through the peaceful English countryside, my daffodils did not go unnoticed. A couple of middle-aged ladies engaged me in conversation about the

War. Having been so cooped up lately, I chatted gladly, even telling them about my mother's death. Their sympathy felt nice. *Ladies like this always know what to say*, I thought, *the Mrs Grimsby sorts*. When I mentioned that Captain Philpott had been a friend of my brother, I was subjected to plenty of knowing glances. *How romantic and charming*, I could see the ladies thinking, moist-eyed. I did not feel romantic and charming, for a strange detachment seemed to have come over me since my mother's death. Even the conversation with Violet had not really sunk in. I thought that she, too, carried some of the same scars, and would not grieve much for the loss of my friendship.

'Those daffs are lovely. Lovely spring flowers,' one of the women said. 'Cheer the poor boy up. Isn't it incredible what those boys have sacrificed for us? They deserve every ounce of gratitude we can give them, don't you think?'

I saw a little flash of envy in her eyes. Perhaps she wanted to be the young girl comforting the wounded soldier. If only she knew how fleeting this errand was, I thought. I was no Florence Nightingale, selfless, devoted.

As I sat there with lowered eyes I felt like an impostor. What the women thought they saw was not in fact real, and I was not forthright enough to explain the mistake. What if I said, 'He was my brother's lover'? Where would their sympathy be then? What if I said, 'I'm in love with a woman, and have just been sacked because of it'?

I pulled out my book with shaking hands and tried to read, feeling the women glancing every now and then at my bent head. *The poor thing*, I imagined them thinking, *so young, barely twenty, and already an orphan*. My God, that was what I was now. Alone in the world.

The train pulled into the station, and I knew that the nursing home would not be far away. I said goodbye to my companions, who fervently wished me good luck and God bless. I stepped out of the train into the warm sun and sniffed the salty air eagerly.

Rex was staying at a place called The Pines. A starched matron met me at the door and led me silently along a corridor to a small room. Pausing outside the door, she whispered, 'Don't tire him too much. He's still quite weak. Were you aware of his disfigurement?'

'No.' I gaped at her.

'Well, we've seen much, much worse. But he had quite a serious head injury — it's healing up fine now, but he's still bandaged. And then, of course, they amputated his foot before he even reached us. His face got quite badly scarred, too, but we're hoping that we won't have to operate again. Go along in now. I'll come and get you when time's up.'

She put her head in the door and murmured something, then gestured to me to go in. Swallowing, I entered the sunny little room.

Rex was lying on the bed with his head partially covered, one leg elevated (I averted my eyes from the bandaged stump) and his hands busy rolling a cigarette. His face was in shadow.

'Rex,' I said softly.

He gasped. 'Caroline! They said you were coming.... I couldn't believe it, I thought they'd garbled the message somehow. Come in and make yourself at home.'

I arranged the flowers in a vase. 'Can you see them?' I asked, for he was so quiet.

'Darling, they're beautiful, there's nothing wrong with my eyes.' I sat down in a chair beside the bed and Rex gestured to me to come closer. I pulled the chair forward. 'My voice is a little weak — my vocal cords seem to have got banged up, along with everything else.'

I laughed nervously and he patted my hand.

'It is comic, isn't it? Good to hear someone laughing in this room.'

I looked hard at him for a moment. Something had changed about his eyes. The pupils were so enlarged that they almost swallowed up the blue.

'Oh, my eyes do look beastly, it's these drops they're giving me for something or other,' he said vaguely. 'I get the most confounded migraines. I feel like a dowager, or something.'

I laughed again, squeezing his hand.

'I brought chocolates,' I said, handing him the box.

'Oh, yum. I'm being fed the most awful pap here. Blanc-manges and so forth.' He pried open the chocolate-box lid and surveyed them gleefully.

'This is like being in the San. at school,' he continued. 'I expect you didn't have the boarding-school experience, Caroline. But I must say, it was one of the few joys of Eton. One always had the most wonderful conversations in the sick bay. They'd leave us alone for hours. I met some of my dearest chums that way.'

He chose a chocolate and ate it with relish.

'Now, Caroline, do tell me how you managed to show up out of the blue like this.'

I had not thought about telling him the truth. But, very simply, I explained that I was no longer working for his aunt, that I had left Dublin after receiving a telegram about my mother's impending death, and that she had died a couple of weeks before.

'I'm so sorry,' he said, pressing my hand, 'so sorry.'

'There's more to it, Rex. Lady Wilcox caught me in a compromising position with one of the ... servants.'

He stared at me oddly.

'One of the servant girls,' I said, blushing.

'Good Lord,' Rex said at last.

'I know it must sound very strange. I assumed it might get back to you sooner or later, so I'd rather you heard it from me.'

He nodded. 'Of course. And do you intend to see this woman again?'

'Yes. I'm going back to Ireland tomorrow. I love her.'

He was silent for a little. 'And does she love you?' he asked.

'I think she does,' I said. 'I suppose I need to know one way or the other. I could just let it go, but ... I don't want to.'

'Well, well,' he said, sighing. 'You seem like someone who knows what she wants.'

I shrugged. 'Do you really think so?'

'Oh, absolutely.'

'You don't seem shocked,' I managed to say.

'Nothing surprises me now,' he murmured. 'I suppose I know what I'm capable of, and what other people are capable of. We English are a strange race, you know. I think the French are right to laugh at us. We're just as sexually active as they are, but we've succeeded in throwing this wonderful veil of propriety and convention over everything. Perhaps I'm just cynical because I'm a public-school boy and an Oxford man. Your brother was certainly shocked at the stories I told him about my schooldays, where he apparently had done *nothing*. But, Caroline ... humour me for a moment. You look so terribly serious, and I'm afraid this is going to make you even more serious.'

'Oh dear,' I said, smiling, but a sadness was spreading over me already.

'It's very simple. I'm wondering if you and I mightn't make a go of it. We like each other, we make each other laugh, we even seem to understand each other. Quite frankly, I'm besotted with you. I know you'll say that I've been flat on my back for months and I've had too much time to brood about things. I just can't think of another girl I'd ever want to marry.'

I got up from the bed and walked over to the window, my face flushing, my heart beating rapidly. Why was he saying this now, after I had told him about Grace? It seemed completely out of character. I had never expected to be proposed to at all, and to be proposed to by a frail young man whom I was fond of threw me into sudden, painful confusion.

I stared out into the vast garden where roses and daffodils bloomed in the flowerbeds, where elderly men sat slumped in chairs taking tea in the sun, smoking, reading newspapers, chatting. Among them a few young men lay or hobbled about on crutches. A dark-haired girl sat by a young man's side on a blanket. They seemed to be laughing about something; she was spreading jam on a crumpet for him. She handed it to him almost maternally. Perhaps she was his sister. It was hard to tell, because of course they wouldn't kiss in front of the others.

I felt tears prick my eyes. Why couldn't Ralph be down there basking in the spring sun? If only I were visiting him now with news of our mother's death! We could have grieved together.... But instead, I had to be strong, I had to be clear.

I turned around and took a few hesitant steps towards Rex's bed. He was looking at me gently, even with some hope, I thought. That was the worst thing, seeing hope in his eyes.

'Rex, why should you want to marry at all? The thing is, I don't. The minute I marry, I'd have to be Mrs Somebody and step into a role that I don't want. It doesn't appeal to me.'

'But even you must need a shoulder to lean on from time to time,' he said, sighing. 'I thought you were like me, Caroline.'

'Like you ... in what way?' I asked.

'That you were able to love both sexes,' he muttered.

'So you already knew?' I did not like the idea of him hearing about Grace and me, of him speculating about my sexual tastes, about whether he had a chance with me. Perhaps the scandal made me seem more vulnerable, I thought, more likely to be open to his advances now that I had been disgraced. That was the way men saw women, wasn't it? They would take advantage of any weakness; it was a scenario that Grace knew well. I had been spared it until now because I'd lived like a nun.

But Rex was looking at me with sympathy. He gestured for me to sit down beside him again, and I did.

'My aunt is a wretched gossip. And a wretched employer, I've no doubt. She volunteered it in one of her recent letters. I'm afraid it's something juicy she can tell her friends at tea parties.... They lead a very dull life, you know.'

'Damn her,' I could not help saying under my breath.

He caressed my hand gently. 'Oh, Caroline, that generation is a complete loss. Let it pass. But think about what I said. If things don't work out with this young woman ... we could have lots of freedom. I'd want that for myself and I'd be happy for you to have it too. It could be the best of both worlds. Will you think about what I've said?'

I looked at his tired face, his forehead lined with pink, raised scars. It seemed so strange that he should be thinking of marriage — and to me? Yet as he stroked my hand I felt myself return to those moments in the wood. They were vivid to me too, shot through with many different emotions. *Perhaps he's right*, I thought for a second; and then the sensation of holding Grace in my arms flashed through me. There was no doubt there.

'Rex, I'd rather we be friends. Can't we just be good friends, like this?' It was hard to see him crumple with disappointment.

'There are so many other people in the world than me!' I told him. 'You're charming, you won't have to search long for someone to love.'

'You simply don't understand how I feel about you,' he said wearily.

'But, Rex,' I ventured, 'it's mostly because of Ralph, isn't it? Let's face it. You would have walked right by me in the wood if I hadn't mentioned his name. You would have thought "nice girl", at the most.'

He stared at me. 'It's not about him any more.'

I jumped as the matron knocked on the door. She came bustling into the room.

'Well now, Captain Philpott. Looks like we've had a lovely chat, haven't we?'

'I'm afraid I've been boring poor Caroline,' Rex said. 'You must release her from me, Matron. She's chafing to go off on her romantic adventure. A quest. How nice. Do you think I'll ever be able to go on a quest again, Matron?'

'I think you're a little overtired, is what I think, Captain Philpott,' the matron said firmly. 'Let me show Miss Singleton to the door.'

I clasped Rex's hand. To my surprise, he held it warmly and brought it to his lips.

'At least you came,' he murmured. 'Bless you.'

~

All the way back in the train I held my book open before me, but I did not read a word. God, what was best? Had I been unnecessarily cruel? I did not think so. I had not told him, either, that I would consider his proposal seriously. But I didn't dismiss it completely; I couldn't. If things fell through with Grace — if she refused to see me, if I could not track her down, if I returned to England defeated and disillusioned — perhaps Rex, with all his charm and intelligence, would be the one to convince me that he could provide a new and liberated life for me.

It would be a different kind of liberation, one I did not trust: I could not imagine being attached to a man and having affairs with women, which he seemed to be hinting was the ideal state for me. For him, of course, yes, it would be wonderful to have a woman at his side and also be able to play the field with young men if he liked. That was the way it was done in his upper-class circles, I had no doubt.

But I wanted something else, and I would try for it, I thought, though the odds were no doubt against me. And there was comfort in knowing that at least one person in the world knew my secret and did not despise me.

Chapter 16

_I_ arrived back in Dublin on the Thursday of Easter Week, 1916. This time it was afternoon when the boat pulled into Kingstown. Along with most of the other passengers, I took the train to the city. Once there, I looked around dazedly at the people milling about in the damp, windy weather. I had a brief impulse to find Grace straightaway, but I felt too tired and demoralised. There were moments when my resolve seemed to drain away and I wondered what I was doing in a strange and hostile place. All I remembered were Amelia's helpful words: Grace's brother worked at a public house called the Cloak and Dagger. I smiled at the name.

I should be enjoying this, I thought: _something is going to happen, and I, of all people, have prior knowledge of it._ But I felt no pleasure in being able to foretell a historic event. I wrapped my coat tighter around me and hailed a cab, glad that I could afford it.

'Is it Grimsby's Wine Merchants in Rathgar?' the cabbie inquired. 'Hop in, Miss. It won't take long.'

I lay back against the cushioned seat, noticing bits of horsehair poking out. The cab smelled of smoke and sweat, a manly smell I did not particularly enjoy. I felt weak. It occurred to me that if Mrs Grimsby did not offer me hospitality I would be well and truly on my own.

We crossed the canal and headed into the little village of Rathmines. Sturdy grey or red-brick houses lined the road; I saw churches, chemists, grocers' shops, a public library. I had a growing feeling of security, and as the street branched into Rathgar I breathed a sigh of relief. It was the kind of middle-class neighbourhood that I recognised from my own London childhood. Children played in front gardens, normal children, not pampered ones like Amelia. I saw dogs, cats perched in windows, policemen walking the streets, a priest ambling along with a young woman at his side.

And Grimsby's, Purveyor of Fine Wines. The cab stopped, and I jumped out. I tipped the cabbie, and he broke into a warm smile.

'Give the missus my best,' he said. 'Tell her Patrick Quinn sends his love.' And he was off with a chuckle.

Heart in mouth, I pounded the knocker of the blue door beside the shop window. *Perhaps I'm mad*, I thought; *perhaps she won't recognise me.* My memory of her was still so vivid!

A stout and cheerful-looking maid answered the door. I gave her my name, and she nodded and closed the door. I was not used to calling on people, and I stood there nervously, clutching my suitcase, wondering if I was about to be told the mistress was not at home.

The door opened again, and this time Mrs Grimsby stood there with an amazed look in her eyes.

'My goodness! Caroline Singleton, of all people! Oh, my dear, you do look done in! Come in.'

'I was hoping you might have a bed for the night, Mrs Grimsby,' I said with cast-down eyes.

'Oh, I see!' Mrs Grimsby gave me a long, appraising look — not hostile, in the tradition of Lady Wilcox, but hard to bear nonetheless. 'Of course you're welcome to stay here as long as you want.'

I breathed a sigh of relief and then, to my embarrassment, dissolved into tears.

In what seemed like seconds, Mrs Grimsby had taken my suitcase and was leading me to a room with a big, cosy bed. I lay down and was asleep in no time. It was as if the world was blotted out.

~

When I woke up, the room was dark. *The bed is so soft,* I thought sleepily. *How lucky I am to have this place....*

There was a gentle rap on the door. I sprang up immediately; I had a fear now of knockings on closed doors. Mrs Grimsby entered the room with a cup of tea.

'You'll have supper with us, won't you, Caroline?' she asked kindly. 'I thought you might need something to wake you up.'

'I do,' I admitted.

I sipped the tea. Mrs Grimsby pulled the curtains and turned on the bedside lamp. It was a curiously intimate scene, I mused; she would do this for a daughter. Yet they had no children.

Mrs Grimsby settled herself in an armchair.

'Now, my dear,' she said comfortably, 'whenever you're ready, I think it might be only fair to tell me what has been happening to you.'

I coughed.

'Well, I had to leave Dublin,' I said, in as normal a voice as possible, 'because my mother fell ill. She died a couple of weeks ago. Lady Wilcox was very kind, but simply couldn't keep me on. She gave me a reference.'

Mrs Grimsby nodded. 'I'm so sorry about your mother, Caroline.'

'Thanks,' I said. 'At least I got to see her before she ...'

There was a curious silence in the room. I felt that my having introduced the story of my mother's death made Mrs Grimsby feel she could not in good taste question me further. Yet something in my words obviously troubled her. Perhaps it was just my tone of voice, my strange weakness and exhaustion.

'Oh, the cabbie who brought me here sent his regards!' I said, trying to be cheerful.

'Was it Patrick Quinn?'

'Yes, it was.'

'Ah ...' Mrs Grimsby said. 'He was one of my beaux, you know, when I first came to Dublin. I was eighteen, a strapping girl. To be honest, Caroline, I have been very lucky. I worked as a barmaid. I worked hard, and Grimsby liked that: he ran the public house, you see. But I had plenty of followers in those days. Grimsby never held it against me. We married late. We both had time to sow our wild oats.'

'I didn't think women were allowed to do that,' I said.

'We are and we aren't,' Mrs Grimsby said. 'As I told you, I was lucky. That's why I have a certain nose for people who are down on their luck. When I saw you at the door I thought it might be something serious. I wondered if you'd perhaps got into trouble.'

'Into trouble?' I blushed, then laughed slightly hysterically. 'No — I ... do I look pregnant?'

'You look as if you're in some trouble, my dear.'

I paused. As the silence lengthened, it grew more agonising. I wrung my hands together. At last I said, 'To be honest, I met someone in the Wilcoxes' household who ... well, Lady Wilcox found us in a compromising position.'

'I see,' Mrs Grimsby murmured.

'And ... I came back to Dublin to find that person, although it may not be possible.'

'Does he love you?' Mrs Grimsby asked.

I bit my lip. I hated to mislead her, yet the truth could not be said without turning her against me.

'I hope so. I need to find out.'

'Well, I married an Irishman,' Mrs Grimsby said. 'It can happen, you know. It does happen. The two races are different, yes, but to me that difference has added a bit of spice. Of course, we're in our middle years now, and all the early excitement has gone, but I've never regretted my decision. I hope it will work out for you, Caroline. I admire your independence; I've always thought it a good quality in a girl, though most don't.'

I smiled.

'Will you stay here as long as you like? When I met you on the boat, I knew you could use a friend, and I want to be a friend to you, if you'll let me.'

'You're so good, Mrs Grimsby. Thank you. I knew I could trust you.'

'Oh, of course you can, my dear. And there's more, isn't there? You can trust me with that too, when you feel ready.'

I looked down, embarrassed. I did not want her ever to know what had really happened. Perhaps this meant I was ashamed.... No: I wanted her to think well of me, and I thought that if she knew the truth she never could. That was a sad little ache that would remain with me, I thought.

'Well, you'll need to freshen up for supper,' Mrs Grimsby said, getting up. 'And it'll be a hearty one. You look as if you haven't eaten in weeks, my dear.'

It was true, now that I came to think of it.

That evening, as I tucked into a huge plate of roast beef and Yorkshire pudding, I plucked up the courage to ask Mr Grimsby (who was as red-faced, portly and genial as his wife) about a few of the names Grace had dropped during some of our talks at Thornley Hall.

Dublin, I soon realised, was a very small city, for Mr Grimsby nodded in recognition at the names, and had a small nugget of information to go with each one. None of them seemed to provoke any alarm or disquiet in him. This made me feel better. Perhaps all that would happen would be a large demonstration of some sort; a few people would be clapped in jail for a few days, and then everything would revert to normal.

'Have you heard of the Countess Markievicz?' I asked.

'Ah, the Countess!' Mr Grimsby said. 'Everyone's heard of her. Used to be a Gore-Booth from Sligo. Fiercely anti-English.

Runs around the city with her gang of small boys called the Fianna. She's well-liked, though. Lives around the corner on Leinster Road.'

'Patrick Pearse,' I said. This was the man Grace seemed to revere most of all.

'Well, he's not a drinker,' Mr Grimsby responded. By this time he was smoking his pipe and looking at me with what seemed like bemused affection. 'Probably the only man of substance in the city who I don't have any business with. But he's a well-known crank. Runs St Enda's, the boys' school. Speaks Irish all the time. Priggish. Don't like him.'

'What about Thomas McDonagh?' I hazarded.

'Friend of Pearse's. He's a poet and teacher. Nice young fellow.'

A poet, I mused. Poets weren't generally involved in armed rebellion.

'And James Connolly?'

'Now, Connolly's a marked man. The English have their eye on him. He helped organise the great general strike here in 1913, when thousands of workers were locked out by their employers and were near starving for months. Finally they were forced back to their jobs without any concessions. He's a trade unionist. Not a bad fellow, but a fanatic. A dyed-in-the-wool socialist, you know.'

There was an awkward pause in the conversation.

'I hope your young man hasn't got himself mixed up in any foolishness,' Mr Grimsby said.

I blushed, pushing the peas around on my plate.

'There's a lot of foolishness around,' Mrs Grimsby said cryptically.

'Yes, people talk a lot of rubbish these days,' her husband agreed. 'I'm surprised at what they get away with.'

'On the whole, Dublin's very peaceful. We wouldn't want you to get the wrong idea.'

I smiled politely, but the impression I came away with was disturbing. There was something hollow about their assurances, I thought. Of course they wanted to believe that nothing was going on, that nothing could disturb their comfortable life. Yet Mr Grimsby was well aware of the currents of dissent swirling around him; he just assumed that it meant nothing, that it was all talk. The English often thought that about the Irish, didn't they? Of course, *he* was Irish.

~

The next morning, I woke up with a sense of mingled dread and anticipation. I would try to find Grace today. The only problem was that Mrs Grimsby might want to accompany me into town.

Over breakfast, I asked her where the public house called the Cloak and Dagger was. It was my only link to Grace, or at least her brother.

Her eyes widened. 'On Thomas Street in the Coombe? Why would you want to go there, Caroline?'

She had taken to calling me by my first name. I wasn't quite used to it yet.

'I have to meet someone there.'

'Your young man?'

'Yes,' I said, since it seemed pointless to hedge. 'We agreed we'd meet today, where nobody we knew would spot us together.'

'Well, he couldn't have chosen a more dangerous place to rendezvous!' Mrs Grimsby said tartly. 'I don't think it's safe for an Englishwoman, or any decent woman. I would never set foot in it myself.'

I shivered slightly. If it were not for my need to see Grace, I would not have ventured this far. But I could not turn back now.

'I'll tell you what, though,' Mrs Grimsby mused. 'I'll get a boy from the shop to go along with you. I just can't think of you going down there alone, being exposed to insults.... Hughie knows that area well.'

I bowed my head. She was very kind. I wondered if I should have covered my tracks better. Yet it was always possible that I wouldn't find Grace; in fact, it was more than likely.

'You're very thoughtful, Mrs Grimsby,' I said. 'The only thing I ask is that I should return alone. I don't want to keep your boy idle for hours. We've so much to talk about....' My face flushed as I said this, as Grace's image flashed into my mind. *Talking, yes. And more than talking.*

'Very well,' Mrs Grimsby said with a sigh. 'But I must say, when I met you on the boat, Caroline, I didn't see you as the type of young woman to get yourself embroiled in this sort of affair. I hope you're not thinking of doing anything rash.'

I said nothing. Her reproaches touched me, reached some part of me that still wanted to please, to be good, to be loved for being obedient and virtuous.

'It's not some sordid entanglement,' I murmured. But my heart was heavy, and I could not meet her eyes.

'Is he going to marry you?' Mrs Grimsby asked. The concern in her voice was hard for me to bear. I clenched my fists.

'I don't know,' I said. 'It's more complicated than that.'

'It always is,' Mrs Grimsby said wryly. 'But it doesn't have to be. Either he loves you or he doesn't. Now if he doesn't, Caroline, you might be better off letting it go. And if he does ... would he ask you to risk your reputation like this? To meet in a dangerous, dirty place, which is well known to everybody in the city as the haunt of conspirators and criminals and prostitutes?'

I bit my lip.

'I hope that isn't an indication of what he feels about you,' Mrs Grimsby said.

I got up, dusting down my dress, unable to bear any more. My face must have looked pale and wretched, because she looked at me pityingly.

'My dear, I'm sorry. I was only saying these things because you're all alone in the world. Your mother's gone, and perhaps you're not thinking clearly.'

I shook my head. 'I don't mind you trying to give me advice, but I can't turn back now. Self-preservation isn't everything!'

I said this rather bitterly. Mrs Grimsby looked shocked. She poured herself another cup of tea. In the awkward silence that followed, I gazed at the solid breakfast table, at the good china plates and cups and dishes of food that Mrs Grimsby and her husband must enjoy every morning. It felt unreal to me, her placid life.

I don't want this security, I thought, *not now. I would give it up so easily for a chance to be in Grace's arms.* And I had to take that chance.

~

The boy Mrs Grimsby had chosen to accompany me turned up at the door a few minutes later. He was a pimply fifteen-year-old with his cap set at a rakish angle, his pale face and glittering eyes somehow a little disconcerting. Probably in the first stages of tuberculosis, I mused, as we sat together uncomfortably in the jostling cab.

'I'm sorry you have to do this, Hughie,' I ventured.

'Ah, don't worry, Miss. Gives me a chance to see me sweetheart on the way back. She works in Arnotts.'

He seemed quite cheerful, whistling a little tune to himself, glancing out the window every now and then.

'I suppose,' I said hesitantly, 'you haven't heard of a man called Jack Sheridan.' As Hughie looked blank, I added in a low voice, 'He's in the Citizen Army.'

'Jack Sheridan!' Hughie exclaimed. 'I know him well, actually. We all grew up on the same street. Course, the Sheridans got out, if you can call it that; they're livin' somewhere along the river now, in a cottage. Jack's a few years older than me. He's a clever fella. A decent skin. What would you be wanting with Jack?'

He fixed his probing eyes on my face.

'Oh ... actually, it's his sister I'm curious about. His sister Grace.'

'Grace Sheridan....' Hughie said in dreamy tones. 'We all called her the loveliest girl in Dublin. You shoulda seen her a few years back, walkin' the streets in her shawl. None of the lads dared bother her, and she certainly acted as if she was too good for them. Course, even then ...'

There was an uncomfortable silence. Hughie shifted in his seat and gazed out the window as if he had suddenly lost his train of thought.

'Even then?' I prompted him. The blood was rushing to my face. I was afraid of what he was going to say.

'Ah, Miss, I don't want to run her down. She was always friendly to me. But there was talk when she started goin' out with the soldiers. Never the Dublin lads, just the soldiers. See, the English soldiers always have a few extra bob for their girls, and Grace had nothin' back then.'

'Soldiers?' I said blankly.

'Yeh. Now, that was a few years ago, d'you see what I'm sayin'? She was a young 'un, only sixteen or so. I'd look down from the window and see them sayin' good night, her and her soldier lover. The gas-light would be shinin' on them and I seed the way he'd paw and fondle her, and she'd laugh, as if she'd already given him so much more. And then the family moved away and I heard tell she went into service....'

I nodded. The cab was crossing the canal and heading into the centre of town. I was stunned, for Grace had never mentioned these experiences to me. The picture Hughie had conjured up was so sordid I could not believe it, and yet it had the ring of truth. I bit my lip hard.

'I knew her when she was with the Wilcoxes,' I told the boy. 'We were friends.'

I hoped this would shut him up.

'Ah, then you're probably worried about what she's been up to since she got kicked out of the Wilcoxes' for improper carryings-on,' Hughie said slyly. 'Am I right, Miss? She was found in bed with someone there, wasn't she? She never let on who.'

I swallowed and did not answer. He whistled for a moment and then said, in a kinder tone, 'It wasn't too surprisin' that she'd go back to her old ways. Jaysus, who would blame her, really?

And she's still lovely. You don't see her staggerin' around drunk on the streets like the rest of them.'

I could not speak. I glanced at the boy, and he seemed startled at my aghast expression.

'Now, Miss, I hope you won't be holdin' it against me that I said what I did,' he said nervously. 'It's the truth, I swear.'

'You must be mistaken,' I muttered.

'Mistaken, is it?' He gave a sneering little chuckle. 'Ask anyone. They'll tell you the same thing. Course, her brother will fight any chap that says it. Poor Jack. Between fightin' them and tryin' to preach violence against the English, he's probably not long for this world, the way things are goin'.'

The cab had turned at Trinity College and was heading up the long hill of Dame Street. 'That's Dublin Castle,' Hughie said, jabbing his finger out the window to my left. A large, fortress-like, greyish building flashed by. 'Since you're visitin' from England I thought you might want to see it.' There was a slight sneer in his voice still, and I wondered what he thought of me and my motivations for seeing the Sheridans. I supposed that if he blabbed to Mrs Grimsby, Jack would be the one he'd peg as my lover. My shock over Grace he would, no doubt, put down to the offended English propriety of a woman in love with Jack.

We finished the journey in silence. I gazed out at the narrow, crowded quarter we had driven into. The houses and shops were mean-looking and the people on the streets looked thin, shabby and exhausted. I too was exhausted, suddenly. The word 'prostitute' — which had never been said — rang and rang in my mind. It was the worst thing that could have happened to Grace; and in the world in which I had grown up, it was the worst fate that could ever befall a girl. Hughie's jadedness made it all the more shocking, somehow, as if Grace had simply fallen into a pattern of behaviour that she could hardly have been expected to avoid. I clenched my hands. I would not turn back now. *There must be some explanation, some mistake....* I would have to hear it from her own lips and make my mind up then. But my heart ached.

'The Cloak an' Dagger,' Hughie said, helping me down from the cab. He paid the cabbie; I supposed Mrs Grimsby had given him the money for it. It was kind of her.

The cab clattered away. I stood there in front of the pub, paralysed suddenly. A bawling noise was coming from inside, punctuated by raucous laughter. I gazed at Hughie as if he would know what to do. He stared back at me for a moment, then muttered, 'I'll run in and get Jack for yeh now. Wait here.' He disappeared into the low, dusty doorway.

Chapter 17

I stood there on the filthy street in an agony of self-consciousness, trying to force myself to be calm and appear confident. Something about meeting Jack was terribly intimidating to me. I knew he was a little younger than I, but it did not matter. If Hughie had unnerved me, I assumed Jack would be far worse.

I did not know what Grace had told him about us. Probably nothing. In that case he would be rude and uncomprehending, but at least the interview would be short. Yet if he did not help me I would lose all chance of finding Grace. It sounded as if Hughie had glimpsed her occasionally on his nocturnal wanderings, but did not know where she lived. I hated to think of him crossing her path, feeling contempt as she swept by. If he, who had once liked her, felt contempt and pity, how much more awful would be the judgement of those who had never liked her — or who loved her? Why had she done it?

Hughie emerged, followed by a young man with short-cropped chestnut hair and a wary expression.

'Thank you,' I said to the boy. He grinned knowingly at us, shrugged, and disappeared.

'What can I do for you?' the young man inquired curtly, after looking me over for a minute. He seemed tense. I had told Hughie not to give him my name, and I sensed that he was not quite sure who I was, but had an inkling.

'You're Jack Sheridan?'

He nodded.

'I'm Caroline,' I said, not sure how formal to be. 'I don't know if Grace told you anything about me, but I worked with her at the Wilcoxes'.'

'The English governess,' Jack said, staring.

'That's right. I was a governess.' It gave me a strange sensation, that I no longer had that role to play.

He paused.

'And what did you want again?'

'To see Grace,' I said wearily. I felt I could not take much more stalling. I tried a different approach. 'Jack, I know I'm a stranger, and I understand why you might not trust me, but you have to believe that Grace would want to see me. We were separated suddenly about a month ago, but I'm certain she intended to keep me informed as to where she was. I'm worried about her and I'd like to help.'

'Help what?' he said with a flash of anger. 'Take her away?'

I shook my head. 'No. I don't have the power to do that. Unless she wants to.'

Jack snorted, but didn't answer. I tried not to get agitated. I saw that he was trying to decide, that everything lay in the balance. He really did not want to help me, to have me meddling in their lives; but something she had said to him, perhaps, forced him to acknowledge me. When he looked at me again, with his strained and troubled expression, I felt that he knew what I had been to his sister.

He sighed. 'All right. Look, go into the snug there. I'll have a drink sent over to you and I'll get someone to fetch her. I'm not telling you where she lives. It's her business if she wants to meet you or not. I can't promise anything.'

My lips trembled. 'Oh, Jack ... thank you.'

'Don't thank me yet,' he said with a grudging smile. It altered his face, and I glimpsed some of his sister's looks and charm beneath his surface toughness. He turned and walked quickly back into the pub.

~

I sipped the hot port that had been brought to me by an unsmiling older man. I supposed that Jack was the apprentice barman. I had never been in a public house, and I settled back uneasily against the plush seat. I guessed that this section of the pub was strictly set aside for women, and I was the only one there. From the next room I could hear the raucous babbling of many voices with rough accents, and the smell of beer and smoke permeated everything. But this room was different — quiet, hushed; it seemed more like the waiting-room of a railway station.

I was trying to remember the good times that Grace and I had had together. It seemed that anything that happened in this place could not be good. Its drab and defeated air seemed infectious. I felt that way too, I mused, as I regarded myself in my compact's small mirror. Was this the end? No doubt. No doubt she would appear briefly, only to tell me that we were finished. It would be a bother to her if I lingered in Dublin, so she would have to tell me that.

I had brought something to give her, carefully wrapped in brown paper. The more I had looked at it, in the house in Camden Town, the more I considered it hers, not mine. The memory of her posing for the portrait on the evening of the garden party, and the subsequent memories of her watching me paint, were very sweet; I would never forget them. Every time I looked at the painting now, though, it stabbed me to the heart. There she was, lying on my bed — beautiful, unattainable, mysterious, promising so much, but revealing, in the end, only what she chose to.

I was still angry and hurting, I realised, over those months in Dublin when she had eluded me. They had made me think of her as someone whom I could never fully trust. The boy's words had raised the spectre of Grace committing acts that shocked me to the core. I thought of Vera and the French novels, her prissy, contemptuous words: 'I don't want to hear about these fallen women, Caroline.' Yet I had read the books and been titillated by them. So why was it different when someone I had loved had done those things? Why had I assumed so thoughtlessly that Grace would be faithful? I supposed it had been because it was easy for *me* to avoid temptation. Virtue was so simple when one had money enough to get by and a clear set of rules that one had never transgressed. My only transgression had been with her.

I swallowed the last of the port. Vaguely aware of a figure at the door, I was about to ask the barman for another, when I gasped. It was Grace.

I stood up. She came towards me swiftly, wearing a dark-green shawl fastened by a silver brooch, her hair looser than it had been at the Wilcoxes', her face thinner. We clasped hands. When I felt her large, warm hands around my pale and cold ones, I remembered why I had felt such a longing for her, what she had been to me. My old hunger returned. It all came clear, and I began to shake.

She threw her arms around me. We embraced for a long time, cheek against cheek. I felt her heart beating, the woollen smell of her shawl. I did not try to kiss her.

We pulled apart without a word. Grace looked at me carefully. I was much calmer, but I saw something new in her eyes: an anxiety, a confusion. She bent her head for a moment and then sat down.

The barman entered silently with drinks for us both. He put them down, remarking, 'Your brother paid for these.'

'Thanks, Mr O'Keefe.'

'Nice seeing you, Grace.' His manner with her was different, almost deferential. I looked at her after he left and blurted out, 'He treats you with respect.'

'Well,' she said softly, raising her glass, 'he's the only man in Dublin who does.' She clinked her glass against mine. I took a gulp of the hot, sweet liquid.

'Is this what ladies drink here?' I asked.

'That's right,' Grace said. 'Would you rather be hoisting a pint?' She smiled at me and I saw that she was trying to delay any explanations, to establish some goodwill between us. I smiled back at her hesitantly.

'How was London? Your mother?' Grace asked, tracing a pattern on the table with her finger.

'She's dead,' I replied. 'At least I got to say goodbye. I suppose when I left I didn't think it was all that important. But I do now.'

She looked at me and sighed. 'God, everything's changed so much. From when we first met.'

'You're right about that,' I said lightly. 'I should thank you for coming to meet me, by the way. I was afraid you mightn't.'

'Of course I had to.' Her voice was almost inaudible. 'I knew you'd think I wouldn't. But I hoped you'd come back all the same.'

'I wasn't sure ...' I began. The words seemed to stretch out endlessly in the dim, dead air of the place. 'The way we'd left it ... I just wasn't sure if you ever wanted to see me again.'

It was difficult to talk. I sensed that Grace was having even more trouble than I. She was sipping the port nervously. Her face began to flush, and she looked as if she was blinking back tears. She swallowed convulsively.

'Caroline, I did. I did want to.'

I had never seen her cry. I reached over and held her hand. Tears began to spill out of her eyes. She wiped them away helplessly. I found my handkerchief and gave it to her.

Her lovely eyes were reddened. She stared into her drink, then looked at me. She looked so sad, so fragile suddenly. I squeezed her hand.

'Grace, what's happened? What's happened to you?'

'If only you were like everyone else,' she said with a bitter smile. 'You see me more clearly than anyone else.'

I was silent for a while. Finally I said in a low voice, 'Look, I don't think I know you all that well, Grace. I want to understand. Everything is different now. We're not working for them any more. We're as free as we ever will be.'

She shook her head stubbornly.

'All right. You don't like the word "free". But listen. What I realised in London is that I really don't have to play by the old rules. I met my old friend Violet; she wants nothing to do with me because she found out what happened between us. I'm not saying we have to go around shouting it from the rooftops; but, Grace, I just want to be with you. I can help. I have some money and I'd be glad to do anything to make things easier for you.'

She looked at me thoughtfully.

'Caroline, for one thing ... you've come back just as ... Oh God, I don't know how much I should say.'

'Don't you trust me?' I asked. It was painful to see that she wasn't sure, that she was wrestling with it.

She nodded. 'It's on. You know what I'm talking about. It's on for this coming Sunday. We've been told to stand by for "special manoeuvres".'

'I see.' I felt suddenly chilled. I looked away. When I looked back at Grace, I saw that her eyes were filled with tears again.

'I'm frightened,' she said with an effort. 'But I can't ask you to stay with me through this. It's too much.'

'Yes, you can,' I said firmly. 'You can ask me. It's what I hoped you'd let me do.'

'If anything happened to you I'd never forgive meself,' she said. 'I've caused you enough harm. I know that.'

'Being with you made up for everything,' I told her. 'I've caused you harm too. You were fired because of me.'

'I don't deserve this, that you'd want to live through this with me. I can't tell you how long it will last or what will happen.'

'I know,' I said. 'I don't expect that. Let me help you, Grace. You look weary.'

'You do too,' she said, making an effort to smile. 'That's terrible about your friend. So Lady Wilcox spilled the beans.'

'Can you believe that? I couldn't believe it.'

It was the old Grace opposite me for a moment, and we were both back in my little room at the top of the Wilcoxes' house. I remembered how she had seduced me then, despite all my feelings of hurt and betrayal. She had stripped naked and pulled me against her. Our bodies had done the rest. And then, ultimately, we had exchanged words of love. I had thought then that it was our last time, that our love had not been strong enough to carry us past our different fates. Lady Wilcox coming in and dismissing Grace so haughtily had seemed to confirm it.

'I hate thinking of her that night,' I murmured. 'I don't know why, but it's so galling to think how she had the power to separate us, just like that.'

'You didn't know,' Grace said equally softly, 'how lucky we were. To have what we had. I knew our luck would run out, though. It always does.'

We stared at each other.

'Grace, are you saying we can only be friends?'

'If I said that ... would you stay?' she asked, looking away, steeling herself, it seemed, for my response.

I nodded slowly. 'Of course. I would still want to stay, even if ... those were the terms.'

She gazed at me, her eyes soft and vulnerable.

'Promise me that you won't ask me to go away with you, though. Stay as long as you can bear it ... but please, Caroline, when it feels time for you to go, please ... just go.'

'All right,' I said, shrugging, feeling the bitterness rise in me. 'I'm resigned to the fact that you'll never come back to England with me, Grace. I haven't forgotten the times I've tried to ask you before.'

She didn't answer, finishing the last of her port.

'I brought this for you,' I said, handing over the picture. She looked at the package in amazement, then started pulling aimlessly at the wrapping. When she had uncovered a little of it, she gasped.

'Why? It's yours.'

'No, it's yours,' I said. 'I'll always remember you, but I'm not sure you'll remember me.'

I had not meant to say this harshly, but Grace's face went dead white. She clasped the package to her bosom as if cradling a baby.

'What must you think of me?'

'Don't say that,' I said. 'For God's sake —'

'Listen, I owe you the truth about what I've been doing lately,' she blurted out. 'But you won't want to stay when you hear.'

I said nothing, biting my lip. Then: 'The boy who brought me here remembered you from the old days, from where you used to live. He told me a few things I didn't know.'

'Was it Hughie Nolan? I bet he did. Oh, Jaysus.'

'It's true, then?'

'I know you'll hate me for this,' Grace said dully. 'And you're right. There was no real reason for me to go back into that life. I could have gone and worked at Jacobs' Biscuit Factory. There's work, even though it's slavery. Maybe I was wrong to think I was too good for that. I thought I could do what I did before. And I didn't expect I'd see you again. I thought you'd surely forget me when you got back among your family and friends.'

'You must have an unrealistic view of my family,' I said wryly, thinking of my uncle. 'And my friends.' Now that she was confessing to me I felt a strange sense of acceptance about the whole thing, not a hatred of her at all. How could I hate her? 'I know. You thought I wouldn't come back; and, to tell the truth, I tried to forget you for a while. But I couldn't, Grace.'

'I couldn't forget you either,' she whispered. 'When I was younger it wasn't much for me to go with a man. Nobody cared — my family didn't give a damn. They would have taken notice if I'd got meself in the family way, but I never did. It was exciting, it was a new thing, and everyone I went with said I was really good.'

She licked her lips nervously.

'So this time, after I got kicked out, me ma didn't have room for me where they're livin' now. I said, "I'll make my own way." Couldn't go back into service. I didn't want to work in a shop, or a factory. I needed time to meself, to read and to work for the cause. I thought, *I'll do it now and then. Nobody will know.* I didn't have you, and I just put a few drinks in me and went out and did it. To be honest, I was working with a friend who's done it for years and said I'd be mad not to do it now that there's so much easy money floating around Dublin from the War. I'm sharing her room. Sheila's in London now for a few weeks. She had to go get an abortion. She knows a good doctor there who does them on the quiet. It'll be safer than going to some butcher here.'

I winced, and she saw it.

'I'm sorry, Caroline,' she said. 'I know it must sound horrible to you. You have to believe it had nothin' to do with how I feel for you. But each time it felt worse. I thought about killing myself. But then there was Jack. He counted on me to be with him in the struggle. I couldn't let him down, I couldn't let the Countess down. I hated being with those men, but they gave me enough to get me through. But I hated myself most of all. Because I wasn't raised to be good like you are, Caroline. I kept seeing it through your eyes.'

I shook my head. 'Grace, I was raised to be conventional. That's all. They did a good job with me, though. I *was* shocked when I heard. I still am, Grace, I can't help it. And English soldiers? I don't understand.'

'I know, I know,' she murmured. 'I can't explain it. I'm too tired. Lots of girls do it — I kept saying that to myself. And the soldiers are the ones with the money. But there's more.... Maybe it used to mean somethin' else to me. Adventure, excitement, passion. I really felt all that when I was sixteen and was goin' out with the first fellas. The money didn't matter then. I needed it, but I didn't do it for that.'

She shrugged, speaking slowly as if thinking aloud. 'But then I met you. And you gave me all the things I'd got from them — but love as well. I'd never felt that strong a love for a man, and I know I never will now. I swear that nobody's ever meant anything to me compared to you.'

She looked at me imploringly.

'I've stopped it, Caroline, anyway. I asked the Countess for help and she got me a job. I've been working at the Irish Women Workers co-operative over by Liberty Hall, making clothes. I didn't have to tell you about the other thing, but I thought you'd find out one way or another, Dublin being the way it is. And it turns out you did.... I'm sorry. I've told you everything now.'

I gazed at her. 'Grace, I believe you. But are you saying to me that you'll never want to be with me again ... that way?'

She shook her head sadly. 'It's me, not you. I feel dirty. I don't feel good enough for you. You have to let me be, Caroline.

Even though you've been a saint about this, it just doesn't feel right to me now. Maybe that will change.'

She got up, clutching her picture. 'I live close by. Will you come lie down with me? I just want you to hold me.'

There was nothing I wanted more either. I followed her as if in a dream.

Chapter 18

When we emerged from the pub into the afternoon, I was astonished to see that the clouded sky had partially cleared. The sun shone through and drops of light rain were falling. It gave me a giddy feeling. 'April showers,' I exclaimed. I had a quick flash of the same joy I'd felt as a child in a London park, when the dismal weather turned to sun and sparkle.

In a gesture that surprised and touched me, Grace took my arm. We walked arm in arm through the maze of cobbled streets, our bodies gently pressing against each other. The craze and chaos of the morning had melted away, and we scarcely seemed to pass anyone. I mentioned this to Grace and she reminded me that it was Good Friday, and that a lot of people would be in church.

'This is a very old part of Dublin called the Coombe, where I was raised,' Grace said. 'Did you know the city was settled by the Vikings?'

'I didn't,' I admitted.

'The Norsemen were here long before the English,' she said cheerfully. She suddenly leaned over and kissed me on the cheek. My heart jumped.

'Grace ... on the street?'

'I'm so glad you came back!' she exclaimed.

'I am too,' I said. I really meant it. I felt content just to be walking down the street with her like this. It was something we'd never done, I realised. We'd never been out in public together. Now we were no longer a maid and a governess; we were two women who had a perfect right to walk together if they wanted to.

'You told Jack about us, then?' I said suddenly.

'I did,' she replied, after a moment's reflection. 'At first, when we came back to Dublin from Thornley, I didn't know what words to use; I wasn't sure if he'd understand. I said you were my friend. But when I got kicked out I told him everything. I said that I wasn't ashamed but that I was afraid it would get around. He said he wouldn't tell a soul. But someone else blabbed — Jones, maybe.'

'I liked him,' I mused. 'He didn't seem the type.'

She smiled. 'Anyway, whoever tattled didn't seem to know I was caught with a woman, so maybe it wasn't him.'

I giggled nervously. It was strange to hear her talk about being caught in bed with me. It seemed like something that had happened in another life. It was not that I had lost my desire for Grace, but that I felt a mixture of emotions now. Desire was one of them. Perhaps it had always been like that for her, I thought: she had not had the luxury of being able to immerse herself in her desire for me. And perhaps it had blinded me to who she really was. Now I saw more. If there were good qualities in

Grace, there were flaws too. The same held true for me, I knew. Perhaps one day we could be comfortable together, like the Grimsbys....

Thinking of them made me start. 'Oh, Grace — I should drop Mrs Grimsby a note. She'll be worried.' I explained briefly who Mrs Grimsby was, where I had met her, where she lived.

Grace nodded.

'A note would be best — it'll reach her by this evening. We'll go to the GPO.'

~

That the General Post Office was a Dublin landmark I had already gathered from the time I'd spent in the city. As Dubliners navigated along the broad artery of Sackville Street, divided by the plinth of Nelson's Pillar, they would judge where things stood by how close they were to the GPO. It was a huge white classical building set off from the street, and it was a public building, so it *was* in a sense theirs.

I looked at the building with an artist's eye, but Grace saw it differently. She whispered proudly in my ear, as we walked through the great doorway, that this was where Patrick Pearse would proclaim the Republic in two days' time. I shivered. The carefree note in her voice was odd. It was as if she were describing the script of a play.

'Will you be here, Grace?'

'No. I'll be with the Countess at Stephen's Green.'

My God, I thought. That was where I had sat while Amelia fed the ducks, where Grace and I had had our brief reconciliation, where my tears had fallen onto her hand. I could not imagine the peaceful park full of soldiers, rifles pointing out through the black iron railings.

'I'd like you to come here on Sunday, though,' Grace said earnestly, in a whisper, as we paused inside the doors. 'I'd like you to listen to him, Caroline.'

Looking at her at that moment, I wondered if she could read in my eyes that I still did not fully believe this was going to happen. *They'll shelve it at the last moment,* I thought. *They'll have to. It's suicidal. Nobody will march out to be slaughtered like sheep.*

'I'll do that, if you want me to,' I said uncomfortably. She touched my shoulder, and I followed her into the vast, sleepy chamber of the post office.

I bought a piece of paper and an envelope from a clerk and stood at the long mahogany counter composing my note. Grace looked around with a knowing, almost smug air. She seemed in excellent spirits. I turned my thoughts to Mrs Grimsby.

Dear Mrs Grimsby, I scribbled.

I have decided to remain away for a few days until I know what to do. Please forgive me for not returning this evening and for causing you some worry. You mustn't worry about me even if you don't hear from me. Things went well today, and ...

I paused. I wanted to warn them, I realised. They were such decent people. But what could I say? Whatever I said would only alarm them further, and probably convince them that I was delusional as well as reckless.

I'm in good hands, I finished, blushing slightly. *All my love, Caroline.* I put the note into the envelope and licked the flap.

Grace came up and stood beside me. 'Are you sure you don't want to go back to Rathgar?' she murmured. 'It's safe, and you'd be much more comfortable. We could meet again after it's all over.'

Her warm breath, her hair, the closeness of her body suddenly overwhelmed me.

'Oh, Grace, no. I've had enough of comfort. I just want to be with you. It's an easy choice, believe me.'

'You'll be alone a lot,' she said solemnly.

'It doesn't matter. I'm alone when I'm with the Grimsbys because I can't talk to them. I had to lie to her, say you were a man.'

For some reason, these words seemed to bring us even closer. She leaned over to whisper in my ear, her lips brushing my cheek, 'But you're glad I'm not.'

'I am,' I said, heart beating. 'Are you glad *I'm* not?'

She laughed softly. Her eyes glowed a particularly soft, sensual shade of green.

'Yes,' she said teasingly. 'It means we can share a bed without being improper. If your Mrs Grimsby ever asks, you can say, "I spent the nights with a woman friend."'

'She knew I was going to the Cloak and Dagger,' I told her, anxious suddenly. 'Could Jack get in trouble? Hughie will tell her that I asked for Jack and that when he last saw me I was speaking to him.'

'Jack won't breathe a word,' Grace said firmly. 'This is his final day there, anyway. He won't be working tomorrow; it's his last chance to see the family and his girl.'

'Jack has a girl?'

'A lovely young thing called Noreen Clarke. It tears him up to leave her. She's not takin' all this very well. She's worried sick.'

~

Tired suddenly, we silently climbed the steps to a tall, dilapidated old brick building off Sackville Street not far from the river. The smell of mould, old food, smoke, and rotting rubbish lingered around the doorway as Grace pushed the door open. She looked at me with a hesitant shrug, as if to say, *I'm sorry, this is all I can offer.* I smiled back, but had to suppress a feeling of dread as I walked inside.

'I live up on top,' Grace said. She seemed eager to get in, to climb the stairs without being bothered by the pale, sickly children I saw lingering at the open doors on each landing. I noticed the yellowed and peeling wallpaper in some faded floral design. Sixty years before, the house might have been quite nice; a hundred years before it had probably been the townhouse of some wealthy merchant family. It held no traces of its former glory.

'As these houses go,' Grace said, panting slightly, 'it's not too bad. At least it's not falling down around us. The draught isn't too strong and it doesn't leak much when it rains.'

She threw open a door at the top of the stairs.

'This is it,' she said rather bleakly.

I walked in. My eyes took in a few things: a large bed, a fireplace, a blackened kettle on the hob, a wardrobe, a small table and a battered chair. A dirty window looked down onto the street.

'You share this room with your friend,' I said in a tone of wonder.

She nodded. 'She was kind enough to take me in.'

'The bed too?' I was suddenly stricken by the thought of them sleeping together night after night.

She nodded again. 'I shared a bed in Thornley as well. I never told you that, did I?'

I shook my head.

'Sheila's just a friend, Caroline,' Grace said wearily. 'I know what you're thinking, but you've no cause to worry.'

She knelt down by the fire and started crumpling newspaper, her face drawn and almost haggard.

'You're hungry, aren't you?' I said suddenly. She had obviously not had the kind of breakfast I'd had, I thought with a pang.

She nodded. 'There's food in the cupboard. Get the tea, it's in a tin.'

I fetched the tea and watched as she hung the kettle over the fire. It would take a while to boil. I buttered some bread at the table and we devoured it quickly, standing up.

'This is the Dublin diet,' Grace said, hardly smiling. 'Bread, butter and jam if you're lucky.'

'Oh, Grace,' I said. 'I'm sorry.'

She turned away instantly, going over to the bed and taking off her boots. She lay on the bed without a word.

I lay down beside her. Turning on my side, I watched her face. The room dimmed as the evening drew on.

'Are you sleeping?' I asked after a few minutes.

Grace shook her head, opening her eyes, which seemed glazed with weariness and sadness. 'I just don't want you to pity me.'

'Oh, Grace, I don't pity you. It's not that. I love you, and I wish your life had been better.'

She sighed. 'Some have it worse. Most women have three kids and a drunken husband by my age. I know my mother did.'

She snuggled against me and I held her close. I thought of how vibrant she had been in the post office and how fragile she was now, like a wounded creature. I stroked her soft brown hair, grateful that I had acted on impulse and returned to Ireland. I would never have forgiven myself if I had stayed on in London and heard that the rising had broken out. Much better that I should be here with her, I mused, so that I could know the worst and maybe protect her from some of it. If she would let me.

'Sheila didn't work out of here,' she said suddenly. 'She worked out of a brothel in Meath Street. In case you're wonderin', we never brought customers back to the room.'

'It didn't occur to me,' I said gently.

'It must seem sordid to you, that's all,' she murmured.

'It's not romantic,' I said, laughing suddenly in spite of myself.

Grace gazed at me and began to laugh too. We shook with laughter. She began to kiss my face lightly, with teasing little kisses. I lay still, smiling, hardly responding to these delicious caresses, for I had taken her words seriously earlier on.

'Caroline,' she whispered, 'kiss me. Just kiss me.'

I rolled over onto her, and our mouths met. We kissed fiercely, her hands loosening my hair so that it flowed down my back. She pushed her tongue deep into my mouth. With a shock, I felt her unbuttoning my blouse, pulling up my undergarment, and then her skilful fingers caressing my small breasts, pinching my hardened nipples. Pinning me down on the bed, she began to suck my nipples with slow, sensual strokes of her tongue and teeth. I trembled and sighed with pleasure, relaxing into her familiar touch.

Finally she raised her head. The room was almost cosy now, the firelight glinting on the walls.

'I thought you didn't want to,' I murmured.

'Let me pleasure you,' she whispered. 'Can I?'

'Yes, but ...'

'Believe me, I want to,' she said softly. Fully clothed as she was, she began to undress me slowly and dreamily, pulling off my skirt and petticoat, unfastening my stockings. When I lay naked in front of her, she lowered herself on top of me, kissing me, stroking my breasts, parting my legs with her hand, pushing a finger inside me, and then, once her thrusts caused me to tremble helplessly against her, sliding her head down between my thighs.

She had built me up into a frenzy. The quick, light movements of her tongue against my intimate parts drove me wild. My legs buckling and my hips moving against her, I began first to moan and then to scream. More loudly than I ever had at the Wilcoxes', I urged her on with my cries. My whole body was aflame.

'Close your eyes for a minute,' Grace whispered.

I obeyed. I heard her moving around the room, pulling something out of a drawer. She came back to the bed. I felt her hesitation, and wondered dreamily what she could possibly do next.

'Do you trust me?' she whispered.

I nodded, eyes still tight shut. I felt her parting my thighs with something blunt, and then the strangest sensation: something slowly pushing up inside me.

I gasped. It was painful for a little while, but I did not ask her to stop. Once it was fully in place, she began to pump the object inside me gently with her hand. I grasped the bedpost, moaning, as her strokes deepened. I scarcely knew where I was. My head was arched back, my eyes flickering open, gazing sightlessly at the ceiling. Minutes or hours could have passed. I climaxed with a groan and my whole body jerked rapidly.

I opened my eyes. Grace was watching me lovingly, as flushed and breathless as I was. We stared at each other for a charged moment. I pulled the coverlet over me, but just as quickly she pulled it back.

'No,' she said. 'I want to look at you.'

'What did you use?' I asked.

'This,' she said with a mischievous little smile. She handed me something I had never seen before: a long, polished, curved object like a male member. It was stained with blood.

'You've made me bleed,' I said wonderingly.

'I know,' she said. 'Are you angry with me? I thought it might be your first time.'

I shook my head, a little stunned.

'It's not mine. It's Sheila's. She got it in England off a working girl there. She has a lot of queer, fancy stuff for customers. Whips and things.'

'It's a dildo, isn't it?' I asked, blushing. I had never said the word, but I remembered reading somewhere that there were such objects, which women used to pleasure each other. *How depraved*, I had thought then; *how shocking*. Yet Grace had shown me what I was capable of.

'Yes,' Grace said, smiling and self-possessed. 'That's what she called it. Did you like it, being fucked that way?'

I felt a twinge of shame at the word. 'Couldn't you tell? I adored it. You're turning me into a slut, Grace!'

She leaned down and kissed me tenderly. 'I loved doin' it to you. I knew I would. I like seeing you that wild, wantin' it that bad.'

I clung to her. I felt childlike, my body warm and tingling, loved and at peace with the world. The kettle steamed away gently over the fire.

Chapter 19

_D_ublin woke up early. Groping for my spectacles, I could see from the clock on the wall that it was around six. Doors slammed along the street as workers left for their day. I heard whistling and shouting. The cry of a baby echoed in the house. Carts rumbled by outside. The sounds were as foreign to me as the smell of the house and the stark quality of the room. _But I am a foreigner here,_ I thought. I had never felt more of an outsider.

Grace was sleeping deeply. She looked very young in her slumber, and happy. Her skin was pink and her hair tousled. I stroked her bare arm outside the coverlet, filled with a yearning to touch her, kiss her. She had undressed last night by the remains of the fire, for the room was growing chilly, and we had kissed chastely, then fallen asleep within minutes.

Was it possible, I wondered, that she would continue to refuse to let me touch her? I did not blame her, but it saddened me, and made me think that it was her way of telling me that we had no future together. Tomorrow, if all went according to her leaders' plan, she would be facing enemy fire; and those guns would be operated by men of my race. To think that she might be killed by an Englishman made the tears rise to my eyes. I lay back and wept silently into the pillow. There had been too many deaths, too many losses. To burden her with my grief would be the most selfish thing of all, of course. I could not do that.

I felt her move towards me, yawning, kissing my neck in greeting. I turned around, hoping she would not see my tearstained eyes. We embraced, our skins soft and delicious against each other. She kissed me and I clasped my hands around her back, heart racing. We lay entangled, kissing, slowly rubbing against each other. She raised herself up on her arms to look down at me, and I put my hands on her breasts, still covered by the thin fabric of her shift.

'No, love,' she said gently. 'There's so much to do today.'

'But, Grace, it's so early,' I whispered. 'We have time.'

'Ah, I'm afraid of you,' she said. 'I'm afraid you'll drive me completely demented.' She laughed, but her eyes were serious.

'Is there some rule that you can't have pleasure?' I murmured. 'You're risking your life for them; are you supposed to be a nun, too?'

She giggled, looking down at me sweetly.

'You're beautiful, though. Don't think it's because I don't want to....'

She bent down and kissed me again with her full, red lips, then pulled away and began to clothe herself.

'I have to spend the whole day over at Liberty Hall,' she told me. 'I'll give you a key for this place. You can leave when you've had enough.'

'You'll come back here tonight?' I asked.

'Of course I will.'

She pinned up her hair jauntily, then looked at me.

'D'you want to see my uniform?'

On the bed in front of me she laid out an entire uniform in dark green. There was a shirt, breeches and a skirt. There was even a cap, with an emblem on it depicting a clenched fist in red.

'Are you ... will you be a soldier, Grace?' I asked, feeling awkward.

'Of course: a soldier of the Citizen Army. But I won't have a gun, Caroline. I decided I wasn't cut out for that. Some of the women have guns. The Countess is a brilliant shot.'

'Are there many women soldiers in the Citizen Army?'

She shrugged, sitting on the bed beside me. 'Maybe about ten. Most of the women involved in this, about a hundred, joined Cumann na mBán. They're the women's group connected to the Volunteers, and they'll be doin' things like nursing, making food, carrying messages for the lads. But I wanted to fight with the Countess and I didn't feel comfortable with the Cumann na mBán girls. They're young ladies from respectable homes, and I dunno ... I'll be close to Jack this way, to keep an eye on him.'

'But it sounds like you'll be in more danger,' I muttered.

Grace looked at me with a proud smile.

'The danger doesn't matter. We all have to go out and strike our blow. There's no safety in this one, Caroline. The leaders are in just as much in danger as we are.'

'I suppose so,' I said. 'You have amazing courage, Grace. I could never do anything like this.'

'Still, you came back,' she said, looking at me steadily. 'I know this isn't your struggle, Caroline. It never has been. I don't hold that against you.'

'But as causes go,' I said, shrugging, 'it's an important one. I see that, but ... Grace, I'm terrified of anything happening to you, that's all.'

I looked away from her, feeling weak and feeble. To my surprise she cupped my chin in her hand, kissing me until my face burned.

'You've raised my morale more than anything,' she murmured. 'Having you here makes it easier for me to go out and fight. I have something to come back to, someone to live for....'

I nodded, stroking her hair, feeling my love for her wash over me. She laid me gently back on the bed and slowly, deliciously, pleasured me with her hands and mouth. The morning sun shone in through the flimsy curtains as I moved under her touch, trembling convulsively, losing myself in the sensations I could never seem to get enough of.

~

An hour later we were walking along by the river towards Liberty Hall. It was a pleasant morning. My body was still awash with the ease that came after being loved so well. I felt a little dazed, but happy — almost giddy. As I followed Grace along the narrow path, she turned and smiled at me now and then. There was an exuberance in her step. I realised what was different about her: the maid's submissiveness, her watchful quality ... these things had been cast off like worn-out clothing. I found the change in her bewildering and exciting. I seemed to catch new facets of her every hour. She had effortlessly taken the lead in our lovemaking in a way that made me think she might have even more delicious things to teach me, if I was willing. But it was a bittersweet revelation. There was so little time.... All I could do was savour the last few hours with her as best I could.

All at once she stopped short, drawing aside. Two khaki-clad soldiers were strutting along the path towards us. Grace leaned back against the river wall, and I saw her fingers were pale as she grasped the grey stone. I fought back a feeling of dread.

'Christ, it's Gracie,' one of them said loudly in a tone of wonderment. He had a pasty face and a little pencil moustache. 'I've been looking all over town for you, my girl.'

She ignored him, staring down at the green, turbid depths of the river.

'Oh, come on, luv, don't give me the cold shoulder!' He reached out and touched her arm, and she shrugged him off angrily, her face still turned away.

A short middle-aged gentleman in a bowler hat and suit walked by us, then came back, his face flushing. 'Stop bothering these respectable women — can't you see they're not interested in talking to you?' he snapped.

'Come off it, mate,' scoffed the soldier, as his friend chortled by his side. 'Can't you see she's a bleeding tart?'

'You blackguards!' said the man in the suit, reddening still further. 'Who's your commanding officer?'

'Ah, to hell with it,' said the soldier, shrugging. As they sauntered away we heard him say to his friend, 'It's not as if there's a shortage of sluts in this town.' Their laughter was soon blotted out by the hubbub of traffic.

'Thanks, sir,' Grace said, turning to the man. Her eyes looked sad and she was barely able to manage a smile.

He tipped his hat to us. 'Pay no attention to those louts, ladies. They're a disgrace to Her Majesty's Government, insulting innocent young women. I can't tell you how many times I've seen it happen and said nothing. But in broad daylight! This is the last straw. I'll be writing to the papers about this.'

He hurried off, still steaming.

Grace turned and stared out at the river again. I touched her arm.

'I'm sorry you had to hear that,' she whispered.

'Grace, it doesn't matter,' I told her. 'It really doesn't matter.'

She looked at me quickly, as if to judge how upset I was. What she saw seemed to reassure her and she met my eyes for a long moment.

'I'm only sorry that I couldn't defend you better,' I said ruefully.

She shook her head. 'Ah, who knows where they'll be in a couple of days' time,' she said after a little while. The simplicity with which she said it was chilling.

She walked on ahead of me. I followed, trembling a little now that it was all over. Of course I felt something, I reflected, but it was better that I hadn't let Grace see it. The shame and embarrassment for her must have been terrible. The only disgust I felt was at imagining them together. And I could prevent myself from doing that, I thought. I would have to. Otherwise, it would overshadow everything.

But her contempt for the soldier had been obvious. That was all I needed to see. I knew, without her having to tell me, that she had felt no pleasure in the act with this man, that she had been completely numb; and that her numbness was still with her somehow — even, a little, when she was with me. That was the saddest result of what she had done.

~

We paused opposite a tall stone building, from the top of which a green flag with a gold harp proudly flew. It was the flag of Ireland flying over Liberty Hall, the trade-union headquarters and the unofficial centre for rebel activities.

'Look,' Grace said proudly, nudging me. 'James Connolly put it up last Sunday, Palm Sunday. The whole Citizen Army turned out to watch. We were drawn up in military formation. It was marvellous.'

'Doesn't it ... show your hand, in a way?' I asked, puzzled.

'Oh, we know they're watching us,' Grace said. 'This place is guarded night and day. They're going to raid us any time now, but we'll be too quick for them.'

She walked across the street, her steps confident again.

I followed her, thinking, *Madness, madness.* It was not Grace and her brother who were mad and deluded, I thought; it was the leaders. They were brazen, thumbing their noses at the British authorities, daring them to strike against them. And then what? *Of course,* I thought, *they want to be persecuted. It's a game, and the harder the British crack down on them, the happier they'll be.* I distrusted this kind of martyrdom instinctively.

As if sensing my reluctance, Grace took my arm and drew me in through the open door. The place was swarming with people. It was like a beehive. Everyone looked purposeful, excited, charged by the drama of the moment. As I looked at Grace I saw it in her face too.

Jack suddenly appeared. He was not in uniform, but he

seemed different: taller and sturdier than I'd remembered, his relief evident as he saw his sister.

'There y'are at last,' he muttered, pulling her aside` and nodding to me. I stood and watched as they talked just out of my hearing. I saw Grace turn pale and her hands go to her mouth. Jack was shrugging, putting his arm around her for a moment; and then they separated, Jack disappearing down a flight of stairs, from where I could hear strange clanging noises.

Grace came back to my side. She stared at me for a moment as if trying to remember who I was, why I was there. Then her face cleared.

'Is something wrong?' I inquired, my tone casual.

She spoke hurriedly and breathlessly. 'Jack told me — a lot of people don't know this yet — did I tell you there was a ship, the *Aud*, coming from Germany with twenty thousand guns for us? Well, it was captured by the British in Kerry yesterday, and the captain blew it up rather than have the guns seized. And they've caught Sir Roger Casement down there and arrested him.'

I tried to recall a conversation at Thornley in which she'd told me about gun-running, and about an Irishman knighted by the British who was trying to muster support for the Irish cause in Germany. *It must be him*, I thought, chilled. *The first casualty of this thing.*

'What will this mean?' I whispered. 'Can you possibly go ahead with the rising now?'

'I don't see what else we can do,' Grace said, her face hardening. 'It's now or never. They'll assume we won't do it now, since there's not a ghost of a chance we can win.'

I remained silent, inwardly tormented. I wanted to beg her to stop, to get out while she still could, but I knew that if anything would kill her love for me, that would be it. It had almost happened before, hadn't it, when I had tried to pressure her to make plans for a future together? She had brought me here to Liberty Hall, and she trusted me. That was something.

She took my cold hand and caressed it for a moment.

'Listen, love, I want to take you down to the basement. I'm going to go ask the Countess if I can. Jack says she's talking to Mr Connolly in his office.'

I nodded dumbly, and she dashed off down a corridor.

Chapter 20

_W_hen Grace returned to me, her face was flushed and her eyes shone brightly. 'Madame says I can take you downstairs,' she told me, and I followed her down the uneven stone steps, unprepared for what I would see.

The first shock was to see so many young boys. They were swarming about the dimly lit room, clad in khaki, chattering excitedly. I assumed they were the Fianna. In one corner a printing press was clacking away, spitting out papers. Against the side of the room men and women worked busily, moving grenades and ammunition from the piles in which they had been dumped and stacking them neatly in large wooden boxes.

'It's our arsenal,' Grace said. 'It's being divvied up, since we're all going to be in different places on the day.'

Jack came over to us, smiling. 'An English visitor is always welcome,' he said to me ironically, but his eyes were friendly. He looked at his sister. 'Isn't it great to be so close? We're almost there.'

'I know,' Grace murmured. 'Can I show Caroline the proclamation?'

'You can show it to her, but don't let her take it out of here. The Countess would kill me if she did that.'

Grace stepped over to the mounting pile of papers, which were being reverently counted by a Fianna boy. Jack was trembling with excitement.

'We have enough weapons here to last us a full week!' he blurted out. 'God, to hold the British at bay for a week ...'

'Jack, does Grace really have to fight?' I murmured desperately in his ear. 'Aren't you concerned for her? I mean, isn't there some way she could stay on the sidelines?'

'There'll be no sidelines,' Jack said, laughing. He didn't even seem to feel contempt at my question. 'No, Grace is in it all the way. That's the way she wants it. She'll be caring for the wounded, preparing food.... Of course, if our forces get low she might have to pick up a gun.'

I stared at him. He seemed so cavalier; he might have been talking about a picnic in the park.

'And afterwards?' I asked.

'Afterwards?' Jack stared at me oddly. It was as if he had not considered the aftermath. 'Well, sure we're all in God's hands. To tell you the truth' — he paused, and then gave a fatalistic little shrug — 'the leaders expect to be shot. For the rest of us, those who survive, it's prison, I suppose.'

I was stunned and felt a shiver go through me.

'Back to work!' Jack said cheerfully, as Grace came towards us with a piece of paper in her hands. She had evidently been reading it, and she had tears in her eyes. She blinked them away.

'Have you read it yourself, Jack?' she asked.

'No time, Grace. It's a shame we won't get to hear it, though.'

'I know. It's beautiful,' she sighed, passing it to me.

'Can you give us a hand now, Grace?'

'I will. I'm sorry it took me so long.'

They wandered away towards their comrades. Ashen, I curled up on a stone slab in the corner and began to read the Proclamation of the Irish Republic.

It was incredible, I thought, holding the paper in my shaking hands. I could barely concentrate, for I felt tension coursing through me, mixed with none of the joyous emotions that seemed to hold Grace and Jack in their grip. Here were lofty words, confident words, and right in front of me weaponry was being sorted and stacked by men and women who were risking their lives in this venture. History was occurring in front of my eyes. But what kind of history? Surely this uprising was bound to fail; it would be only a tragic little footnote in the long tradition of British dominion over Ireland. Would nobody step in and stop it?

I began to read. In bold type I saw a phrase in Irish. Then:

THE PROVISIONAL GOVERNMENT OF THE IRISH REPUBLIC TO THE PEOPLE OF IRELAND. *Irishmen and Irishwomen: In the name of God and of the dead generations from which she receives her old tradition of nationhood, Ireland, through us, summons her children to her flag and strikes for her freedom.*

Having organised her manhood through her secret revolutionary organisation, the Irish Republican Brotherhood, and through her open military organisations, the Irish Volunteers and the Irish Citizen Army, having patiently perfected her discipline, having resolutely waited for the right moment to reveal herself, she now seizes that moment, and supported by her exiled children in America and by gallant allies in Europe, but relying in the first on her own strength, she strikes in full confidence of victory....

I put it down, unable to read further, although there was much more. *These fine, impressive words might send my lover to her death,* I thought bitterly.

As I often did in moments of confusion and pain, I took out my sketchbook and began to draw. It would be a challenge, I thought, to sketch that room and its occupants as they went about their tasks.

And so this was what I was absorbed in when I felt a hand on my shoulder. I started.

'What have we here?' said a tall woman in uniform, laughing. 'A war artist?'

I gazed up into merry blue eyes dancing behind spectacles. Her accent marked her as an Englishwoman. It was the Countess, I was sure of it. A gun hung at her belt. She was lean, elegant and oddly beautiful.

Grace trotted over from the corner of the room. 'Madame, this is my friend Caroline.'

'Hmm,' said the Countess, picking up my book. 'Quite talented, I see.'

I flushed.

'She's painted a picture of me,' Grace said proudly.

'Well, you must hold on to that, my dear,' the Countess told her with a smile. 'If your friend becomes famous one day, it may be worth quite a bit of money. You never know.'

Grace nodded, her face bright with pleasure.

'Did Grace tell you I went to art school myself?' the Countess asked. 'First the Slade, then Paris. I would have kept on with it if it weren't for my damned eyes.'

'I'm thinking of applying to the Slade,' I told her nervously.

She nodded, handing my work back to me. 'You should.

What a pity you can't ask me for a reference. Well, you'll get in without my help, I'm sure. Stay here as long as you like, Caroline; Grace has vouched for you.'

'Thanks,' I muttered as she strode away; I was aware only of the curious power and vigour this woman had, and her charm. It was this charm, I thought, that turned Grace into a sweet, malleable young girl at her side. Men would die for her, for a sign of her approval.

Grace turned back to me, her face afire.

'Isn't she wonderful?'

'She's a fine woman,' I admitted. 'I've never seen anyone like her.'

Pleased by my words, Grace smiled at me, and I felt myself melting, looking towards her yearningly.

'You've been so patient, my love,' she said quietly. No one could hear us over the noise of the press and the clink of weapons, I was sure of that.

'It's our last day together, isn't it?' I asked, a lump in my throat.

She nodded. 'Yes, but there's tomorrow morning to lie in together. I won't have to leave till afternoon. Don't worry, I haven't forgotten you.'

'I should hope not,' I said, smiling.

'I must get back to it,' she told me. 'Jack says he'll take you home when you're ready to leave.'

I nodded, looking into her curiously bright and loving eyes. Over the din of the room I could hear the Countess exclaiming in approval at what the workers had done. Grace turned and walked back into the throng.

~

In the afternoon, tea and sandwiches were brought in — provided by the Countess, Grace whispered to me. We sat close together, legs touching, as the Countess joked and laughed with her little band of followers. She inquired whether the guns had been kept oiled according to her instructions. She described the first-aid kits that the Cumann na mBán girls had spent all week making, and how Dr Kathleen Lynn would make sure they got medical attention if they were wounded. The level of nervous excitement in the room was overpowering. These were all general comments: she said nothing about where they were going to be on the day. 'And of course,' she said, beaming, 'I'll be your second-in-command, under the able leadership of Michael Mallin here.' The pleasant-looking man beside her nodded at her words. As I looked around at the eager faces, I thought, *They're all drunk with it. For the first time in their lives, they have something to die for.*

I felt strangely comfortable there. A few curious looks were cast in my direction, but it was as if the Countess's presence — and perhaps the fact that she had talked to me earlier — gave me the benefit of the doubt. Grace's warm body next to mine was also reassuring. *If Violet could see me now!* I thought at one point during this strange little tea break. *She'd certainly call me a traitor to my people, wouldn't she?* How had I got this far? It had all seemed to happen in gradual stages, so gradual that there was no point at which I had had any real desire to turn and flee. Even the soldiers today, I thought, even that sordid scene had not really diminished my love for Grace.... I was allowing faith and trust in Grace to build up inside me, like these fresh-faced young Dubliners in front of me who hung on every word from the Countess's lips. Would they ever feel betrayed? I did not think so — at least, not by her, nor Pearse, nor Connolly, nor any of the others.

'I'm going to need you all for a few more hours, and then I'll let you get back to your families and loved ones,' the Countess announced. Everyone rose to their feet, and I whispered to Grace that I should probably return to the upper room. She nodded, gesturing to Jack. He came over to us.

'You'll take Caroline home?' Grace asked.

'I will, of course,' Jack responded. I cast one last look around the basement, realising how quiet and bare it was now that the press had stopped and the weapons were all safely stowed away. My last sight of the Countess was of her standing in the centre of the room, absent-mindedly caressing the head of a Fianna boy. I followed Jack up the stairs.

When we emerged onto the street the sun was setting, glinting in the windows of the shops we passed. Jack stretched, yawning. He seemed quite at ease with me now. He led me home by a different way, up streets that were dank and drab, where the men and women who passed us were in tattered clothes and stared at me with hostile eyes. A man came to the door of a public house and flung out a bucket of filthy water so that it splashed my skirt. Jack barely seemed to notice, humming, intent on his own thoughts. I was immensely grateful that I had not had to walk back alone.

'Long day for you, what?' Jack inquired suddenly.

'Yes,' I admitted shyly. 'It was strange to be so close to the Countess. She's quite a character.'

'Ah, that's true, but we've all grown up around her. She has a heart of gold, that woman. But she's as good as any man in a fight. Best of both worlds.'

'Maybe, yes,' I said, blushing. 'Look, I'm sorry I asked about Grace earlier. It was impertinent. I shouldn't have interfered.'

Jack shrugged, looking at me kindly. 'You've every right in the world, from what I hear.'

I looked away, embarrassed.

'I'm glad you're around, Caroline — mind if I call you that? For Grace's sake, in case anything happens to me. I can count on you to stand by her, can I?'

'Of course,' I murmured.

He nodded, relieved to have got that sticky business over with. I stood on the steps of the house.

'Is this the last time I'll see you?' I asked.

'It shouldn't be. I'm calling for Grace tomorrow.'

'All the same ... good luck,' I told him. I held out my hand and Jack clasped it in his.

'And the same to you. It can't be easy. I'm grateful you didn't take her away.'

'How could I have done that?' I asked, puzzled. 'It was never a hard choice for her, I know that much.'

'You're wrong,' he said, looking at me directly. 'It was very hard on her. I knew she'd do the right thing, but I wouldn't have blamed her if she'd left with you. She's had so little happiness.... I told her, "Get through this thing with me and then you can go off to London with your English girl."'

I gasped, my face burning with sudden shock. 'Jack, are you serious?'

'Of course,' he said. 'Grace isn't really cut out for this, you know. Not the way it's going to be if the rising fails. It'll be guerrilla warfare then, slow, bloody and brutal. I don't mind giving years of my life to it, but I don't see why she should.'

I sat down on the grimy steps, clasping my hands to my knees.

'You're surprised at me sayin' that, aren't you?' he said gently.

'She's never promised me anything,' I blurted out. 'I don't think she's sure of anything.'

Jack shrugged. 'Grace never gives promises; she doesn't like going back on her word. Don't despair of her, though. Sure, she's distracted most of the time, thinking of you. She's sweet on you, believe me. She wouldn't have gone to meet you yesterday if she didn't mean to stick with you. Don't you know that?'

I could say nothing more, breathless and near tears as I was. I had been keyed up for the whole day, pushing away emotion, and his words — so welcome, yet strangely shocking — pierced my defences and caused me to unravel.

'There's always hope,' Jack said softly. It was his way of bidding me farewell, for when I looked up he was far away, a small figure on a darkening street heading back to Liberty Hall.

Chapter 21

$\mathcal{I}$ woke with a start to a loud banging on the door. Grace stirred in her sleep, murmuring sadly. She had come in exhausted very late last night, and I had gone back to sleep after exchanging a few words with her. She said she'd taken a tram with Jack to see her family. They'd told their parents about their involvement in the rising. Her father had laughed drunkenly and her mother had cursed her. It was all coming back to me now.

Again, a pounding on the door. 'Grace, it's me. Jack.'

Her eyes opened. She rubbed her face. It was sweet to see her like this, so sleepy and unselfconscious.

'What does he want, for Jaysus' sake?' she groaned, looking at me comically. 'There's hours yet.'

She leaned over and kissed me, then crawled out of bed, pulling a wrap around her.

I watched her step out of the room, then put on my spectacles. It was nine o'clock in the morning of Easter Sunday, 1916.

I could hear their raised voices, but the door was thick and garbled the sounds. I yawned. Jack's words had soothed me last night. I felt a strange fatalism. Nothing terrible was going to happen. Jack seemed to think Grace would get through it. It was out of my hands. I'd done my part. It was when she left me later in the day that the real pain and uncertainty would come, for I would know nothing of her well-being.

Grace came back in, pale, slamming the door behind her. She sat down on the bed, shaking. I put my arm around her.

'MacNeill tried to stop the rising!' she said indignantly. Hope swelled in my heart, but I said nothing.

'He's countermanded the orders for the Volunteers to march today. He put a notice in the papers. The bastard!'

'What will happen?' I asked.

She looked at me. 'The leaders are meeting at Liberty Hall now. Jack says it's a sure thing that they'll go ahead with it tomorrow. But they have to send messengers around the country, telling the local Volunteer groups to come out and fight despite what MacNeill said. It's a disaster.'

'Oh, Grace,' I said gently. 'I'm sorry.'

She put her head on my shoulder for a moment. 'It's just so hard. I was all ready to go out, and now ...'

I stroked her hair.

'How's Jack taking it?' I asked.

'Ah, he's grand.' There was bitterness in her voice. 'He'll be spending the day with Noreen, listening to her swear undying love, I suppose. There's nothing like this sort of thing to bring out the passion in a girl.'

'Why are you so cynical?' I asked, despite myself, for I had grown fond of Jack. 'What's wrong with him getting a bit of affection?'

'I dunno,' she said sullenly, shrugging. 'Maybe it was just hearin' me ma last night, cursin' me for bein' wild and unwomanly to be involved in a thing like this. Jack just stood there playin' the gallant soldier boy, with her weepin' all over him. Da claps him on the back and says, "Take care, son. We're proud of you." His friends'll be standin' him free drinks over this, is what he's thinkin'. But me bein' involved? They're ashamed.'

'Forget them, Grace. Anyway, I know how much Jack cares about you.'

She nodded, relaxing a little. 'He likes you too. I'm glad.'

We were wrapped in each other's arms.

'This way I have more time with you, anyway,' Grace said in a whisper. 'God, Caroline, I just wish it could be over.'

'So do I, Grace,' I said. 'So do I.'

'Show us what you drew yesterday,' she said suddenly. 'I didn't have time to really see.'

I pulled my sketchbook from my bag and she lay on the bed in her flimsy gown, leafing through the pages.

'You did one of the Countess,' she said, marvelling. 'Ah, you got her there, Caroline. So is it true about you going to art school? You never said that to me.'

'I know. Grace, we haven't had a lot of time to talk about the future.'

She nodded. 'That's been my fault.'

'Well, it's nobody's fault,' I said, hesitating. 'But yes, I want to. It's a way to make something of my life. It's unconventional, I know that.'

'But, sure, the Countess did it back in 1900 or something,' Grace murmured.

'Yes, but the Countess Markievicz is an aristocrat,' I said gently. 'They can generally do what they like.'

'You don't trust her, do you?' she said sharply.

I paused, biting my lip.

'I think she's sincere,' I answered.

'That's not what I asked,' she persisted.

'I think, perhaps, she's a little bit selfish, because she's leading others into danger for an idea — an idea that's captured her, of course, and she's willing to pay the price of her convictions, but ...'

Grace sighed. 'Well, there's nothin' I can say to that. No great arguments. Perhaps you'd rather me and Jack piss our lives away like our parents have.'

Again, the bitterness in her voice. I could see how tightly wound she was and I did not know what to say.

At last I said, 'I've been honest with you, Grace, that's all.'

She nodded, looking intently at me. Then, very softly, she said, 'I've wanted you to be honest with me. I can depend on you for that. That's what I love about her too.'

I gulped. 'The Countess, you mean.'

She smiled. It was as if even hearing the name gave her pleasure.

'And what about the Countess?' I asked lightly. 'Does she have a husband, or children, or any loved ones to be with today?'

'She's staying with friends,' Grace said. 'Her husband left years ago to cover the war in the Balkans as a foreign correspondent. She has a stepson, but he's in the Ukraine. Her daughter's living with her grandparents in the country. The Countess left her there a long time ago. She thought it would be better for the child.'

I could not help a small thrill of satisfaction. It was exactly as I had thought: this woman had already given up her personal connections. No wonder she could pour herself heart and soul into an abstract cause! But it was different for Grace. She was torn, as any warm-blooded human being would be. I loved her for that, though I wasn't sure she would forgive me for seeing it.

'Well,' said Grace, getting up, 'time for breakfast, I suppose.' She dressed quickly, not looking at me. *Perhaps she's determined not to touch me at all today*, I thought. Sighing, I began to dress too, in the same clothes I had worn the previous day. Everything else was at the Grimsbys'.

'Look, Grace,' I ventured, 'why don't we get out of the city for the day? There must be places that you liked going to as a child....'

She beamed suddenly. 'All right. Let's take the train to Bray and walk along the sea front.'

'Fine,' I said, shrugging. 'I have no idea where that is.'

'South, along the coast of Dublin Bay. You'll love it,' Grace said. She seemed full of quiet satisfaction. I marvelled at her change of mood, but I felt better myself.

~

The train wound its way, high up on the track, along the picturesque curve of the bay. I gazed down in awe at the miles of perfect, empty coastline, the sparkling blue sea still too cold to swim in. We passed through town after town, none of them familiar to me. I smiled at some of the names: Booterstown, Monkstown — Kingstown, of course, where I had caught the train a few days before. The passengers seemed merry too, the little girls in their Easter bonnets, plump matrons clutching babies.

Grace was very quiet. She sat across from me, lost in her

thoughts. I looked at her sometimes, thinking of her parents' shabby treatment of her, and wondering how they could not be proud of their daughter. My eyes lingered on her cast-down lashes and her full lips. A young, buxom blonde girl and her beau sat nearby, flirting, giggling and generally announcing their love to the world at large. Once I caught Grace glancing over at them crossly. She caught my eye and grinned.

The courting couple got out at the same station as we did. We watched them trot down the path together, arm in arm.

'Stop looking at them,' said Grace, nudging me. 'Are you envious?'

I couldn't help laughing. 'It's just so easy for them, that's all. They'll probably find a nice quiet spot and start fooling about. He'll seduce her ... she does look ripe for it, doesn't she?'

Grace gave me a strange look. 'I see you don't have much faith in the virtue of Irish girls.'

'Well, do you?' I said, smiling.

She sighed. 'Caroline, I'm sorry, I have more things to worry about than whether that stupid young thing is going to yield herself today.'

I held my tongue. We passed out of the station and crossed the tracks, finding ourselves on a long esplanade filled with strolling couples and families. I leaned over the sea wall and watched children and dogs running along the beach, all in high good spirits, it seemed.

'So you came here as a child?' I asked.

'Yes, when Da was working,' Grace said. 'We couldn't always afford the fare.'

She had wrapped herself in her shawl, even though the sun was shining brightly. She seemed worn out.

'I'll get us some ices,' I said practically. Returning with an ice for her, I felt that she was near tears.

'Grace, what's wrong?' I asked after a while.

'Nothing, really,' she mumbled.

'You can tell me.'

'Well, it's just ...' Her eyes were fixed on the distance, and suddenly she started. 'God, is that ... Yes, it's little Miss Greystones.'

'What?' I said blankly. Following her gaze, I saw the unexpected figure of Vera Lee coming towards us rapidly, an earnest young man at her side.

'Are we close to Greystones?' I muttered.

'It's the next town down, more's the pity. Perhaps she won't recognise us.'

But she had. 'Caroline! Caroline Singleton!' Vera announced breathlessly, stepping towards us. 'I'm just back home for the Easter holidays, but I thought you'd returned to England.... What a surprise! And is your friend — she worked at the Wilcoxes' too, didn't she? I always remember a face.'

'This is Grace,' I said, blushing.

'Oh, *Grace*. Of course.' Vera turned her beady eyes on me. 'I heard you'd left the Wilcoxes' employ suddenly. I was quite stunned.'

'These things happen,' I said, shrugging.

'But the circumstances! Forgive me for alluding to this, but I heard the ugliest rumours. Not that I believed them for a second.'

'They're all true,' I heard myself saying bluntly. Grace gave a surprised laugh. I had never actually seen anyone's jaw drop so convincingly as Vera's did then. She looked at me blankly. The young man at her side gazed at us both with a puzzled air.

Vera flushed. 'I ... yes, well, it was nice seeing you. We should be going. Come along, Charles.' They hurried off, Charles's arm draped protectively over her thin shoulders.

I breathed deeply, looking into Grace's gleeful face. The incident seemed to have revived her. She jumped up.

'Let's paddle.'

~

We stood at the edge of the sand, the cold sea streaming up over our feet and ankles.

'Well, that was horrid,' I said, still somewhat agitated.

'The Vera thing, you mean? Don't take it too hard. You said the right thing anyway.'

'You didn't care?' I asked her. 'It didn't bother you that I said that?'

Grace shook her head. 'No, I was proud. I was proud you talked back to her, didn't let her fluster you. You were brave.'

She placed her hand on my shoulder, and we stood like that, leaning against each other, looking out to sea.

Later, as we sat on the beach eating sandwiches, I said, 'I think I know what's wrong. You think I'm weak. You compare me to the Countess and you wonder what you're doing with me.' I added in a lower voice, 'Even though you love me.'

Grace swallowed. 'No, it's the opposite. I do love you, and I wonder what you're doing with *me*. If I went back with you to England after all this is over, people would look at us the way that Vera did just now. They'd think, *She's so common.*

What's Caroline doing with her? You'd be ashamed of me in the long run.'

'Well, I've never been ashamed of you yet!' I snapped, the blood rushing to my cheeks.

'No, but you've doubted me. And I don't blame you, I've given you plenty of cause.'

'Oh, Grace, for God's sake,' I said. 'That's the kind of person I am. I have doubts about most people I care about.' It sounded feeble, I thought, and yet it was the truth. 'Yes, I've had some doubts, but I'm also learning to trust you again.'

'I'm afraid,' she said, forcing the words out. 'I'm afraid you'll cast me away one day when you meet someone of your own class ... like Captain Philpott.'

'What?' I said, flushing. 'What does he have to do with it?'

'Well, you liked him,' she said miserably, like a child.

'Yes, months ago, and that was only because he knew my brother. Perhaps I do care for him a little....' I paused, steeling myself. 'Grace, I went to see him in England. I didn't tell you because it didn't seem to matter.'

Her face paled with shock. I cursed myself for not telling her before. But why should it bother her so much?

'I don't love him,' I said firmly. 'I told him that.'

'But he loves you?'

'Well, he thinks he does. It's just because he's so ill. He wanted to marry me, but I told him it was impossible. It's just a fantasy, nothing more.'

'You see?' Grace said with a forced smile. 'And if I wasn't around to pull you off course, you probably would have.'

'No. That's nonsense. I would never marry a man just because I liked him! It wouldn't be fair. And besides, he's a different class from me, Grace. Lady Wilcox would have a fit if I married him. His family would disinherit him. Look, to them I'm as common as mud. I'm a little nobody with a few pennies scraped together, an orphan; I'm completely pitiful and inconsequential.'

'I see you've thought about it, though,' Grace said grimly.

A flush of anger rose to my cheeks, because, after all, she was right.

'Very well; use that excuse if you want!' I said bitterly. 'I'm sure you'll have to come up with some reason not to be with me. You can tell yourself I was mentally unfaithful to you for a few minutes if that'll do the trick.'

I had never spoken to her like that. Hating myself, I pulled on my boots. I turned and began to walk away in the direction of Bray Head, hoping she would follow. The mountain loomed up before me and I began to scramble up the hilly path towards the summit. I tried not to look at the happy picnicking couples sprawled on the slopes.

Once I reached the top I paused, panting, looking out over the water towards the city of Dublin. It was incredibly quiet and beautiful there, with tufts of heather and gorse bushes all around. I breathed the fresh sea air and felt calmer. It would be better, I thought, not to go back to that dreary house. I could stay in a nice little hotel here — or go back to the Grimsbys. Mrs Grimsby would receive me with open arms, I knew that. She would pamper me and tell me I'd made the right decision....

It was the expression in Vera's face that haunted me — the way that, all of a sudden, it had gone blank. I had been written off. It had happened with Violet, but Violet had made the decision before she even met me. With Vera it had happened there and then. It was so humiliating to be rejected by someone like her, someone who had once seemed to admire me in a curious way. She had admired me but she hadn't known me. I was afraid, suddenly, that I would never again be accepted by any respectable women once they knew. Grace didn't mind, because she had always scorned Vera. But I minded. I couldn't help it.

I heard steps approaching and looked around. I felt a pang because she looked so weary. She came straight up to me and said, 'I'm sorry.'

'No, I'm sorry,' I told her.

Her arms slid around me. 'You'll do what you think best, won't you?'

'Grace,' I said, kissing her, unable to stop. 'Oh, Grace....'

Our faces were burning. We held each other tightly.

'I didn't mean to attack you. It was because of Vera,' I murmured. 'The way I felt when she walked away like that, judging us ... didn't you feel anything?'

'Any shame, you mean?' she said in a low voice. 'Ah, I'm used to it. You're just not used to it. You have to cover it up.'

'Grace,' I said, hesitating, hardly knowing where my words were coming from, but knowing I had to speak them, 'I do love you, but it's hard to stop thinking about you being with those men for money. I wish I *could* stop thinking about it. Maybe that's what you meant when you said that I'd be ashamed of you after a while. I'm ashamed of myself, really, because I can't let it rest.'

She nodded. 'I knew I'd probably lose you because of that.' She said it so matter-of-factly that I gasped.

'But you did it anyway,' I said.

'I had no choice.'

Our words were stark, simple. The wind whipping around us seemed to blow our words away, as if it wanted us to stop fighting, be kind to each other. When I looked in Grace's eyes I saw that she wasn't angry, wasn't denying anything, wasn't begging me to forgive her; she was just leaving me with the decision.

'It's part of who I am, even though you don't like that,' she said very softly, her eyes cast down.

I didn't answer.

'Are you thinking I'd do it again? I'd never do it again. I can be faithful, you know, Caroline. I feel like I have been faithful.'

Tears began to form in her eyes. I bent and kissed them away, tasting the salt on my tongue. I suddenly felt that she had said enough. A little bit of cold, hard anger that I had never even known I was clinging on to seemed to blow away in the wind.

'Let's go home, love,' she whispered. I nodded. It was lovely to see her smile. It spread a warmth through me.

I remember very little of that journey back to Dublin. We were both tired, but gentle with each other. We sat side by side on the train, our hands clasped together under Grace's shawl. It was strange to feel my heart beating as we entered the house again, to watch her longingly as she went upstairs in front of me. Once we were in the door, she put the kettle on and suggested that we wash. We lugged containers of water from the tap in the courtyard up the stairs and emptied it into a tin tub Grace pulled out from a little alcove. Then the boiling water was poured on top of that.

'Most Dubliners bathe like this,' she said, yawning, her hair flowing as she settled into the tub. She began to rub herself with a big cake of yellow soap. I tried not to stare at her breasts, full and delectable as I remembered.

'That soap looks vile,' I joked, and offered to scrub her back. She leaned forward and I gave her a gentle massage with the sponge. Then she leaned back. She looked beautiful, lying there, and I just sat and regarded her. She smiled at me.

'Sorry for earlier,' she said. 'I just want what's best for us both.'

'This is what's best, isn't it?' I asked.

Grace stood up, water streaming down her legs. She was such a goddess, I thought, so absolutely stunning. A towel soon covered her, but she insisted I should wash too.

'You might as well,' she murmured, 'although you never get dirty, Caroline.'

I slid into the warm water, aware of her eyes on me. 'I'm so scrawny,' I apologised, but she only laughed.

'It's true, you're thinner again since you went to London. What'll we do with you at all?'

She sat on the bed and waited for me to join her.

I came and stood beside her. She patted me down with the towel, and then, to my delight, stretched out on the bed, nude.

'I like the way you were looking at me just now,' she murmured. 'Kiss me.'

We kissed. I was lying on top of her. The feel of her bare skin under me was delicious. I had forgotten how good it was. She moaned, clutching me tight.

'Does this mean you want me to make love to you, Grace?' I asked, teasing her rosy nipple with my tongue.

'Oh yes, please,' she gasped. Her hands were everywhere. I began a slow seduction, savouring her, enjoying her cries of pleasure. I wanted to drive her mad, make her forget what lay ahead. And after she had cooled down, I thought, I would begin again.

Chapter 22

$\mathcal{I}$ woke up late, to find the sun shining into the room. Grace was sitting on the end of the bed. When I put on my spectacles I saw that she was already dressed in her uniform, hat on head. She looked handsome, serious, and quite unlike the girl who had given herself to me for hours last night.

'You look lovely,' she said, leaning over to kiss me. 'All warm and sleepy....' Her face and her lips, in contrast, were cool. I threw my arms around her.

'Oh, Grace.... It's funny: I never really imagined this moment would come.'

'I know,' she said. 'I hate to leave you, Caroline.'

'But you'll come back,' I said tearfully. 'Won't you?'

She sighed. 'I'll try, but I don't know when. Will you be here?'

'Yes,' I said. 'I won't go back to Rathgar. Grace, it will only be a few days, won't it?'

'I don't know,' she said. 'I just don't know.'

She released me gently and stood up. I got up and threw on

a wrap. At that moment there was a knock on the door. I swallowed. So this was it, so soon.

'It's Jack,' Grace said. She opened the door, and I heard Jack say, 'Are you ready?'

She stepped back to embrace me. It was a terrible feeling, not knowing if I would hold her again. There was a sensation of panic at the pit of my stomach, a fluttering. I wondered if she had it too.

Jack coughed politely at the door. He was smoking a cigarette, his head turned away.

We kissed again. Grace whispered, 'Thanks for staying with me, love. Thank you for last night. Don't worry about me. I'll be back soon.'

She released me and I had to sit down on the bed, for my legs trembled. Standing by Jack at the door, she said, 'Remember — go to the GPO at noon. Be there for us.'

I nodded. Jack took her arm. He was pale and his face looked drawn. I guessed his heavy coat concealed a rifle.

'Goodbye,' Grace murmured. I smiled at the two of them, not wanting to speak for fear of how my voice would sound.

'Come on,' Jack said hoarsely. The door shut behind them. I listened to their boots clattering down the stairs. Then the house was still.

~

I lay on the bed, still not dressed, looking at the clock. The minutes were ticking by agonisingly slowly. For Grace and Jack, though, fear and exhilaration pumping through their bodies, things would be moving very fast. They would be at Liberty Hall now, drawn up in battle formation with their comrades. They would be marching in the direction of Stephen's Green, following the Countess and Michael Mallin through the sunny, deserted streets of this Easter Monday. Pearse and Connolly and a large band would be marching towards the GPO. A man called de Valera would be at Boland's Mills. I remembered his name because Grace had said he was a maths teacher, of all things, a tall, skinny man with glasses who always rode a bicycle. And there were other places, other names, but I had forgotten them.

The place where Grace had lain beside me was still faintly warm. I buried my face in the sheets, tears seeping out of my eyes. I was glad to cry, finally. *Oh, God,* I thought, *what is to become of me? Of us?* I could not live with this uncertainty, this creeping sense of panic and dread. And then, perhaps, to be rejected at the end of this ordeal because Grace could not see herself living in England with me ... was that to be the end of our story?

Our angry words on the beach came back to me. I did not blame her for questioning me about Rex Philpott. Why had I said that I cared for him? Next to Grace he meant nothing at all. Surely she could see that. In the throes of our passion last night she had told me that she could never tire of me, that she would always love me. She had even said — and I felt a little thrill of happiness, remembering it — that she never wanted to be with anyone else. That she had had enough experience of love — too much, in fact — and that only with me had she found true and complete bliss.

I'd told her that I wanted to be with her for the rest of my life. Marriage didn't matter to me. Respectability didn't either —

although I considered living with a woman to be perfectly respectable, really. Grace had giggled at my words, saying that I was sweet, but that I didn't know how hard the world was, how censorious. Like Vera, sweeping away from us with her nose in the air. Then I'd told her that the world would change, that I believed a time was coming when there would be more freedom for women than we could dream of. 'They'll be smoking, driving cars, drinking and wearing trousers,' I had prophesied, while Grace laughed tenderly, indulgently. Hadn't I already seen a girl in London with cropped hair and trousers? I continued. Hadn't I seen a woman bus conductor? 'Ooh, I bet you liked her,' Grace had whispered, pulling my head down once again between her breasts. I was sure that beneath the starched fabric of her uniform her breasts were swollen and her nipples tender today. I smiled at the thought. What was wrong with that?

I glanced at the clock again. It was 11.30 already. *All right.* I got up and began to dress in the unbearable loneliness and quiet of the room. I needed to get out of there, suddenly. At least, though I would not see Grace and Jack, I would see other Volunteers and Citizen Army soldiers. Grace had told me that there would be a mixture of them inside the GPO, for, after all, James Connolly the labour leader was there. But Pearse would read the Proclamation, since he was the movement's fiery, eloquent speaker.

Nervously I stepped out of the room, locking the door behind me. I slipped the heavy key back into my bag. As I went downstairs I noticed all the doors were closed. Perhaps the families were lying in. The streets were equally quiet, and the men who passed me were cheerful, whistling, even eyeing me, I thought. Once I turned the corner into Sackville Street, though, I was aware of a little crowd gathered further up the street. I hastened towards them.

The first things I noticed were the flags being raised over the GPO by some green-clad Volunteers. One was the tricolour; the other was a green flag with the words 'Irish Republic' emblazoned on it in gold. Looking at the building, I could see that windows had been broken and that there were rifle butts pointing out. It gave me an eerie chill, but the faces of the Dubliners standing near me seemed amused or scornful.

'What the hell are they doing in there?' one man muttered to no one in particular. 'Sure, I was only in there a minute ago buying stamps, and they kicked me out. What stunt are they pulling now? Jaysus, it's like the night last year they pretended to take over the Castle. That was a bloody laugh. The soldiers'll have them out in no time.'

Suddenly a short dark-haired man in uniform emerged; standing on the portico of the GPO, between its tall pillars, he quickly began to read the proclamation that I had looked over at Liberty Hall a few days before. As he read, I tried to imagine what Grace would feel if she were here instead of me. Would her legs tremble, her heart pound? Would tears rise to her eyes?

I listened respectfully; but, glancing around at the crowd, I saw nothing in people's faces except stony incomprehension and disbelief. They were silent, mostly, but it was not the quiet that comes from a rapt audience of believers.

'The Irish Republic is entitled to, and hereby claims, the allegiance of every Irishman and Irishwoman,' Pearse declared.

'Wha'?' the man next to me asked incredulously. As Pearse finished by invoking God's blessing and protection on the cause of the Irish Republic and her soldiers, the men around me were sniggering and shrugging. When he stopped speaking, there was a long, indifferent silence.

I saw a sturdy middle-aged man in uniform step over to him and clasp his hand. I faintly heard his words: 'Thanks be to God, Pearse, that we have lived to see this day.' Visibly drained, Pearse cast one last look at the faces of the crowd, and both men walked back into the building.

'That was Connolly,' said the man next to me, yawning. Suddenly he gasped, 'Ah Jaysus, look out!'

We all rushed across the street and flattened ourselves against the opposite wall. A company of men on horseback dashed up the street. As they reached Nelson's Pillar, a long volley of gunfire broke out from the GPO. At least four soldiers dropped to the ground. The others wheeled around and galloped away.

'Mother of God!' the man said. 'I don't believe this.' Stunned, he lit a cigarette and offered me one as an afterthought. Shakily, I accepted.

'Those men are dead over there,' reported one of the bystanders who had gone over to look. An uneasy silence fell on the crowd. People seemed unwilling to leave.

'Ah, they'll still have the rebels out of there in a few hours,' someone muttered.

'Where's the police?' another one said.

A young boy, running up, shouted, 'A policeman was killed on Stephen's Green! They say the Countess did it.'

Another man walked into the crowd and said, 'Listen, lads, I hear the police have been taken off the streets. These boyos with guns are too much for 'em. They'd slaughter 'em.'

A murmur arose from the crowd, which was growing larger.

Women and children were wandering up, their faces pinched and eager.

'Let's get the grub here, then,' a youth said, gaily pitching a brick through a confectioner's window. I watched in amazement as half the crowd poured into the shop, the broken glass ripping their clothes and cutting their flesh. Jars of sweets and boxes of toffees and chocolates were thrown out onto the street, where children fell on them with cries of glee. It was all happening extraordinarily fast.

The shoe shop was next. A group of old women attacked the plate glass and waded into the shop. Boots and shoes flew through the air. Warning gunshots rang out from the Post Office, and some in the crowd reacted angrily, making obscene gestures and shouting curses at them. Finally, a few minutes later, a group of Volunteers, guns in hand, dashed across the street and into the store, herding the trespassers out.

'Get out of here, all of you! It's too dangerous,' shouted a young Volunteer.

The crowd jeered at him. 'Well, it's you lot that's made it dangerous, isn't it?' queried a man with impeccable logic.

'Ah, fuck the lot o' yez!' an old woman screeched. 'I got me boots!' She waved them tauntingly in the air. The Volunteers ignored her, heading back to their post.

A chocolate bar had fallen at my feet. I unwrapped it and started nibbling on it without thinking. I began wandering away from the GPO, towards home, for I knew that soon the British would send in reinforcements and the street would become a battleground.

Chapter 23

_____

$\mathcal{I}$ lingered at the corner of Sackville Street, listening to the sporadic sound of gunfire coming from all quarters of the city. I felt completely dazed by what I had seen. It was the first time I had witnessed death at such close quarters. The sincerity of Pearse, the killing of the soldiers and the orgy of looting whirled around in my brain. I could not make sense of any of it.

Suddenly a hand touched my arm. I gasped.

'Miss Singleton ... Caroline, is it?' Hughie's freckled face was lit up with a kind of unearthly glee.

'Hughie! What are you doing here?'

'Same as you — lookin' around,' the boy replied. 'I was just over at the Green, matter of fact.'

'What's happening there?' I asked, clutching his arm.

Hughie pulled out a cigarette. It was obviously his moment to be suave and manly, and I waited impatiently, frowning.

'Well, the rebels are digging in at the Green and barricading all the roads around it,' he said, exhaling a puff of smoke. 'There's English officers firing at them from the roof of the Shelbourne

Hotel. Meanwhile there's posh ladies taking afternoon tea and chatting inside. Course, they can't get out, so they're stuck there for the duration. What do you think of that?'

'Has anyone been killed?'

'A policeman was, earlier. Then the Sinn Féiners killed a man who wandered up and seized hold of a cart. He wouldn't let go. The Countess was furious that they shot him. Turns out he was on their side, but was bein' an eejit for some reason. I don't think any of the Citizen Army lads have been shot yet.'

'Oh God, Hughie,' I muttered.

I hardly expected any sympathy, but to my surprise he put his hand on my arm again.

'Don't go down there, Miss. It's pretty bad. There's dead horses lying around the streets. A stray bullet could get yeh at any minute. I thought about joinin' them, but then I thought, why would I? I'm in enough trouble at home as it is for being sacked from Grimsby's.'

'Why did the Grimsbys sack you?' My voice sounded shrill and uneven.

'Ah, don't worry, it's not your fault. Sure, it's true the missus was angry at me for not bringin' you back, but then she got that note you sent and she seemed all right after that. I've been taking the odd bottle of booze home for me and my girl, that's all — everyone does it. But himself caught me at it and said it was the last straw, threatened to box my ears even. Never mind. I don't give a damn if oul' Grimsby and his fat wife call me a jackeen and throw me out. I can do better than the likes o' them. I'll show them.'

He pulled a little bottle of brandy out of his jacket and handed it to me with a flourish.

I looked at him blankly.

'You might need this. You never know. Medicinal.'

I smiled at him. 'Hughie, I'm a woman and a foreigner in this city, as you know. I can't move about in it the way you do. Would you be willing to meet me here at the same time every day for a few minutes — just to let me know what's going on?'

He considered for a moment.

'Yeh, all right, for Jack's sake. It's wrong of Jack to leave you stranded like this.'

'Hughie, Jack and I are just friends,' I murmured. 'He has a sweetheart.'

He winked at me. 'Friends. Yeh. Well, you can count on me. Jack's quite the man, isn't he?' He shook his head, baffled at Jack's stupidity. 'To have two girls after him — and then to run off and get involved in a thing like this. The fella needs his head examined.'

'It's for his country,' I said, shrugging.

Hughie gave me a withering look and spat eloquently into the gutter. 'I tell you one thing: the British are going to have to rip apart every building they're in to get them out. By the end of this thing, the people of this city will be howling for their heads.'

'The soldiers'?' I asked, confused.

'The rebels'. Shoot the whole bloody lot of 'em. That's what people are saying already.'

'But they don't mean it,' I whispered.

'Time will tell,' Hughie replied, tucking another cigarette into his mouth.

~

I remember that it was very cold that first night. I built up the fire and sat by it, sketching in my book. I also kept a diary, for I wanted to be able to tell Grace of the events I saw or heard about, and I sensed that by the time she came back to me too much would have happened for me to be able to reel off a string of stories. It was strange that the little pockets of rebels were so cut off from one another. It must be terrible for them. I knew that one of the functions of the Cumann na mBán women in this struggle was to cut across enemy lines with messages. If only Grace had decided to do that.... But I was proud of her as she was. I thought about her and Jack huddling in the cold park somewhere, and my heart sank.

I awoke to the distant *pock-pock* of gunfire and the sound of rain spitting against the window. I lay in bed for a while, then got up and made myself a cup of tea. *Even if I wanted to return to the Grimsbys now*, I reflected, *I couldn't*. The city was paralysed: no deliveries, no public transport. It would soon be a problem to get food and fuel, no doubt.

I took a gulp of Hughie's brandy and sat down to try to read. It was a novel I had brought with me, entitled *The Voyage Out*, by a new young writer called Virginia Woolf. Apparently she was a member of the same 'Bloomsbury crowd' that the young art student at the Slade had referred to. I found it bewildering, for the people, when they talked, seemed very clever, and yet their words seemed to slip by with no fixed meaning. A young Englishman called Terence was looking at his fiancée's books in a villa in a small town in South America. They had just got engaged, and were having a conversation like no other discussion I had ever read in a novel between two young people. Yet the words calmed me, pleased me somehow with their lack of relevance to the situation at hand. I dozed on the bed for a while and then realised it was time to meet Hughie. I threw on my clothes and went out.

Sackville Street was a mess. The windows of most shops were broken; those that weren't were protected by thick shutters. I stood on the corner, trembling, as angry gunfire exchanges went on up the street. I glanced at my watch. It was three o'clock. I ducked under a striped shop-awning to shelter from the rain.

I waited for twenty minutes. Finally a small figure dashed across the street towards me. Hughie was soaking wet.

'D'you want the latest?' he cried. 'The Countess and the Citizen Army fellas have left the Green. They did it early this morning. There's dead and wounded. They're holed up in the College of Surgeons, firin' back out the windows at the soldiers shootin' at them. They'll be all right now till it ends. Would you believe I saw a Cumann na mBán girl holding up a bread van?'

I smiled at him, and he rewarded me with a cigarette.

'Yeh, they're short of food, but so's the whole city now,' he said philosophically. 'But you're not going to like this, Caroline....' He paused for effect.

'What?' I whispered.

'You'll hear it soon enough,' he said.

He was right. A couple of minutes later, as I continued pumping him for information, a massive boom rang out.

'What is it?' I gasped.

'Ah, that's an eighteen-pounder,' Hughie said. 'Artillery, wha'? The British are after bringin' four of them in from Athlone, a fella told me. They'll be bangin' away at the GPO, that's for sure.'

'How awful,' I said, shivering. But at least Grace and Jack were safe!

'Can you come tomorrow, Hughie?' I asked him.

'I don't see why not,' he said, shrugging. 'Best be off now, though. See ya.'

And so we parted ways, the thunder of the big guns ringing in our ears.

~

The next day, my interview with Hughie was even shorter. I had woken up in the early hours of Wednesday morning and lain shivering in bed. The city was being pounded relentlessly. It brought back to me the misery my brother must have endured in the trenches. A terrible stony anger had come upon me. By the time I reached my rendezvous spot, near the corner of Sackville Street, I was dizzy from the smoke and fumes. Peering around the corner, I saw houses burning close to the GPO, which itself still looked more or less intact. Weeping and moaning women passed me.

Hughie sidled up to me with a dirty face. We stood in silence for a moment, and then I offered him a gulp of his own brandy. He wiped his mouth and sighed.

'Well,' he said bitterly, 'they've destroyed Liberty Hall.'

I looked at him open-mouthed.

'The English general, Sir John Maxwell, had the gunboat *Helga* come down the Liffey and fire on it for hours, even though 'twas empty. It's still standing, but they say it's pounded all to pieces inside.'

I burst into tears. Hughie stood beside me in the rain, his hand on my arm.

'Yeh,' he said, sighing, 'they're going to burn them out.' He gestured in the direction of the GPO.

'I suppose it'll be too dangerous to meet tomorrow,' I muttered.

'We'll do it anyway. God knows I can't sit at home all day listening to me ma wailing and carrying on.'

~

On Thursday Hughie told me that there had been a raiding party sent out from the College of Surgeons, and that a Citizen Army boy of seventeen had been killed and a girl badly wounded; but her name was Margaret something, he assured me. And anyway, the Countess was doing well: she was up on the roof, picking off snipers like a professional soldier.

He told me that a handful of Volunteers had kept British reinforcements out of the city for a long time before they had been overpowered.

'They're brave lads,' he declared, as the guns pounded on the street. 'Brave lads. They're outnumbered twenty to one now.'

~

That night was terrible. The gunfire continued all night, along with sporadic shots that I feared were from officers picking off people on the street who were out after the curfew. Screams and confused shouting thwarted my attempts to sleep. I heard rough English accents and listened to them with dread. The soldiers were patrolling everywhere, taking back the city, street by street.

Towards dawn, I heard a man pounding on the door downstairs. 'Let me in! Ah, Jaysus, let me in!' he begged. Someone clattered down the stairs of the house; but before they could open the door and pull him to safety, I heard an English voice shouting 'Hands up!' and then 'Get the bastard!'

I crept to the window and looked down. In the eerie pre-dawn glow the man was on his knees, the officer holding a gun to his head, while the rest of the soldiers stood by as if frozen.

The man was quite young — just a boy, really. His mouth was moving; it looked like he was saying a Hail Mary. Acting out of some instinct I had not known I had, I unlatched the window and let it slide down. The cold, smoky air streamed in.

The soldiers below looked up, hands on guns. They saw I was a woman. I leaned out.

'Don't kill him,' I said loudly. I tried to make my voice sound like the Countess's. *What would she say?* 'He's not armed!'

'He's violating the curfew,' the officer said curtly. 'We have orders to shoot to kill.'

A lorry pulled up.

'You don't mind if we arrest him, do you, Miss?' the officer called up, his voice thick with sarcasm. The soldiers began joking amongst themselves and I saw the boy's body relax. He looked up briefly at the window, his face pale as milk in the ghostly light, and I thought: *He'll always remember this, and so will I.*

They herded him roughly into the lorry. I pushed the window closed, shaking. Sleep still did not come, but as I lay on the bed I felt a rare moment of peace and gratitude.

~

On Friday, fear hammered at me as I walked the streets, drying my mouth, making my hands tremble. Sackville Street was a lake of fire. I had never seen such desolation. Flames were licking the roof of the battered GPO.

Hughie and I met at the corner, as before, but hurried away from the burning street. A British Army officer rushed up and ordered us back further. 'Clear out, you fools!' he yelled at us contemptuously. Then, to another soldier, he commented, 'What is it about these people? They've been blundering into the line of fire all week.'

'But it's our city,' Hughie said softly, as if to himself, looking at the soldier.

~

For all of those nights I could barely sleep; I lay awake reading, by the light of a candle, in the dingy room. I was waiting for Grace's step on the stairs — yet how could she come? I prayed that the Countess would let her go. *But even if the Countess did that*, I thought, *out of a brief impulse of mercy, Grace would insist on staying till the bitter end.*

On Saturday Hughie told me that the rebels in the GPO had evacuated to houses in nearby Moore Street the night before, and that they were now trapped. Connolly was badly wounded and had been carried out on a stretcher. 'They'll have to surrender,' he said, his eyes red-rimmed with exhaustion. The firing was dying down all over the city and a curious sense of desolation and bitterness had taken its place, as if rising from the smoking ruins.

'I tell you what, Caroline,' Hughie promised, 'when I find out that the Countess and her men have surrendered, I'll come find you. Maybe you'll be able to spot Jack marching by on his way to the Castle — that's where they'll all end up, I s'pose, till they decide what to do with them.'

I told him my address, and he nodded.

'Just wait there for me.'

Chapter 24

I lay on the bed, fully dressed. It was Sunday morning. Mass bells were ringing all over the city, interspersed by the odd gunshot. The rebels had held the authorities off for a week, as Jack had hoped. I was not sure what I felt about any of it. I longed to return to the little house in Camden Town, to my books, to the vast anonymity of London. I sensed that more heart-break lay in store for the people of Dublin, and for Grace too. I was not even sure that she was still alive, but I trusted Hughie's words. But to see her marching as a captured soldier ... God!

Still, I thought, *so far she has not hated me for being English....* I had bought a paper the day before and had been shocked by reports of an atrocity committed by a British army officer, Captain Bowen-Colthurst. He had apparently cracked under the strain of his duties and had arrested a well-known Dublin intellectual, Francis Sheehy-Skeffington, who had been trying to stop the widespread looting, and two journalists who had simply been walking in the street. He'd taken them out on patrol in Rathmines that night, and they'd watched him shoot dead a boy walking out of a Catholic church. Then, in a fit of mad rage, he had had them all shot up against a wall at some barracks, and had buried their bodies in quicklime. He'd proceeded to arrest Skeffington's wife and son and search their home in an attempt to find some incriminating evidence against the man he'd already killed. He had been relieved of his post and an inquiry was in progress. I felt profoundly ashamed of what 'my people' were doing.

I heard a tap at my door. Hughie summoned me quickly. I ran down the stairs after him and we hurried down the street, turning left on Sackville Street and crossing over the bridge. I looked down the river to see the frail shell of Liberty Hall, still standing, but scarred with deep holes that I could spot even from that distance. I stood there sadly until Hughie tugged at my arm.

We waited at the corner of College Green. I could not see anything unusual except a few grim-looking passers-by.

'Are you sure they're coming, Hughie?' I asked breathlessly.

'I ran and got you the minute I saw the woman with the white flag go into the College of Surgeons,' Hughie explained. 'Pearse and his lot have already surrendered. They're in the hands of the British now.'

'I suppose they can't expect mercy,' I said in a low voice.

'Nobody knows,' Hughie said, shrugging. 'That's the worst of it. But, sure, they can't kill them all. They're rounding up everyone connected to it now. Did you know that three hundred and eighteen rebels were killed in Dublin, and over two thousand wounded? That includes ordinary citizens, too, 'cause they're counting us all together.'

'That's nice of them,' I said with a grim laugh.

'And millions of pounds' worth of damage to property,' Hughie muttered. 'It means James Connolly was wrong, then.'

'Why?'

'Someone told me he said that, because the British were capitalists, they'd never destroy their own property the way they just did.'

'Poor Connolly,' I said with a sigh.

'Here they are now,' Hughie exclaimed suddenly.

I strained to hear. Yes, I could hear marching feet. Soon a tiny band of men and a few women, ragged and exhausted-looking, some bandaged, came up Grafton Street under the watchful guard of a few British officers with pistols in their hands. I saw the Countess in front, clad in breeches, deep in discussion with Michael Mallin. They did not look despairing; more like people who had fought a good hard fight. But where were Grace and Jack?

'There's Jack, at the end of it,' Hughie said suddenly. 'See?'

Stunning me, he shouted, 'Jack!' and then, to my even greater astonishment, his voice cracked and hoarse, 'Fair play to you, Jack!'

Jack scanned the crowd. When he saw us, a smile crossed his weary face. Would he smile like that if Grace were injured or dead? An officer glanced at us, but, seeing only a woman standing with a boy, looked away indifferently.

'Shoot every one of them,' an elderly man standing near us cried out, as if affronted by Hughie's hailing a rebel.

'And isn't it terrible to see a woman wearing breeches?' someone muttered behind us.

The battalion turned the corner of Dame Street and headed up towards the Castle.

'I don't understand,' I said to Hughie. I felt my voice quivering. 'Why wasn't Grace with them? I don't understand.'

'Well, there's only one possibility,' Hughie said thoughtfully.

'What, Hughie?'

'I'd say to you now,' he muttered, looking wise beyond his years, 'to go home. Just go home and see what happens.'

It was strange that I should cry now, but I started to weep uncontrollably on Hughie's shoulder.

'I know, I know,' he said, patting my back. 'It's hard to see your man carted off to prison. You must have wanted to go up and embrace him. That's why I called out, so you could see his face.'

'You've been so sweet to me, Hughie,' I wept. 'So good.'

'All right, all right,' he said, looking embarrassed suddenly. 'But listen, don't be gettin' all mushy on me now.'

I laughed into my handkerchief.

'Just go home, Caroline,' Hughie repeated.

'Goodbye, Hughie,' I said to him. I held out my hand and he took it hesitantly. He was not used to shaking hands with women, I supposed.

'You've been a brick, as they'd say in England,' I told him.

'Em ... thanks.' He looked strangely flattered, as if nobody had ever complimented him before. 'So long, then.'

He moved off in the direction of home, pulling his cap down over his ears. My feet were leaden as I walked back across the river. On a whim I made my way to the GPO, and my tears flowed again as I stood in front of that once-fine building. It had been savagely pounded; it was pitted with bullet-holes and blackened by smoke. Unsmiling British troops stood on guard at the doorway.

I turned away, my heart aching. I could not bear much more of this.

~

I trudged up the stairs, pausing at the door to fumble for my key. Something seemed different, but I could not imagine what. Perhaps it was just a blackened mark on the door that had not been there before. I walked into the room and screamed.

'Shut the door,' said Grace from the bed. She was lying there in a blouse and skirt that I did not recognise. She was pale and thin, and looked feverish.

I slammed the door shut. Running to embrace her, I held her in my arms as her face burned against me.

'You've got a fever! Grace, how did you get here?'

'I escaped,' she said weakly. 'I don't know why. It was at the last minute. We'd smashed holes in the walls of the College of Surgeons so that we could occupy neighbouring houses too. I was there with Jack when I saw a woman coming in with a white flag. Jack begged me to go. He saw I was ill and he said, "I don't want you in prison, Grace. Go back to your friend and get out of the country." I said I wanted to stay with him, I couldn't desert the Countess now. He told me that the Countess had said that I didn't have to stay, that I'd done my part. I didn't believe him, but suddenly ...' She broke into tears. 'Ah, God, Caroline, I wanted to leave.'

She sobbed for a long time as I held her in my arms.

'Grace, you did the right thing. I saw Jack just a few minutes ago on the way to the Castle. He looked happy. I'm so glad you're here, Grace.'

'So the woman in one of the houses gave me her clothes, and I crept through the streets....'

'It's been a terrible week,' I murmured.

'Thank God you're here. Thank God,' she said, kissing me gently. 'How have you borne it, all this time?'

'I met Hughie Nolan each day and he told me everything that was going on. He seemed to have some uncanny knowledge of things that were happening. So I heard about you and your friends leaving the park, and the Countess shooting snipers from the roof....'

'We had a mass last night,' Grace murmured sleepily. 'It was beautiful. The Countess joined in. We prayed for the dead and the living. It was so peaceful. We didn't know, you see, what the morning would bring. We thought we might have to fight till the death.'

I watched her drift off to sleep, hardly believing that she was back with me. It seemed like a miracle.

Chapter 25

_____

I nursed Grace with beef tea (for the shops were open again) and sips of Hughie's brandy. She accepted everything trustingly, like a child. She asked to see my diary of the rising, and mused over the words and sketches. She seemed deeply interested in everything I had seen, especially the looting of the shops and the things I had heard people say. The news about Liberty Hall stunned her, as it had me. She wept at James Connolly's comment to Pearse on the steps of the GPO, and groaned when I said he was badly wounded.

'They didn't tell us that. They were trying to spare us, I suppose.'

Apparently a few messages had got through to the College of Surgeons from the GPO, but mostly they had been cut off. She described nursing Margaret Skinnider, the girl who had almost been killed in the raiding party. They had had to tear off her uniform, and Margaret had cried only because she had been so proud of her uniform. It was very touching to hear Grace describing incidents like these.

'But then,' Grace said, smiling, 'the Countess had to go out and shoot the sniper who'd got Margaret.'

Meanwhile, Dublin had been placed under martial law. The authorities had rounded up three thousand five hundred people, and the city waited anxiously to see what the British would do. Nearly two hundred people were tried by courts martial held in secret. Nothing was known about the judgements until the executions were announced to an increasingly horrified public.

I dashed out to get the paper every day. The first news came on Wednesday morning: Patrick Pearse, Tom Clarke and Thomas MacDonagh had been executed by firing squad at Kilmainham Jail, where the ringleaders were being held. It was not unexpected to me, at least, because they were signatories of the Proclamation. Grace wept bitterly as I told her. She was still in bed, weak and coughing, and each death I related seemed to hit her hard. I knew what it was that she feared most, what it was that would break her spirit completely.

The next day four more executions were announced. They had shot Patrick Pearse's brother Willie — a particularly petty act, it seemed — and Joseph Plunkett, who had married his fiancée the night before in his cell. 'But he was dying of TB!' Grace raged.

The following day it was the turn of Maud Gonne's ex-husband, John McBride, who had not even known about the rising, according to Grace, but had joined in once he heard it had started.

The paper had other news. The Countess Markievicz's death sentence had been commuted to life imprisonment, 'solely and only on account of her sex', as the court put it. She had been moved to Mountjoy Prison. Grace read the news and lay back in bed, her eyes closing and tears seeping between her lids.

'Aren't you glad, Grace?' I asked gently.

'Oh yes, Caroline, but I know she would rather have died with her friends,' she whispered. 'Prison is cruel for someone like her.'

On 10 May the papers published a picture of the Countess huddling in the back of a van with a female wardress, on her way to prison, her face thin and sad.

On 12 May, James Connolly was executed, strapped into a chair because he was too weak to stand. Fifteen men had been executed in all, including two nineteen-year-old boys whom Grace knew vaguely, for Jack had been friends with them in the Fianna, and Michael Mallin, who had led the Citizen Army forces at Stephen's Green.

After that, Major-General Sir John Maxwell seemed to realise that things had gone too far. He commuted seventy-five other death sentences and pronounced a massive internment policy — eighteen hundred men and five women would be sent to a camp in Wales. The Countess would be made to serve out her prison term in England too.

'Jack will be among them, then,' Grace said dreamily. She was better now, but still seemed very drained and passive. She sighed in my arms. 'Oh, Caroline, at least he's alive.'

~

The next morning she got up, dressed, and stood by the window. I watched her from the bed.

'What are you doing, Grace?'

'Looking out at the city, that's all,' she said with a smile.

She turned and walked over to the bed, gazing down at me. I could not read her expression.

'You've been so good to me, Caroline.'

'Grace, it's nothing,' I said, shrugging. 'I wanted to be here to help you, that's all.'

'And you got used to it here,' she mused.

'Yes, I got used to Dublin. It's easy when someone you love needs you.'

Grace sat down on the bed, looking at me seriously.

'It's time for me to do the same for you, then. If you could put up with this, I should be able to deal with life in London. At least I'll try.'

Years later, she would still tease me that my face had paled completely when she said that, and that I had looked as if I were going to faint.

'Grace, are you sure?' I gasped.

She laughed at my expression. 'God, Caroline, you knew I was going to make up my mind one way or the other. Didn't you have any faith in me at all?'

I flung my arms around her. She seemed happy at my joy, which I could not conceal.

'Darling,' I whispered.

~

That morning, our last in Dublin, we took a cab to the Grimsbys'. Grace insisted on coming with me. We sat hand in hand in the back. A million things were going through my mind. Grace nudged me as we passed the College of Surgeons, then leaned over and kissed me on the lips. Her eyes were bright again, and the sight was beautiful to me. I had got her back, and no matter what happened next, we would at least have some time together, free from all of the pain and misery that seemed trodden into these streets.

'I won't miss it here, you know,' Grace declared, squeezing my hand, as if to convince herself as much as me.

'You can always go back for as long as you want, Grace,' I answered. 'The two countries are very close. I'm not going to chain you to me.'

'The way England's done with Ireland,' Grace mused. 'And it hasn't worked. But England doesn't know it yet.'

~

The Grimsbys' shop looked completely unharmed, and the house was the same. I expected Mrs Grimsby to be frosty, after all that had happened; but when she came to the door, perhaps it was the unusual sight of happiness glowing in my face that softened her expression. She led us into the parlour and left us there while she fetched my suitcase.

'I just wanted to say goodbye, Mrs Grimsby,' I told her, swallowing nervously. 'There wasn't anything of value in the suitcase, and I didn't have to come back for it, but I couldn't leave Ireland without thanking you for your kindness.'

'You're looking quite well, my dear,' she said, glancing from Grace to me. Grace stood beside me calmly, self-possessed as ever.

'Yes, I feel well.' I actually felt so elated I could have done a dance on her Oriental carpet, but I didn't tell her that.

'We feared the worst, Grimsby and I. Were you caught up in that terrible rising at all?'

'In a way,' I said, blushing.

'And your young man?'

'Well, really, Mrs Grimsby, there is no young man.'

'No young man?' she echoed.

'It was me that Caroline came back for,' Grace said.

'Oh.' Mrs Grimsby turned pink and looked away from us for a moment. There was an agonising pause.

'Well,' she said briskly, 'I suppose in the end it boils down to the same thing. Two people trying to make a go of it. That's all.'

Her English common sense had come to the fore, apparently. I gazed at her, hoping for a sign of warmth, approval, the things she had always offered me before.

'I'm sorry I didn't tell you earlier.'

'My dear,' she said with a sigh, 'I have to admit I was worried for you when I thought you were making a fool of yourself over a disreputable young man. But now that I see you with this nice girl, I don't see that there's anything to worry about at all. Shall we have a drink?'

She waved Grace and me towards the soft, wine-coloured sofa, which we sank into as we sat down. We leaned back against the cushions, and our arms and legs touched. Over our drinks, which were strong and plentifully replenished, Mrs Grimsby began to wax nostalgic. I was tipsy immediately, and later wondered if I had imagined some of what she said that May morning.

She told Grace that she looked on me as her daughter, the

child she'd never had. And why had she never been able to have children? she asked rhetorically. Well, because she and Mr Grimsby had always been more like friends and companions. He was a very nice man, but there had never been any passion. All the passion she'd felt had been for a special friend with whom she'd lived for years and years. They'd both been barmaids and had shared a room, and this had led to that; and even though they went out with men whenever they felt like it, they decided to commit to each other and never let a man come between them. And then one day her friend had been taken ill quite suddenly, and had died and left her alone in the world. So when Mr Grimsby proposed, she accepted. He had asked her many times before, and she had never said yes to him, even though he was wealthy and she would have been able to stop working, at least behind a bar. But she liked freedom, and she liked to come home to her friend at the end of the day. It was like a marriage, really. So in a way she felt she'd been married twice.

'Women can do that, you know,' she pointed out to us, and both Grace and I looked bashful — perhaps one of us even giggled. A giddy, delicious feeling had filled me; I was half-concentrating on what Mrs Grimsby was saying and half-thinking about the future, the happiness that I knew Grace and I were destined to enjoy.

'So, yes, it's best to give it a try and not worry too much about what the world thinks,' Mrs Grimsby continued with a sigh, 'even though in the end the world usually wins out. Just like in this rising. Those foolish, idealistic young people held out for a little while, for as long as they could, but the end was inevitable.' She did feel sorry about the deaths, though. It was a tragic thing. It seemed that every generation had to try. But the power of the

British Empire ... well, some things just couldn't change. If it did happen, it wasn't going to be in *her* lifetime, that was certain. But she could see from my friend's eyes that she didn't believe it. Well, that was all right. Young people always had their hopes; that was the best thing about youth.

Epilogue

July, 1927

'Excuse me, is this where we get the boat to Saorstát Éireann?' I heard Grace say to a ferry employee standing at the dock. A mischievous smile played across her lips. She looked fresh and lovely in a pale-green knee-length chiffon dress with a matching scarf, her glossy brown hair waved in the latest style.

The young man glanced at her. 'Beg pardon, Miss?'

'The Irish Free State,' Grace clarified loudly, relishing the words.

He nodded, reddening slightly under her mocking glance. 'That's right.'

I touched her arm as he moved away. 'Torturing the English?'

'Only a little,' Grace said. 'Only what they deserve.'

She smiled at me. Her hazel eyes were bright. Yet the night before, I thought, still holding on to her arm in one of those unconscious gestures that got us stared at on the street sometimes, her eyes had been red with weeping.

Jack had telephoned with news of the Countess Markievicz's death. She had died, practically a pauper, in a hospital ward full of poor Dublin women, but much prayed over and loved. Her last years had been spent living humbly among the people, her wealth and beauty gone, her generosity of spirit intact, while her political foes ruled the country she had helped to free. Jack told us that hundreds of thousands were expected to line the streets for her state funeral. Grace wanted to be among them, and I was willing to go back with her, for Ireland no longer seemed to pose any threat to me, to us.

For a while we had both tried to forget Ireland, it seemed, intent on establishing our life together in Camden Town. The past was always with us, though. It was strange to think that it had already been six years since Rex had given us the news that Thornley Hall had been burned down by the IRA. Sir John and Lady Wilcox had been in Dublin at the time, and they had moved permanently to England, like so many others of their class, after the Treaty was signed. Rex did not keep in close contact with them, though he was able to tell me that Amelia had become a flapper, moved with a fast set who danced to jazz at wild parties, and seemed intent upon leading an aimless youth.

Lady Wilcox was a shadow of her former self, according to Rex. Despite all her past dissatisfaction with the Irish, she apparently found life in England terribly disappointing. She often gave Rex an earful about both her erring daughter and her servant problems. It was now considered quite appropriate to treat servants with respect, and this had been a difficult adjustment for her; they were forever giving notice. Sir John had retreated from public life and was supposedly writing his memoirs, which involved spending long hours away from his wife. Grace and I often wondered if we would be in them. It would have pleased me if the Wilcoxes could have seen the life Grace and I were leading now.

The 20s suited me; for once I was in tune with the spirit of the times. My flat-chested physique was now the 'in' thing, an irony I never failed to appreciate. Like so many other women these days, I had had my hair bobbed, and I smoked with a holder, something Grace found terribly affected.

I had got my wish, and studied art, and I now made a decent living at it, designing book jackets and magazine covers. Grace worked among London's poor — there were plenty of them around us in Camden Town. Her latest job was working in a clinic that provided what were euphemistically called 'family planning' services. Only to married women, of course — a rule Grace hoped would change someday.

We had stripped each room in the little house of its thick, age-darkened wallpaper, and painted it in light, cheerful colours. Where heavy drapes had once hung, we put up venetian blinds. Grace proved to have great talents for cooking and gardening. Domestic peace — such as my mother must have once had with my father, in the early days of their marriage — reigned over the house again.

Among our small group of friends were other lesbians and homosexual men, most of whom I had met through art school. Rex had become a great friend. He had helped me enormously by recommending my work to various contacts he had in art-world circles. He was something of a dilettante, always with a new adoring young male companion by his side. Sometimes he asked me a little sadly how Grace and I managed it, how we stayed so committed, so devoted.

I really didn't know. All I could say was that we had been through difficult times together in the past, and that we knew things about each other that nobody else ever would.

I could have told him that, all through the terrible struggle for a Republic in Ireland, I had feared losing her. I sometimes sensed the pull that Ireland had for her, even if we passed two women with Dublin accents gossiping in the street. In our early years in London Grace pored over newspaper accounts of Black and Tan atrocities, of Michael Collins and de Valera running the country unofficially, of Sinn Féin setting up a separate government, of independence from England — which came such a short time after the Rising, really, only five years; but they were exhausting years; and I often saw in Grace's eyes a mixture of sadness that she was not there and relief that she had somehow escaped it.

And then, as the English ruling classes left Ireland in droves, their great houses burning to the ground, it hurt me somehow to see the triumph in her eyes; just as it was hard to see the anguish and bitterness she felt as the IRA forces, including Jack, continued to fight on in a futile, bloody struggle after the Treaty was signed. Now they were battling their former fellow soldiers, who they believed had sold the country out to the British — for wasn't the North partitioned? After a time, Jack was captured, like many of his comrades; but he was one of the lucky ones.

Slowly the people of the twenty-six remaining counties seemed to accept the loss of the North, the fact that their greatest leaders had been killed or had died, that they had treated one another with great brutality. Slowly everything settled into place in the grim aftermath of the Civil War. Jack got out of prison and married Noreen; they had a baby.

It was around that time, two years ago, that Grace had gone back. She wanted to visit her brother, she said; and I tried not to let her see how worried I felt. I was afraid that she would have a taste of the new Ireland and decide to stay — that the good times we'd had together would not be strong enough to hold her, compared to the emotional ties she felt for her country. I knew she was planning to see Countess Markievicz, and perhaps the Countess would embroil her in some plot or scheme.... We parted at Euston Station and I went home sobbing. The little house seemed unbearably empty, drained suddenly of life.

But, to my relief, one morning about two weeks later I heard the key scraping in the lock. I rushed down the hall and we embraced for a long time. Grace told me of her shock at seeing the Countess dependent upon the charity of friends, her clothes patched and carelessly thrown on, gaunt, suddenly looking her age....

'She was thrilled for me, Caroline, when I told her about our life here,' Grace murmured later, as we lay in bed together.

I imagined the scene: the two of them sitting over a pot of tea in a sparsely furnished room, a fire burning weakly in the grate, the Countess huddling in a coat to keep warm.

'She said, "You're well out of it, my dear. It's best not to look back at all the hopes we had for poor old Ireland ... too painful. There's nothing wrong with making your life in England. Happiness is so rare; cherish it." And of course,' Grace said, half-laughing, half-crying, 'she thoroughly approved of my job at the women's clinic!'

The fact that the Countess was so isolated and powerless made it very clear to us both that Ireland's increasingly conservative, Catholic regime offered very little freedom and opportunity to women. Grace was bitterly disappointed by it. Yet her bitterness never extended to me. Perhaps that was the secret of us, ultimately. Grace didn't hold me responsible for any of it. She liked her job, liked the ordinary people she met on the streets of London, liked the fact that we could jump into our little two-seater and motor all over the English countryside if we chose. Things had been easier between us ever since she had returned from her trip to Ireland. Sometimes we just seemed like friends, and that worried me, for I was not sure that one of us might not eventually go elsewhere to seek passion. But at times like last night, when she had grieved for the Countess, it was me whom she wanted to hold her. And after the sadness had come love — love which never seemed, these days, to have the intensity of our encounters in Ireland, but which had something else: a sense of permanence.

The ferry loomed above us, horn booming. Grace glanced at her wristwatch.

'You're keen to be off,' I said.

'And you're enjoying the delay,' she noted tartly. 'Lost in your thoughts, as usual.'

I glanced around. We had been early; but there was still only a small group of travellers standing around in the sun. They all looked Irish. It was no longer common, these days, for English people to go over for day trips or business. The country was proudly self-sufficient, determined to show that it could stand alone.

'It's strange to be on our way back, that's all. The first time I went over it was 1915. It was raining, cold, the War was on. I was so scared, Grace, going off on my own. It's different now, with you here.'

'You're very different, Caroline,' she said, leaning close to me so I could smell her perfume, her lips curving in a smile. 'Sure, we both are.'

'All aboard for the Irish Free State!' the young man she'd talked to earlier shouted. The words shocked me: suddenly it was all real.

Grace smiled at my startled look and took my arm. We walked up the gangway to the boat together.

Also from Wolfhound Press

Once Upon a Summer
Patricia O'Reilly

It is 1959. And the class of 4A at Rose Horn's convent school
in Dublin have discovered boys. And dating. And kissing.

Rose dreams of love — and of exchanging her thick lisle
stockings and bulky school uniform for the daring black chiffon
numbers of the gorgeous Rita Hayworth. When her mother
discovers Rose's secret trysts with Frank Fennelly,
she banishes her to spend summer in the depths of Kerry —
far from temptation, she believes.

But beneath the peaceful exterior of Fenit village,
with its close community and simple pleasures,
lurks a wild web of social undercurrents. Here Rose meets
heart-throb Mikey Daw, and she is drawn into the adult world of
broken promises, hidden secrets and bitter tragedy....

0-86327-795-0

Also from Wolfhound Press

That Girl from Happy
Judy May Murphy

Janie Jay Kelly has gone.

Aimee, Sammy, Fat Molly and Boots are left at Happy —
each with a void to fill.

Against the backdrop of contemporary New York City,
Judy May Murphy paints a fluorescent, tangy, grown-up
alternative to *The Wizard of Oz*.

Through a mixture of flashback, drunken revelation and
confession, *That Girl from Happy* sweeps you along in an
enigmatic whirlwind of obsession, insecurities and gritty zest.

0-86327-820-5

Also from Wolfhound Press

The Honey Plain
Elizabeth Wassell

Dermot O'Duffy has a reputation as a philanderer. His marriage to the flame-haired Fiona is foundering. Then along comes Grania — a young painter who challenges his antics — and together they embark on a rollicking affair around Ireland, just one step ahead of a posse including Fiona, her angry father and an oily popinjay called Doyle.

'A realistic novel with a mythological presence; a satiric-comic novel with a serious feel; and a rattling good yarn bristling with ideas … a touching love story, well wrought and well told.'
Brendan Kennelly

Sleight of Hand
Elizabeth Wassell

New York in the 1980s is at once vibrant and squalid — the rich take cocaine, and drifters line the streets. Young Manhattanite Claire Browne is an innocent amidst the urban clamour. An art historian, the only child of unhappy parents, she lives in her dreams and in the beauty of the paintings she studies.

Then brash reality intrudes in the person of *enfant terrible* Simon Brady, a once-great artist, now suffering a crisis of confidence. For him, Claire's naïveté is inspiring, even as he infects her with his cynicism and anger. But Claire Browne is tougher than she looks and is determined to find her own path to the truth....

Peopled with vivid characters and informed with an original sensibility, *Sleight of Hand* is a richly entertaining novel of ideas.